The Meadow

John S. Hall

iUniverse, Inc.
New York   Bloomington

The Meadow

iUniverse books may be ordered through booksellers or by contacting:

iUniverse
1663 Liberty Drive
Bloomington, IN 47403
www.iuniverse.com
1-800-Authors (1-800-288-4677)

ISBN: 978-1-4401-8670-7 (pbk)
ISBN: 978-1-4401-8671-4 (ebook)

Printed in the United States of America

iUniverse rev. date: 4/20/10

To Jim Facos:

A friend and teacher for whom I'm profoundly grateful.

—— CHAPTER ONE ——

Huntersville, VT, 1970

On a spring morning around five o'clock, if you ride out our way on Murray's Flats, fog will be hugging a hundred-acre piece of land we all call "the meadow." The meadow mist lies motionless and silent as a cloud. Underneath the white hazy cover, the land sleeps—waiting for the sun and the rain, waiting to burst from its winter's rest, waiting to grow whatever seeds are nestled in its warm soil.

Passing by with the window rolled down, all you'll hear is the muffled echo of a milking machine pump. It's a soothing sound, seeming as though life has put on a big smile. But as Cooner Clapton, the wisest uneducated man I know, says, "There's a heap of change comin' and it ain't goin' to be good."

He's referring to Uncle Bill being sick, and having had to sell his cows last year. My grandfather Thad Murray wants to sell his cows, too, because, he complains, "There ain't no money in milkin' just twenty-five head." Cooner works for Grandpa Thad and lives in the farmhouse with his wife, Addie, and me.

To make matters worse, Buster Erickson, the biggest sleaze-bag in town, is eyeing to buy Uncle Bill's meadow. Now, how can I, Dusty Murray, just a kid thirteen, stop change?

Cooner says, "Holdin' back change ain't possible. It's like tryin' to stuff a bale of hay into a paper bag. Change can tear life to smithereens." He just turned sixty. He's medium height, with broad shoulders and big strong hands, work worn and calloused. His thinning hair is under a denim cap most of the time. A leathered face and brow show his age; but on meeting folks, he breaks into a broad smile as his alert eyes brighten, and sagging jowls disappear. He's a great guy—like a dad to me.

My real first name is Marcus, but everyone calls me Dusty. Addie started calling me that when I was little. I'd play with our old dog on

1

the banks of the Blue River and come in the house loaded with dust. She'd say, "Goodness, you're dusty."

"Yeah, I'm dusty. Dusty Murray." We'd both laugh.

The meadow's my big worry. Who will end up owning this beautiful land is anybody's guess, but it's important to me because I want to farm someday right here at my Grandpa Thad's place. I'm short and skinny for my age, and some think I'm not cut out for the hard work of farming, but that's my definite plan.

"Yup, good land is scarcer than deerflies in January." Cooner pauses and rubs his forehead, lifting the visor of his cap. We're sitting outside the kitchen door at the farmhouse on old rusty chairs. "The best lies along rivers. It's flat, stone free, and by gum does it ever grow crops." He sniffs and reaches for his red-checkered handkerchief. "Just like the land right here hugging the Blue River."

The meadow has been farmed by my family for over two hundred years, but my Grandpa Thad owns only five acres that surround the barn. "I'm curious. Why was he left such a small part of the meadow?"

Cooner, who got his nickname from his lifelong coon-hunting ability, pulls a package of Union Leader from his back pocket and rests it on his knee. "I've asked myself that question hundreds of times." He packs in a big wad. "I'm told that when your great-grandfather drew up his will, he gave the five acres, a strip of pasture across the Blue River and these buildings to your Grandpa Thad. He gave ninety-five acres, the pines, plus the old homestead to your Uncle Bill."

I turn toward Cooner. "Must be my great-grandfather didn't like Grandpa Thad."

"Maybe so. Your Grandpa Thad has never said and his brother Bill has never said. Sometimes family secrets are hidden forever, but I do know the two ain't spoken since the reading of your great-grandpa's will some fifty years ago." The hinges in the folding chair squeak as he leans back and watches clouds floating over the meadow. The meadow seems to stretch as far as my eyes can see. "Ask your grandpa what took place."

"Ask Grandpa Thad? He's a grump!"

"Anyway, it ain't goin' to make a scat of difference." Cooner's voice sounds resigned as he continues to gaze skyward.

"It will! Someday, I want the meadow for *my* farm! Since I'm a Murray, maybe Uncle Bill will leave me the meadow. "

"Boy, that might not be possible." He turns and places his big hand on mine and gives me a sad look as the tobacco juice starts to trickle down the deep creases at the corners of his mouth. He spits and reaches for his handkerchief and wipes his face. "What you want in life and what you get ain't always a match."

CHAPTER TWO

The school bus squeals to a stop. I dash down the aisle and jump, clearing the steps, but stumble before landing on my feet. Laughter pours behind me. On the run, I charge through the kitchen past Addie who's standing by the sink with her back turned. I head for the bathroom and yank the door closed behind me. The slam rattles the bathroom mirror. Addie's surprised voice filters through the door: "Goodness, what's the hurry?"

The mirror tells it all. There's a bright red outline of lipstick lips on the side of my face where Orla O'Neil planted a kiss. When the bus stopped at her house, on leaving, she bent and sucked on my cheek with a loud *smack*. Everyone seeing it laughed. I mumbled, "The little witch!"

In the bathroom, I eventually feel warm water flowing from the faucet. A soaked washcloth, soap, and hard scrubbing remove the mark. My reflection of a light complexion has turned red on the kissed side of my thin face. I surmise it's the scrubbing that's given me the pink cheek. Running a brush through my short blond hair, and taking one last look, I return to the kitchen. Addie has a glass of milk and a plate of three cookies waiting for me. It's sort of a late afternoon ritual, having a snack and visiting with Addie. I pull out a chair and take my seat. She's sitting at the corner of the table waiting to hear how my day went.

A full-length apron wraps around her barrel figure. Her puffy cheeks broaden with a warm smile as she questions, "Why the big rush?"

"Orla gave me a lipstick kiss and left the bus, laughing. Everyone thought it was a big joke, especially when I turned so everybody could see."

"She's always liked you."

"Yeah. What a way to show it." I swallow a big gulp of milk and bite into a cookie.

"Orla's growin' up and doin' it on her own."

"Yeah, well it's hard for me to feel sorry for her." My words flow through a mouthful.

"You ain't met her mother. You might's well say she ain't got one. The woman's gone all the time." Addie leans forward with her arms and elbows on the table.

"Yeah, that's what Orla tells me." I swallow more milk. Another cookie leaves the plate.

"Mothers are important. I'm sorry you never got to know yours." Her fingers tuck loose hair behind her ear.

"Well, I have you." I'm chewing the last cookie and wash it down with the remaining milk.

Her hand rests on my forearm. "It's been a blessin' raisin' you."

"Thanks, Addie." I push my chair back. "Those molasses cookies were great." I glance at the kitchen counter—several are cooling on racks. I reach and grab one.

"Goodness, you'll spoil your supper." She pushes me gently away from the counter. "Go change, and do your chores."

I head for the stairs. I like my little upstairs room with a single bed, bureau, and a small school desk with a chair. The room's so narrow I can reach the back of the chair while lying in bed. My best clothes hang on the back of the door. A large window at least four feet wide stretches from the floor to the ceiling. I can see the whole farmyard, the meadow, and all the way up the flats to the old Murray homestead where Uncle Bill and his daughter Maggie live.

There's also an old captain's chair I often sit in. It's placed in the alcove in front of the bay window where I can enjoy the view of what I think of as my world.

A large picture of Napoleon hangs in our homeroom at school. He's sitting on a white horse, surveying his kingdom much the way I do mine in my captain's chair. I sort of feel connected to Napoleon because he was a very small man, but he did big things. I'm skinny and small, too, but it won't stop me from dreaming and hopefully accomplishing a lot.

The land, the cows, and the barn are my life. Percolating through my whole being are the smells of newly mown hay, pine sawdust, and contented cows. Inside my head, in some remote place, the farming desire lingers like a satisfying taste. When I'm at school, I feel an invisible tether, an indescribable urge, pulling me back to the land and the barn.

Grandpa milks a small herd of Holstein cows that Cooner says are some of the best around. They're big with huge udders. They just eat, sleep, and make milk. Grandpa takes great pride in his cattle.

They're stabled in a red barn with white trim. It has a wooden silo at the end—the style of barn and silo that artists place in their Vermont landscapes. The Blue River winds its way in back of the farm buildings. The barn sits away from the road, close to our small white farmhouse. Grandpa fixed up the buildings years ago when my great-grandfather gave him the place. He built these two dormer windows on the front and barn-side of the house. They're way too big for the size of the house. In fact, they make the house look so top-heavy that from a distance it appears as though the house could tip over. Grandpa isn't much into style; but since the windows came free from an old demolished mansion, he used them for his house. Cooner, who usually never speaks ill of anybody, laughs and says, "Thad would take anything that's free, even if it's castor oil."

Grandpa keeps the front of the buildings painted to keep the place neat, but the backsides, out of view, never get painted.

I've thought a lot about farming right here where I live—maybe starting with a baby calf. It would be all my own. I'd grow up with my first cow, but it's hopeless to even wish it. I would never dare ask. Grandpa ignores me, and I avoid him. But I do like looking at dairy magazines and dreaming that someday I'll own a herd of beautiful Holsteins.

Last Saturday night around six, the setting sun was filtering through the windows, filling the barn with golden light. I'd bedded the cows, fed the calves, and swept the aisles—all things I like to do. Chores aren't a chore for me. They're as natural and automatic as buttoning my shirt or closing a door.

Cooner had finished milking and left for the house. There were a few minutes before supper to brush some cows—something that's fun for me. The light in the barn was fading as time passed. The sun had nearly set. Most of the cows were resting. Grandpa often worked in near darkness to save on the cost of electricity. He was in the feed alley, sweeping hay to the cows. I could hear the *swish* of the broom. Suddenly I was aware the sound had stopped. I noticed that he was leaning on the broom handle watching me; but I couldn't see his face, just an outline. He spoke in his low thunderous voice. "Uh…gettin' rid of all that winter hair?"

Hearing him talk made me jump. "Yeah—yeah, they like it."

The *swish* continued. That was the most he'd said to me in recent memory. I think he was pleased I was brushing his cows, but of course he didn't say. He lives in back of the house in a small apartment. I don't go there.

I never knew my father and mother. They got killed in a car accident when I was a baby. Cooner and Addie moved into the farmhouse when Grandpa hired them. They raised me, taught me right from wrong, and still care for me as if I was their own.

Just down the flats from Grandpa's farm, Maggie Murray lives with her papa, my great-uncle Bill, at the old Murray homestead. Maggie's my age, tall and slender, and almost always smiling. She's a friend to everyone. I've liked her forever. Uncle Bill and his wife Rosie adopted her as a baby when they were in their fifties; but Rosie died soon after, leaving Uncle Bill to raise Maggie.

Maggie's fraternal twin sister, Orla O'Neil—my pain—lives across the road from the Murray homestead. She might as well live with Uncle Bill and Maggie because she's almost always at their place. Maggie and Orla's birth-mother Zelda O'Neil, Rosie's sister, is a businesswoman who owns a string of flower shops. As far as Cooner knows, she's never had a man in her life. He knows a lot about folks in town, catching the news while on trips to the country store. He's told me, "As a teenager, she had a fling with a carnie she met at the trestle."

Zelda, younger than Rosie by more than fifteen years, couldn't handle twins. Cooner says she couldn't even handle Orla. Bill, with help from Addie and Cooner, really raised both girls.

Orla gives me the creeps. Those dark eyes of hers can fill with incredible mystery. She's read *The Legend of Sleepy Hollow* so many times she has it almost memorized. She loves to talk about the Headless Horseman who rides in the dark of night looking for his head—filling her mind with stuff like that. And her eyes, I swear they have the power to stare down and derail a train if she had a mind to.

For as long as I can remember Orla has said, "I want to be a Murray, too." She could have been if Uncle Bill and Rosie had adopted her with Maggie; but it will never happen, especially now with him being sick.

Orla telling me she wants to be a Murray sends my insides into a deep chill. She wants to marry me someday just so she can be a Murray. At this point, Orla being who she is and just a kid of fourteen, I can't imagine marrying her because I don't like her. She loves to boss me around, and her mysterious powers make me feel uneasy.

I remember just two or three years ago, visiting Uncle Bill and Maggie. Cooner and I had been looking in the pasture across the Blue River for a calf. The fence follows the Blue for some distance. The pasture's narrow, only two to three hundred feet wide in most places. The calf's mother had come to the barn with afterbirth hanging, showing she'd calved. After morning milking, we went out and searched under the willows and along the river in thickets of swamp elders following the fence line but found nothing. Cooner said, "Well, I'll be. We ain't seen a single sign. I've got to go back to the barn and finish chores. Maybe Maggie can help us."

Maggie and Uncle Bill's place is across the river, the meadow, and Murray's Flats. I offered, "I'll walk over and ask."

"Okay. You'll be back for dinner?"

"Yeah, if we find the calf." I slid under the fence and crossed by a white stone at the water's edge. Cooner had told me the rock was quartz, bigger and obvious, resting among the surrounding grays and browns in the river. The Blue River was just a trickle as it quietly wove its way downstream. Flat stones were laid years ago for crossing by ox cart out of an old gravel pit. The crossing made for good footing, since warm sun had dried the slipperiness of the stones sticking out of the water. On Uncle Bill's side of the river, I swung my leg over a rusty, sagging, barbwire fence that hadn't seen a caring hand in years. Uncle Bill's a nice guy, but as Cooner often comments, "He ain't no farmer."

The meadow rose from the river's edge to a level plateau. The pasture is brown and beaten, not at all like Grandpa Thad's across the river—deep green, growing lush grass and clover.

The sun was hot. Uncle Bill's skinny cows were working hard to find a belly-full. Poor things, they were all on the move, heads down in search of some withered grass that might have fought its way to daylight. After walking a considerable distance through paintbrush and sensitive ferns, bent and burdened by the heat, I jumped over the roadside fence, crossed Murray's Flats, and walked into the drive. In back of the house, I climbed the weathered wooden steps and knocked. The old screen door sagged on its hinges. While waiting, I looked at rusted holes in the screen big enough for a crow to pass through. Maggie came to the door. "Dusty! What a surprise!"

"Cooner and I have been looking for a lost calf."

"Come in." She backed from the doorway. "Have a seat." Her honey blond hair rested in shoulder-length curls. She has a slanting smile with a dimple on one side of her face that usually turns red when we meet.

"Hi, Uncle Bill."

He sat at the table, drinking coffee, and immediately stood to shake my hand. I liked the way he made me feel at ease and comfortable. He's a tall, thin guy, with a kindly expression. He doesn't look the age of Cooner and Grandpa who seem hardened by their years and the weather. He sat down, resting his arms on the table. He wore the same blue shirt he always wears—long sleeves and frayed at the collar and cuffs. He turned my way and motioned for me to take a seat. "So, you can't find a calf?"

I pulled out an old wooden chair from the table and sat. "Cooner and I have been looking." Without asking, Maggie placed a glass of orange Kool-Aid and a piece of cake in front of me.

"Thanks, Maggie."

She smiled and turned her back to wash some pots and pans. I could hear the TV from the front room and the familiar theme song of "The Munsters," Orla's favorite show. Eddie Munster was our age. His smile showed fangs, and he sported a wizard's haircut which made him look as if he was from outer space. If Orla wasn't so stuck on wanting to be a Murray, I swear, she'd like to hook up with this kid. They'd make a great pair.

Having heard me, she came charging into the kitchen. She wasn't more than eleven at the time. The neck of her shirt was pulled up, covering her hair. "Wooo, I'm the Headless Horseman."

None of us reacted.

She reappeared through the opening in her short-sleeved jersey, collected her black hair and pushed it away from her brown face. Her black lashes and black eyebrows framed her dark stare. "Hi, Dusty." Her voice had her usual sickening whine. She pulled up a chair and sat beside me.

"Hi." At the moment, she embarrassed me. She was in her other world, way beyond anything I cared about. I hated that I even knew her.

Slumping her shoulders, she said, "Everyone around here is so serious. What have you been up to? I'll bet it's more exciting than this place. How boring!"

"Trying to find a lost calf isn't boring."

She pulled something from around her neck. "See the locket Bill gave me that Rosie wore."

"Gee, that's beautiful." I opened it. "Whose picture and hair?" Both were under inlaid glass.

"My grandmother's." She closed it and turned over the circular gold piece of jewelry—the size of a half-dollar. "See the initials OO. That's me. Orla O'Neil, my grandmother's name."

"Neat!" I passed it back to her. "Don't lose it."

"Don't worry. It will be with me forever and it will give me power."

Maggie, with her back turned, laughed.

Uncle Bill lifted an eyebrow. He drank from his cup and placed it in the saucer. "If you don't find that calf today, the coyotes will take it tonight. The mother and her pups will have it stripped clean by morning. I hear them howling and yapping most nights across the river on the ridge."

"Yeah, I know. I don't know what more we can do. We've looked everywhere."

Maggie continued working, not commenting, cleaning the sink with a dish cloth.

Orla sat with elbows resting on the table. Her dark brown eyes glared at the locket in her hand. "I see something white and hard that might be a rock and a tree."

Orla grabbed my forearm. "Let's go and find that calf."

"You don't see anything. Anyway, there're a lot of willows. The quartz stone is by the river. We all know that." I watched her serious expression. She gazed intently at her locket, claiming it to be the source of her power. At least that's what she was trying to make us believe.

"I see a lone tree. Walk from the stone to the tree. You'll find the calf." She got up. "Let's go."

"I told you we've been looking for the last two hours." I thought of what Uncle Bill just said about the coyotes killing it tonight. "Maggie, can you come?"

"I've got too much to do right here." Maggie snickered. "Go with the little witch; she'll cast a spell and *whoosh,* the calf will appear." She continued to scrub the sink with cleanser in one hand and the dish rag in the other.

Orla snapped, "You'll see! Maggie's just jealous that *I* have powers she doesn't. So there! You may be a Murray, but I can see things most people can't."

"Yeah, right," Maggie said.

I checked Orla's eyes and her stare sent a shiver through me.

She was headed for the door. "We'll see."

Uncle Bill warned, "Stay clear of that old gravel bed. Years ago a man got killed in there, buried in an avalanche of gravel."

I followed Orla through the door. "We shouldn't be anywhere near the gravel pit. It's a ways beyond the pasture."

Outside in the heat and hot sun, she clung to my arm with a sweaty hand grabbing my wrist. As we walked, she swung her head to face me. Since I was knobby-kneed, and skinny, my legs and feet strayed off an even path. I stepped on her foot and started to stumble. "Gosh, Orla, let's just walk normal."

"I like being close."

"Well, it's too hot." I was only going with her because I wanted to find the calf before the coyotes did. Uncle Bill was right. I'd seen what a mother coyote and her young could do—stripping the poor thing like surgeons, leaving only hide, some bones, and a skull. Orla made up the white stone and tree, just so she could be with me. I knew the way she thinks, figuring how we can be together.

"I like you lots, Dusty."

At that point, I didn't want to be blunt. Maybe she could help me find the calf. "We can be friends, but don't hang on me. It's too hot."

"Okay."

After we crossed the river, she sat on the white rock which was just outside the pasture fence. She squinted toward the ridge, on the edge of the dug-out section of the old pit. "See that lone tree?"

"Yeah." I stood with my hand shading the bright noonday sun. "That's a stray pine not far from the upper edge of the pit. It's next to Grandpa Murray's pine stand. The calf can't be way up there. It's outside the pasture, and the bank's too steep."

"Well, from this stone, head toward that pine." She sat with a smug expression, a fistful of her black hair pulled over her shoulder, rubbing the ends with her other hand. The sun brightened the gold locket, resting against her shirt.

"If I follow a straight line to the tree, I'll be in the pit."

"Walk from this rock to the tree. Do as I say."

I started walking. "There's no calf in this pit. I'm way outside the fence!"

She continued to sit, looking as though she was directing the universe. "Keep going!"

I did for about ten more feet. What a surprise! I found the calf curled in a ball, hidden behind a big boulder that had rolled from the gravel bank. I looked closely across the fence and saw clear dried birthing fluid that Cooner and I had missed. Apparently the calf wobbled or rolled under the bottom wire of the fence and walked behind the stone to bed down. I yelled, "I found the calf!"

"Of course—I told you!"

That was a few years ago. She hasn't changed.

—— CHAPTER THREE ——

I'm pushing my bike pedals hard. Hard enough so after a few turns, it feels like I'm pumping air. My feet are ready to fly off the pedals. I ride into the Town Hall yard and skid to a stop. It's spring—the last 4-H meeting of the year. Shirley Iverson is our leader. She's sure nice—like a second mother. Since I don't have one, except for Addie, I think of her that way. As Shirley's getting out of her truck, I notice her all-white hair glistening in the afternoon sun. She's slender, medium height, and always has a ready smile. Her hair is no match for her age of about forty. Her brown eyes blend well with her tan and the dark brown blouse and blue jeans she's wearing. "Hi, Shirley." I take the box she's carrying. "What's going on today?"

"Oh, a surprise." She grins, causing a slight curl at the corners of her mouth. She moves, acting youthful and full of energy. "How have you been?"

"Good. Cooner and I planted a few acres of corn a couple a weeks ago in Uncle Bill's meadow." I hold the box under my arm and open the door for her. "Other than that, nothing much has happened."

"Thanks. You have the calf yet that you've wanted?" She walks through the doorway, pausing for my answer.

"No."

"It's time you got one." She continues walking toward the front of the hall as I follow. "4-H can teach you a lot about raising a calf."

"Yeah, I know, but it's Grandpa Thad." I place the box on a table in front of the room. Kids are entering as I help set up the U.S. and 4-H flags, plus the podium with the gavel.

"Well, I think a project of owning a calf is important. Something you should be doing." She bends and places the box under the table.

"Maybe so, but not at Grandpa's place."

"Ask if you can have a calf!" When Shirley stands, she automatically resets the silver barrette she always wears.

"You don't know him."

"No. I've never met the man."

"That's because he never leaves the farm."

"Talk to him!" She says it with force, almost as a command.

"There's a reason folks call him Mad Thad."

"I'd like to meet him someday."

"Come to the farm."

"When I get a chance, I will."

Her eyebrows jump when Orla comes through the door. She's plastered on white makeup to cover her naturally dark coloring—contrasting a lighter face with black mascara. The dark mascara accentuates her already spooky eyes. With her black hair, a black low-cut blouse, and dangling earrings, she looks ready for The Grand Ole Opry, not a 4-H meeting. We both take a seat. Maggie hurries in at the last minute.

Orla, our 4-H president, opens the meeting with a gavel: *bang, bang, bang.* "The meeting will come to order."

I notice Shirley wince, but she says nothing. Orla wasn't elected out of popularity, she demanded the position. We all, like fools, voted for her.

She pauses and stands with one hand on her hip as if she's at a fashion show. The room is silent. She's making us twenty kids gawk at her with her chest out, acting like the Queen of Sheba. She could be, too, because at fourteen she looks more like twenty and obviously loves the fact. I'm thinking: okay, we all know how weird you are.

She finally says, "Let's all stand for the salute to the flags." She leads us in the Pledge of Allegiance and the 4-H Pledge. She smiles my way, enjoying her role as the grand director.

After reciting the pledges, she checks the order of the meeting. "I guess we *have* to sing a song."

Maggie, our song leader, walks up front with her big smile, faded jeans, and a powder-blue T-shirt with three yellow daisies on the front. "Let's sing *This Little Light of Mine.*"

We sort of mumble the words from our song books while Maggie carries the tune. Her voice is beautiful. I notice Orla doesn't join in. She's acting busy, glancing at the business meeting booklet. She doesn't even thank Maggie and calls for the secretary's report of the last meeting, which is my responsibility.

I begin, "April, 1970. . ."

After my report, Shirley stands and announces, "We've been asked, along with other clubs, by the Fair Director to have a special 4-H display. I'm excited about this opportunity because we, The Huntersville Hustlers, have a lot to be proud of."

We all cheer.

"I want all of you to work especially hard on your projects so we'll be ready by fall."

"So is this the surprise?" I ask.

"Yes. That's another reason for you to have a calf. We've been provided a big space to display projects; and as usual, there will be the 4-H cattle show."

After the meeting, Shirley comments, "I'll make it a point to meet your grandfather."

"Thanks, Shirley. Good luck." I jump on my bike, wondering how a Shirley and Grandpa visit might go. Not too hot, I'll bet.

—— CHAPTER FOUR ——

As I ride down Murray's Flats toward home, I'm eager to see what's going on at the farm. The cool breeze flutters through my blond hair and slides down the front of my shirt, giving me a snowball-down-the-shirt chill. The "Dusty" nameplate wired to the back of my seat clatters in the wind. My chin is nearly touching the handlebars, with my sleeves filling with air. My light jacket looks like a balloon with puffy arms. It makes me feel twice my size, bigger than anyone I know. Even though I'm due to have my fourteenth birthday, I'm the shortest, skinniest boy in my eighth-grade class.

I keep pumping my bike. My legs are beginning to ache so much they feel like they're ready to fall off. Sitting back to relax, I check the corn growing in the field at the side of the road. It seems to be jumping out of the ground.

It was fun planting it. We borrowed Uncle Bill's equipment since we helped him with haying the previous summer. The two-bottom plow, hooked by a three-point hitch, pulled easily through the light sandy loam. After the seven acres were finished, I harrowed the land. It smoothed as easily and level as the road on Murray's Flats. Grandpa's Massey Ferguson "50" had plenty of power to do the work.

The week of May 10, Cooner greased and oiled Uncle Bill's two-row, horse-drawn corn planter. He cut off the pole and pulled it with the tractor. I sat on the planter seat. Every time a kernel of corn dropped, the seed hopper, the size of a milk pail, clicked. The blade of the shoe below the hopper separated the soil for the seed. The wheels of the planter pressed and closed the opening. At the end of the row, my job was to lift the marker arm with a rope. When Cooner turned the tractor, straddling the line in the soil, I dropped the marker for the return pass. In two or three hours we had the corn planted.

Cooner told me that our corn would grow on one of the best pieces of land anywhere. He should know because during his coon-hunting days, he traveled the country far and wide. He told me with the voice of regret, "In another year the meadow may be growin' houses instead of corn."

Grandpa Thad says he's losing money on his cows. That's why we're growing corn: so we can feed the herd corn silage and make lower-cost milk. It was Cooner's and my idea to grow the corn in hopes of keeping the cows.

Finally, I stop pumping and just coast on my bike. My lungs feel like they are blowing flames. Slobber covers my chin; I swipe my sleeve across my mouth. Suddenly, a thunderous *burrr* blasts my ears. A car zips past so fast, it feels like I'm tied in place. My one hand on the handlebars jerks the front wheel into the rough, and in a split second the bike is headed toward the ditch. The front wheel stops dead when it hits a big stone. I fly off my seat and over the handlebars, sailing headfirst into the corn. I land facedown on soft dark soil. For a few seconds, there is no question but what I'm dead. After a while, I blink my eyes. My body has just flattened a bunch of three-inch-high corn plants.

With the palms of my hands pressed in the ground, I sit up and check—no blood. Licking my lips, I spit and spit to rid my mouth of grit. Without realizing there's still some back on my tongue, I gulp down a little of the stuff. Feeling the dirt going down causes me to cough a couple of times. Pulling clods off my face, I look at the soil as it crumbles in my hand. It has to be saved. This stuff is like magic. Although the soft loam I'm holding is only a handful, it's worth more than gold. It can grow a corn seed in May into a huge plant by September. This soil is greater than all the great natural wonders of the world I've been studying about in geography. If this stuff can grow a corn plant so fast, I wish it could do the same for me, but really, what a joke.

It must look strange, a dirt-faced kid sitting in a corn field. But it feels more okay to me than it would to anyone else because this meadow is a part of me. It's had the name Murray tied to it for as long as land records have been kept. At least that's what Cooner tells me.

Down the road at the farm where I live, squealing tires blast my ears. In seconds, a black Ford screeches to a stop where I took my swan-dive with no water. It's Eddie LaQuine; we kids call him Snaky.

He's just turned sixteen, and just started racing his hot Ford on the flats. What a jerk!

He wears his hair Elvis-style. He dumps plenty of hair-goop on it, and you can smell the stuff a mile away. "Hey, Dusty, you eatin' dirt for supper?" He lets out a donkey laugh. "How do you like my new mufflers?"

He swings his door open and shows me a lever he pulls to make his car sound ear-splitting loud. He floors the engine, *burrr*. The car shakes and it sounds like it could explode.

His eyes are almost black, with black bushy eyebrows. When he talks or smiles, he shows gold caps on his front teeth. The comb in his shirt pocket is in continual use. He slides it straight back through his thick hair, leaving a greasy mat. He automatically drops the comb into his pocket, and slams the door while popping the clutch. Black rubber smoke rolls off the pavement. He leaves about ten feet of burning vapors that rise from the cement.

I mumble, "Snaky! I can't stand him!" Again, I can hear, off in the distance, squealing tires as he pulls into the old Murray homestead. Snaky's the biggest pea-brain in town. Maybe in the whole U. S. of A. I think he likes his nickname, but for different reasons. He thinks it's cool and sorta scary, but I like it because there isn't anybody I know that is as lowdown as Eddie "Snaky" LaQuine.

He works part-time for Uncle Bill, who needs the help because he's ailing. I stand and brush more black dirt off my shirt, mumbling that I'm lucky not having to be near the creep like last summer when we were both helping Uncle Bill with haying. I jump back on my bike thinking about what Cooner said: "With Bill ailin', the meadow might not always be farmed by a Murray." The seeds of change were planted a year ago when Uncle Bill sold his cows.

— CHAPTER FIVE —

After my spill, I ride into the yard and follow a path under a maple tree that grows on a mound at the edge of the lawn. Lifting myself off my bike seat, I let the lower leaves brush my muddy hair. It makes me feel tall, but I'm just dreaming.

Slue, Cooner's dog, is tied at her doghouse by the corner of the barn. He got her as a pup, a few years back, and trained her for coon hunting. Having seen me, she starts to bark and whine. I jump off my bike, and slide my hand over her smooth head and along her back. "Have you missed me, Slue?" She answers with a low-throated whine. She's a black and tan, known at one time to be the best coon dog in town. Cooner says that a good coon dog needs to be kept tied.

He'll never admit it, but he won't ever go hunting again. He's lost interest in it, and besides pelts aren't worth much. The night a big male coon almost drowned Slue in a deep pool of the Blue River was the last time he went. He told me, "I thought Slue was a goner, but she struggled free, retchin' water."

I unsnap her chain and push my bike to where Cooner's working in the shed in back of the barn. Slue wags her tail, rubbing against my leg as we move along. Cooner's getting the haying equipment ready for our first cutting. He stops his work and pulls a stem of orchard grass growing beside an outside post of the shed. "By golly, this grass is gettin' ripe." He bites the soft end. "It pulls easy, but it ain't stayin' that way long."

Slue flops down in the shade and rests her head on the cool ground. Cooner glances at her. There's a pause as he munches. The stem of grass sways with the movement of his mouth. He pushes the visor of his cap with his thumb, and rubs his forehead. "You ain't makin' this a habit. I told you before, coon dogs ain't s'pose to run free."

"Okay." I'm not about to remind him that he'll never go hunting again. I change the subject, and pull a head of grass. "I like chewing this stuff."

He pulls his hat back in place, and stares me up and down. "What in thunder happened to you? Looks like you've been rollin' in dirt."

"I took a spill on the flats when Snaky—er—Eddie passed me. He must've been going ninety miles an hour. That loud muffler of his—the jerk!"

"He's a wild one all right. With the likes of Eddie racin' on the flats, it's a dangerous place to be."

"Yeah, I know."

Cooner's expression changes as if a big storm cloud has just covered the deep wrinkles on his face. "I saw your Uncle Bill today. He sold all his hay by the bale to Buster Erickson, the crook." *Crook* sort of flows from his mouth in a whisper as an afterthought. "Bill's mighty sick."

"I know. Maggie told me."

"She needs your help," Cooner says. "Eddie will be loadin' hay. Be sure to count the bales as they leave the barn. I don't want Bill cheated."

I throw my head back. "You mean I've got to help Snaky?" I stare in disbelief at Cooner as his mouth, with those deep lines on either side, sets firmly in an expression of determination. "Maggie just told me her papa was sick. She didn't say she'd be loading hay."

"Well, she wouldn't. Sometimes it's best to do things you ain't been asked." He spits and bites onto more stem of the grass. "Sick as Bill is, he ain't able to leave the house."

"Okay, I *guess* I can help."

"Go wash up, change your clothes. I'll put your bike in the back of the pickup. You'll get there faster, but you be careful comin' home."

He spits chewed grass, ending his sentence with authority.

I watch the stream of green juice soak into the gravel. Then I hear his urging, "Get goin', boy!" Slue jumps up and follows.

I run toward the house. Cooner's words hit me like a big soft pillow. They get me going but they never hurt. I run through the entry and into the kitchen. Addie is standing by the kitchen counter, rolling out pie dough. "Hi, Addie."

She moves to the sink, rinses her hands of flour, and turns. She smiles, but her round puffy face quickly changes. "My goodness, look at you!"

"Yeah, I took a spill." Slue flops on the kitchen floor.

"Were you hurt?

"No."

"Thank heavens." She continues her baking. With her back turned, I glance at her gray hair pulled in a tight bun. Her fleshy arms and hands move quickly on the handles of the rolling pin, flattening the pie dough. Without stopping, she says, "I'll have a snack for you after you change, and bring those dirty clothes down from your room. I'll put them soaking." The *clank* of the rolling pin continues as I climb the stairs to my room. I hear her say as she's working, "Thad will throw a fit if I have to buy new clothes for the boy."

Although the Thad Murray place is the neatest farm around, it really isn't much of a farm. Grandpa Thad rents most of the hay land he needs around town.

A good many times Cooner, Grandpa Thad, and I will stand at our fence line and look at all that land that belongs to Uncle Bill. It usually only grows dried-out grass, goldenrod, and ferns. Grandpa will grumble, "Bill ain't much of a farmer."

On hot summer nights, he'll sit in a lawn chair at the end of the barn just gazing out over the meadow. It's a restful place to be because our end of the field rises slightly, making it possible to see the whole hundred acres. The Blue River sweeps around on the edge of the meadow. The river has willows growing along its banks. The trees make a perfect place for all sorts of birds to nest. Kestrels swoop and dive, hunting for field mice. Deer come down from the hills at twilight, cross the river, and feed. The only commotion on Murray's Flats, besides Snaky, comes on a Sunday night. That's when the dirt-track races let out. For an hour or so the flats are jam-packed with cars.

But Grandpa always keeps his sights on the meadow—brooding with a scowl, looking as though he could bite your ear off if you even dared come near him.

Cooner told me, "He don't sit there to enjoy the scenery. He's just nursing his fifty-year-old grudge."

—— CHAPTER SIX ——

Cooner and I climb into his old Chevy pickup. Slue is right behind and leaps into the back. The truck chatters in reverse—sputters and bucks as we move slowly forward onto Murray's Flats. Cooner, wearing his usual bib-overalls, is not himself. The deep weathered lines at the corners of his mouth turn down. He rubs his forehead. "Your uncle Bill and I have had a lot of good times over the years. Poor guy, I hated to see him today—the way he acted and all. Funny thing, we being close all these years, then this happens."

"How come you never worked for him?" I look his way. "You're good friends."

"I wanted to. I wanted it bad—to get my hands on that meadow and grow the crops I know it can." He glances over the passing scenery. "Bill was never the farmer your Grandpa Thad is. He was always sayin' he couldn't afford to hire me."

I add, "He needed help when he and Rosie adopted Maggie from Zelda, didn't he?"

"He sure did, especially after Rosie died. Thinkin' back on the situation, I guess it was a blessin' I never worked for him because workin' for somebody and bein' friends ain't the same. It might have loused up all the good times we had." He slows for a bird in the road. "Besides, Addie and I had you to tend to, and sometimes Maggie and Orla."

I look over the truck's dashboard, which is littered with dusty chewing gum wrappers, a box of shotgun shells, and rusty bolts, nuts, and nails. The odd collection vibrates as we rumble along. Over the loud hum of the motor, I ask, "What will happen to Maggie if—well—you know?"

"I've been thinkin' about that. Maybe she can come and live with us."

I smile. "I'd like that. What about Grandpa?"

"I wonder. The hate he has for his brother runs as deep and hard as if a spike was driven clear through his heart."

"Just because he hates Uncle Bill, he doesn't have to hate Maggie."

"You're right. Maybe he don't. We'll see."

The truck continues to chug along. Cooner's in deep thought. I guess he's trying to figure out a way Grandpa can get to know Maggie. Even though she lives at the end of the flats, she might as well live in China as far as Grandpa's concerned. Seems impossible to say, but I don't think he'd know who she is even if they bumped head-to-head. Our neighboring only goes one way on Murray's Flats: the way we're headed.

I glance out my window. Slue's bracing herself against the wind with eyes shut, and ears snug to her head, loving the breeze bath.

Cooner clears his throat and says, "I'll have to talk to Addie. She could put on a little extra at mealtime. Well—well, we're gettin' ahead of ourselves." Then he frowns. "Now, don't take any lip from Eddie— stand right up to him."

"Yeah, that's easy to say. Just remember, Maggie claims he lifts weights."

"But you're twice as smart." Cooner turns to me. "That's what counts."

He's always saying I'm smart, so much so that I halfway believe him. I do well in school, better than most kids, but I still wish I were bigger and stronger. Cooner keeps telling me I have to be patient, that I haven't gotten my growth spurt yet. That might be true, but if ever I get a sucker punch from Muscleman Snaky, I'll probably be going to my own funeral.

—— CHAPTER SEVEN ——

The truck enters the yard of the Murray place, passing between two giant elm trees that grow on either side of the drive. I remember the few times I stayed overnight. If there was a wind, the limbs would whip and sway right next to the spare bedroom. When the breeze was strong enough, the tip ends would brush the window, sounding like bird claws scratching glass.

The buildings badly need painting. They're weathered and sad. The house and barn stand big and tall though, and underneath the shabby look you can tell that at one time someone had taken pride in the place. That someone was my great-grandfather, Marcus Murray, the guy who built the buildings. Cooner told me that he had been a real good farmer. I'm proud to know that, because my great-grandfather's name is my given name—Marcus Jacob Murray.

Snaky's sitting behind the wheel of Uncle Bill's truck, trying to drive. He's jerking it back and forth, grinding gears, and racing the engine as smoke pours out the exhaust. I park my bike and hear the back door slam. Maggie is running down the steps. "Dusty! What are you doing here?" Her long wavy blond hair drops off her shoulders.

"I've come to help load hay."

"Gee, that's great!" She stands with arms and elbows raised, wrapping her hair into a folded roll, and covering her head with a bandanna. She's a good head taller than me, even though we're both the same age.

As she tucks hair under the checkered cloth, protecting it from hayseed and dust, she walks toward me with a big, friendly grin. She always has that smile even with her dad being sick. It must worry her, but it never shows.

The screen door slams again. Orla leans over the railing of the steps. "Hi, Dusty." Her voice has that usual sickening quality. Hearing her whining tone puts me on guard. It's similar to calling the hens, catching the closest one for a chicken dinner. She has a plan. At the same time, she glances in Snaky's direction, dying to be noticed. She's wearing a V-neck sweater. Snaky drives the truck close to the steps and blows the horn. He's laughing in the cab as Orla quickly stands erect and giggles. She throws her shoulders back and walks to where Maggie and I are standing. "Dusty, want to go swimming at the trestle after you load hay?" Her dark brown eyes zoom in on me, demanding me to say yes.

I turn away from her beckoning stare and glance at the gravel underfoot. Her eyes remind me of winter nights I slept at Uncle Bill's. The wind howled and the limbs of the giant elm cast moon shadows across the darkened room. When a big blow hammered against the house, shadows of the lacy twigs skittered over the musty walls. Watching those shadows scared me half to death.

At the moment, she's staring at me, waiting for a reply. I imagine those eyes have those dark creepy shadows, trying to break my resistance. My throat goes dry and my jaw stiffens. "I—I can't. I've got to help at home."

Her eyes open wider. She glares and stamps her foot. "Oh darn! You don't have to work all the time."

I quickly grasp for an excuse. "No, but—but I—I've never been to the trestle."

She leans toward me, exerting her power. "How about Saturday? We can go then!"

Maggie quickly remarks, "Saturday? We?" She glares at Orla. "You know I have housework."

"I wasn't asking *you.*" She turns her back on Maggie. Orla lightly pushes my shoulders, grabbing my attention. "It's time you grew up and did things with just me for a change!"

She knows me like I know the walk to the barn. This growing-up thing is a tender subject, and she senses when to use it like a crowbar to pry on my resistance. I feel cold chills just thinking of striking off with Orla, but at the same time I want to show everybody that I'm a big kid—that I can handle a new adventure on my own. Without any further thought, the words pop out of my mouth. "Okay, I'll go after I do my chores."

She jumps off the ground, wearing a smirk of self-satisfaction. "Give me a ride on your bike. I can't wait!"

I want to blurt, "I can wait." I recall the last time I went swimming with Orla, when we were little kids. That day was also the last time Orla and Maggie were allowed to come to my place. The swimming hole is up the river in back of the barn. Cooner dug out a pool in the middle of the Blue for us kids to use. In the summer, the river runs shallow, making it handy to sit on rocks and splash around in the knee-deep water. I was wading in the pool with Orla and Maggie. That was the summer all three of us were entering first grade. After a while, Orla had the idea that we should take off our bathing suits. She had heard the term *skinny dipping* and thought it would be fun to try. So she took off her suit. Her skin was as brown and smooth as chocolate milk.

Maggie sat on a rock at the opposite end of the pool, swishing the water with the flat of her hand. "I'm not doing it!"

Orla demanded, "Come on, Dusty, take yours off!"

"No, I won't!" I held tightly to the band of my swimsuit.

"Come on, take your suit off." She flashed those domineering eyes at me.

I was out of Maggie's reach, but hoping she would say something. But she continued splashing the water, acting disinterested.

Orla wouldn't let up. "Come on, Dusty."

I gripped my suit tighter. "No!"

In a flash she yanked my hands away and pulled my trunks down to my knees. I screamed, "Orla!"

"Orla, stop!" Maggie was on her feet wading toward me. Our old dog started barking. Before Maggie could reach me, I howled again, "Orla!"

My cry for help stirred the whole Thad Murray place. I tried, but I couldn't get her to release her hands.

Finally Maggie slapped Orla and she let go. I looked up. Addie, Cooner, and Grandpa Thad were standing on the bank with horror written all over their faces. I started crying while pulling up my suit.

Orla was laughing, but not for long.

Grandpa Thad spoke sternly, sounding as if he was rescuing me from the devil. "Get those girls away from here! I don't want them around the place."

I don't think he even knew who they were. He ignored them most of the time. However, being an adult of his age, and not familiar with kids, I'm sure he believed he'd just witnessed disgusting behavior. I heard the pickup doors slam, and the truck left the yard. That was the last time the girls were at the Thad Murray place.

Now, years later, I'm understandably nervous mulling over Orla wanting to swim at the trestle. For one thing, I'm sure that no one will see me bare naked. And I certainly won't be changing anywhere near her. I quickly say, "I'm sorry you can't come with us, Maggie."

Maggie scowls. "Orla, that's only a place for big kids."

Orla whines, "Maggie," and throws her shoulders back. "I'm just as grown-up as anybody."

Even though Maggie is trying to protect me, the thought of not being old enough bugs me. The desire to be an adult sweeps away all my fears. I want to go to show Maggie I can manage any situation.

I firmly remark, "I'm going!"

Orla flashes a smile of satisfaction. "I'll see you Saturday around ten." She leaves and walks across the road to her house.

I turn to look, and notice the hay barn door is open. Snaky has driven the truck near the door, but it's not yet in any position for loading. He's acting all business, fiddling with ropes gathered from the truck and thrown on the ground. They'll be needed to tie on the load. I chuckle to myself as I watch Maggie. She swings the truck door open, jumps in, starts the engine, and backs within inches of the haymow door.

Snaky clears his throat and walks past me as if I'm invisible. He wears a silver chain clipped to his pants. It loops below his beltline to a big leather wallet he carries in his back pocket. I sneer, thinking that it's just for show. He thinks he's a big shot.

He swaggers toward the truck, acting important like he'd just invented sunshine, saying to Maggie, "I was plannin' to get the truck closer to the door after I got the hay ropes all set."

I mumble under my breath, "Yeah, right, you can't even drive a baby carriage." Without expecting it, I let out a big snicker.

He must realize the truth about his ability to handle the truck; but just the same, when he hears my reaction, he jams his comb through his Elvis-style hair. With comb in hand, his squinty eyes and face are in an ugly twist within inches of me. Then I smell his sickening sweet hair goop. I have an urge to hold my nose and open my mouth in a big gag; but instead, I back up and turn my head. He doesn't say anything, but his ugly expression is scary.

I remember all too well that previous summer during haying. He stood in the truck, loading, and I was on the ground throwing the bales. Often, when I went for the next bale, he'd show me his peach tattoo. Standing on the back of the truck, shirtless, with a tan as brown as the earth, he'd flex his upper right arm saying, "Look, Dusty." Then he'd laugh that stupid donkey laugh of his. It was amazing to watch. With his muscle relaxed, he has a tattoo that looks like a dried apricot. That day, as his muscle bulged, the tattoo turned into a full-blown, pink-and-red juicy peach. With his fist clenched as solid as a hammer, he'd laugh and say, "Anyone that messes with Snaky gets my peach punch."

Presently, as I expect, Maggie takes charge. "Snaky, you throw the bales to me at the door and I'll throw them onto the truck. Dusty can build the load."

She's speaking for my benefit. She knows placing the bales is the easy job. Running his comb through his slick hair, he sneers, "Let the little dirt-eater get up in the mow. I'm buildin' my own load."

Maggie loses her pleasant expression. "Okay, but cut the talk. Dusty's here to help!"

I adjust my eyes to the dimness of the haymow. The light through the cracks in the boarding casts a soft yellow against the brown hay. I start grabbing the thirty-pound bales by the strings, throwing them to Maggie where she stands at the door. The bales stir a sweet hay scent as they land at her feet. The pleasing smell fills the mow. Hay dust can be seen where rays of light bounce off the tiny particles suspended in the thick haymow air.

Cooner has no need to worry over the bale count. Maggie takes care of that; I can hear her whispering, "Fifty-five—fifty-six—fifty-seven."

Thankfully, last summer Uncle Bill had adjusted the baler to make small thirty-pound bales, because, as it was, I was doing plenty of grunting when I picked them up. I thought Uncle Bill made the bales small because he was sick, and maybe, too, he thought of me. I hated to admit I was weak, but I would have found it hard to handle the hay if the bales were any heavier. Uncle Bill and Maggie are the same in the way they do nice things for me without making a big deal over it.

All during haying, Uncle Bill drove the tractor as the plunger of the baler pumped, dropping bales in rows. He was well enough then to drive a tractor even though he looked pale and thin, wearing his fishing hat and a worn work shirt. He humped over the steering wheel like he was holding on for dear life. Having sold his cows that spring, he had no cattle to graze the meadow. He was able to hay more land than usual, hoping to raise enough money to pay his taxes.

In between loads, Snaky would take a minute to visit with Uncle Bill, probably telling him some news or his latest joke. I remember seeing him leaning on the tractor fender, and both of them laughing. That amazed me. It didn't matter who it was, Uncle Bill visited with anyone, even the likes of Snaky LaQuine.

Snaky kept reminding me that we were handling midget-sized bales. When I'd go for the next one, sliding my hands under the strings, he'd show me his peach. After a while it got to be pretty disgusting. With one hand, he'd throw a bale the length of the truck like it was some powder puff—then he'd flash me his dumb smile and say, "Look at that."

I looked, all right, at the silver chain dangling at his side. It glistened from the bright sun. I wanted to jump up and grab it, pulling him off the back end of the truck. Then to add to my misery he asked, "How about goin' to the races with me next Sunday?"

He laughed, showing his gold teeth, already realizing I couldn't go, knowing he'd struck a sore subject with me. All my friends went. I didn't give him the satisfaction of an answer. He kept being nasty. "What—do Cooner and Addie think you're too good?"

At that instant, I felt like walking away. Snaky was really making me mad, because he was right. Cooner and Addie usually let me do as I wanted; but they had some rules, saying the race crowd's too rowdy with a lot of drinkin' goin' on. But all my friends say they have a good time, and I know they don't drink. I'd see my friends, riding their bikes past the house on a Sunday, heading toward the races. Late in the afternoon after the races finished, they'd return, traveling faster on their bikes than the line of slow-moving traffic.

Snaky was being a jerk of the highest order. Maybe he says mean things to me because he's strong and I'm weak. Maybe, too, it's because I'm Thad Murray's grandson, and he's a LaQuine. Grandpa has never been very friendly with anyone, especially the LaQuine family. They live in a junk heap of a house. Cooner said, as a kid, when Snaky's father came home drunk, Snaky got a licking whether he needed it or not. Maybe it's true, but I still hate having to work with the guy.

Last summer, after the truck was half loaded, Maggie looked out the window and saw my face. It must have been about as red as Slue's tongue. I could feel the sweat dripping off my chin and my soaked tee-shirt stuck to my back. The truck door flew open, and Maggie strutted to the back of the truck. "Snaky LaQuine, you get down here and throw the bales up to Dusty."

He did just as she said and jumped to the ground. With my back turned, I climbed up into the truck with a big smile. Maggie can rule with her voice. I like that. The rest of the summer, she saw to it that Snaky and I took turns picking up bales.

Now, loading the hay from the barn, Maggie continues to whisper, "Hundred and twenty—twenty-one—twenty-two. We're just about loaded, Dusty."

I close my stiff hands and feel the burning from the bale strings. My fingers have turned soft since last summer. Maggie is out on the load telling Snaky where to place the last few bales. She yells to me in the barn, "We'll take one more to top off the load."

Snaky is bent over, pushing a bale in place with his back to the door. I look at his rear with that silver chain dangling. I want to show him that I can throw a bale from the barn, out the door, and onto the middle of the load.

I think of watching big kids throw the shot-put at high school. They spin, twist, and with the ball in their hand, throw it forward. It flies in an arch as if it's as light as a snowball. I want to try the same with a bale, to show Snaky.

Standing with my back to the door, I hold one knee high. I draw a deep breath and puff up all my strength. Turning and throwing the bale, my arms fling open and it leaves my hands so slick and easy, I can hardly believe it's me. Bull's eye! Without my intending it to, the bale hits Snaky's rear. He lets out a *huff* and dives forward, landing flat-out on the hay. With his face smashed in a bale, a mumbling line of words and threats comes out of him that would scare the biggest of kids. For a moment, I stand in shock.

Maggie smiles. She adjusts her bandanna, waiting for Snaky to stand. I quickly close the door, climb down the haymow ladder, shut off the light, and run out the barn door. Pumping my bike hard, I'm on Murray's Flats in a matter of seconds. I yell, "I'll see you tomorrow night."

Snaky screams, "Yeah, I'll see you tomorrow night, too."

All the way home, I laugh. However, I shudder a little, too, admitting to myself that, by accident, I've done a dumb thing. If he ever gets a hand on me, I'll sure have a bumblebee-sting-in-the-butt day.

After whizzing into our yard and following the bike path worn in the grass under the maple tree, I park by the barn door. Slue barks and whines. I let her free and walk into the barn with her following. Cooner's milking, squatting by a cow, about to take off the milking machine. He slips the cover off the forty-pound pail and looks down. It's full. "Your grandfather's got these cows milkin' like thunder. I don't see's they can do much better feedin' them corn silage."

"So, why did we grow corn?" I sit on a stool with Slue resting at my feet.

"If your Grandpa can feed corn, he won't have to buy as much cow grain."

The twenty-five cows stand in contented fashion. They search with their muzzles. Grandpa has just grained them. They're hoping for any morsels they might have missed. Their black-and-white coats shine like polished cars.

The barn smells fresh from the pine sawdust bedding. Cooner looks up with a mouth full of tobacco and spits a stream of juice into the gutter. "You loaded the hay okay?"

"Yeah, Maggie counted. We got on about a hundred and twenty-five. The best or worst of all—I fixed Snaky. I smacked him in the rear with a bale. He flew like a leap frog on top of the load, spreading out as flat as a cow flop."

Cooner spits again. "Now you're happy?"

"Yes and no—more like scared. I wish I didn't have to help load tomorrow night."

"You aimin' to let Maggie do it alone with Eddie?" He bends by the cow he's just prepared for milking, and attaches the four teat cups. "Can't you spend an hour helping?"

"Yeah, I guess." I know he doesn't understand how scared I am of Snaky.

—— CHAPTER EIGHT ——

After school, I ride my bike to Uncle Bill's, climb the back rickety steps and knock. Maggie comes to the door. "Hi, Dusty, you're early." She swings the screen open, reaching full length with her arm and hand.

I fidget a little and walk in. "I thought I'd get here before you-know-who."

Uncle Bill's at the kitchen table, wearing the same worn-out work shirt. He stands and shakes my hand. I can feel that his hand is softer and weaker since I last saw him. "How are you?"

"Fine, I guess. I'll know better after Snaky comes."

"Oh, don't worry about him. Eddie's a good guy."

I'm not about to argue, but Snaky doesn't act like a good guy to me. Uncle Bill sips from a cup of coffee. Every time his shaky hand lifts his cup, it rattles against the saucer. "Have a chair and sit down." He pulls a Kleenex from a box by his elbow. His hand wavers toward his nose. "I appreciate you stopping by to help Maggie."

Radio tunes are blaring from the front room—Orla again. I can't imagine why she hangs around the homestead, even though she lives across the road. The two girls are exact opposites, and Orla treats Maggie as if she's her worst enemy. She comes to the door leading into the kitchen, wearing her red V-neck sweater. Sliding both hands and arms halfway down the door casing, she swings her head and body forward in a bent position as if about to dive into the water. Her sweater looks about two sizes too small. "Remember Saturday afternoon, Dusty. We're going swimming at the trestle."

Uncle Bill turns to face her and jerks his hand on the cup resting on the saucer. It rattles slightly. "The trestle!" He turns again. Orla is still suspended in a revealing position, similar to a Greek goddess hood ornament on an expensive car. The locket swings from her neck. He remarks, "Oh, my gosh!"

That's all he says. His face turns to a brilliant red. He clears his throat, and resettles himself in the old wooden chair while asking, "How's school going?"

"Oh, fine." I sit facing the window and the barns.

"Cooner tells me you want to be a farmer." His withered hand holds a paper napkin to wipe his mouth again. The redness fades. His eyes are sunken. Before I answer, I glance at the blue veins on the side of his thin gaunt face and bald head.

"Yeah, just like all the Murrays."

"Farming isn't what it used to be." He lifts his cup. "I hope you do well in school. That's one thing that will help the most."

Maggie pours me a glass of milk and places one of her doughnuts on a saucer. I thank her, then ask Uncle Bill, "Do you suppose someday all of the meadow will belong to one farm?"

Uncle Bill lets out a big laugh and says, "By golly, Dusty, you're thinking. Good for you! Farms are getting bigger. By rights, it should be all one farm."

My face turns red. I dare to say, "Someday, maybe it can be, and I can have it as a part of my farm." I don't want Uncle Bill to think I'm greedy, wanting something that isn't mine. But lately, I've been thinking how unfair it was that Grandpa Thad was only given five acres and Uncle Bill owns ninety-five. I'm bringing up the subject because of what Cooner said, that Uncle Bill might be forced to sell in order to pay the taxes. I wish he might make right a fifty-year-old injustice by giving Grandpa Thad some of the meadow. But really, the way Grandpa acts, he doesn't deserve it.

Uncle Bill's smile fades. "I hope I can hang onto the farm. Buster Erickson is supposed to buy all the hay. I should make enough to pay the taxes." Maggie sits with us and listens. "He's asked me if I'd sell the farm, but I'm not planning to. The meadow and pine stand should be yours someday."

"Gee, really? That would be great!"

After Uncle Bill has come right out and said what he wants for me, I feel guilty for bringing up the subject. I feel badly that I hadn't wanted to help Maggie, all because I'm a wimp, worrying over Snaky.

The squeal of tires, and a loud *burrr* comes from the driveway. A flash of black darkens the kitchen window. Uncle Bill remarks, "Eddie just got out of work for Buster Erickson, loading hay trucks."

Orla whizzes by us on a dead run. She barges out the screen door, slamming it behind her.

Uncle Bill jumps, rattling his cup again. All I see is a streak of red sweater. She's wildly waving at Snaky.

A knot forms in my stomach, remembering the fun I had with the bale of hay. But it isn't fun any longer. Maggie gets up from the table and bends over, looking in a cupboard for gloves. Without my asking, she tosses me a pair. "Thanks." I stand from the table and hurry toward the door. "I'm headed for the mow."

Outside, Snaky yells to Orla, "Hi, gorgeous." Passing her, I charge for the barn, turn on the lights, and climb the ladder to where the hay is stored. Maggie and Snaky are in the truck, throwing the ropes on the ground, getting ready to load. He notices me at the mow door. "There's the little dirt-eater. You ready to come down here and face me like a man?"

Maggie frowns. "Hey, you leave him alone! He's come to help."

I smile and exhale a sigh of relief.

— CHAPTER NINE —

Saturday noon, I'm having lunch with Cooner and Addie. The house walls, floors, and woodwork have a worn appearance. If Grandpa spent money on paint, I'm sure Addie would gladly use it. If she isn't cooking, she's scrubbing and cleaning, or knitting for relaxation.

When I brought home my eighth-grade picture, she tacked it over the sink, along with seven wallet-size photos, one for every grade. She placed them four over four, outlined with a two inch wide red satin ribbon, cut and sewn at angles to look like a perfect frame. The only other picture in the kitchen is one of Cooner and Slue, taken the year Slue won the coon dog trials. That picture sets on top of the refrigerator.

Cooner and I are at the table. Addie is washing dishes at the sink. Out of the blue, I announce, "Orla and I are going swimming at the trestle."

Addie turns, slack-jawed, to her husband. Cooner settles into his old captain's chair, and blurts with tension in his voice, "The trestle!"

"Yeah, what's wrong?" My elbows are on the table with my chin resting in the palm of my hand.

"That's where all the big-shots hang out. You ain't ready for that, and besides you can't swim." He reaches in his back pocket for his tobacco.

"Did you ever go there?"

"Yup, and I learnt more than I had any right knowin'."

"Like what?"

"Well, for one thing, the gypsies are comin' to town. They travel with the carnival and swim at the trestle. They might be there today. If they are, they'll take over the place. It's quite the crowd. You'll see everythin'—beyond belief."

"What's the problem, if they aren't there?"

Addie dries her hands on a towel, and chimes in, "Orla's mother got in all kinds of trouble the summer she hung out at the trestle."

"Like what?"

"Well—well, she started traveling with the carnival crowd."

While in deep thought, Cooner slides his thumb over the package of tobacco. "It's the whole place. It ain't good."

I sit up straight in my chair. "Well, I'm going," I declare with confidence to override any objections.

Addie and Cooner trade glances. He continues, "I'll tell you—bein' around train tracks is dangerous. The last time I was at the trestle a train had hit a heifer. Bill was with me and spotted the carnage first. 'Course her parts were strewn down the tracks for more than two hundred feet. We spotted just the end of her tail first, then the hind quarters up fifty feet, followed by the most ungodly sight of guts, heart, and liver. The front end was up yonder more than a hundred feet. Stink, man did it ever stink! Green flies were layin' eggs all over it. Thousands of maggots were making some parts look like they were crawlin'. The sight would make most folks gag." He stuffs a pinch of tobacco in his mouth. "I'll warn you, if you stand too close to a fast-moving train, I've heard tell of folks being sucked right onto the tracks. Yup, sucked in like a vacuum cleaner. Trains are dangerous. If you go, and I ain't suggestin' it, and you hear a whistle, stay clear until it passes."

I stand and shove my chair in place. "Well, I'm going."

"Who's goin' besides Orla?"

"No one."

I can see Addie stiffen. Cooner grimaces. "Beside all the other reasons you shouldn't go, land sakes, well—you don't fit with the likes of Orla. "

"Cooner—I'm going. I'll be back tonight for chores." The two pair of eyes follow me with looks of shock as I walk out the door.

Cooner raises his voice from inside the house. "All I can say is don't do anything stupid."

"Don't worry."

I pedal my bike up Murray's Flats with hesitation nagging at me, since Cooner and Addie don't want me to go.

Riding along, I absorb every bit of the meadow, seeing it spread out all the way to the banks of the Blue. It's amazing to see how fast our small patch of corn is growing. The sun is hot, but it has taken all morning for the heavy fog to lift over the lowlands. A lone goose honks several times, flying toward the Blue. Probably its mate is setting on eggs in a swale at the river's edge.

I slowly continue on my way toward Orla's. Not in a hurry to get there, I sit back. Beyond the Blue, high on the ridge, stand Great-Grandpa Murray's pines. The dark green is in sharp contrast to the light green leaves of the aspens. On the slope in the foreground is an old heifer pasture that Uncle Bill once used. It has long since grown up. From where I am, it seems like the landscape of pale green pasture juniper, brownish red maple leaves, light green aspens, and dark green pines resembles the many colors of one of Addie's braided rugs.

I recall the one time I was at the pines. Uncle Bill traded the use of a tractor and a manure spreader for Cooner's help to thin Marcus Murray's ten-acre, white pine stand. Everyone refers to the trees as my great-grandfather's even though he died a long time ago. However, to Uncle Bill, they represent his father. It's as if Marcus Murray himself is standing on the ridge overlooking the valley, taking pleasure in the results of his hard work. Cooner once said, "Thankfully, the trees ain't actually Marcus Murray, because he'd run tears, seein' his farm as it is today."

Cooner and Uncle Bill were up there logging in late summer just before I entered fifth grade. Cooner brought me along. Uncle Bill was there with Maggie and Orla.

That day, the three of us kids walked alone into the deep darkness of the woods, looking up into the treetops, admiring the beauty of this wonderful place that had been started by planting small trees. Cooner said they were at least a hundred years old. They towered toward the sky. Rows of trees with huge long branches overlapped the adjoining rows of trees with similar branches, letting in only small amounts of light. The place reminded me of being in a big empty hay barn with all the doors closed.

We ran back to be with Cooner and Uncle Bill. They were getting ready to start cutting. Uncle Bill stood straight and tall, with high color and a gentle smile. This was before he got sick. He spoke to the three of us with pride in his voice. "These trees have been well cared for and they'll be here for many years to come." He paused and gazed into the towering pines. "Back over fifty years ago when Thad and I were kids, my father brought us up here with pruning saws to cut the lower dead branches in reach of the saw. He told us our work would allow us to someday cut top-quality logs with no knots."

As I remember, later that night, Cooner said, "That stand is as much a gravestone as the one in the cemetery, and watchin' over it is like layin' Memorial Day flowers on Marcus Murray's grave."

We had a lot of fun running between the rows of trees, away from the sound of chain saws and the skidding tractor. Because of an accumulation of pine needles, the ground was as soft as feathers. Blue jays darted from limb to limb screaming *jaaay, jaaay,* upset because we had found their safe haven.

The scent of pine drifted our way, coming from the sawdust spilled by the saws. We played hide-and-seek, using the tree trunks, which was easy in the dull darkness of the closely growing trees. After we ran low on energy, we scooped up needles and made thick beds that were as soft as any mattress. We all agreed that Marcus Murray's pine stand was the greatest place we'd ever seen.

To keep us at a safe distance from the logging operation, Cooner loaned me his jackknife. "Why don't you kids carve your names on that bull pine that ain't no good." He pointed toward it, standing alone. "Stay clear of the edge of the gravel pit. You don't want to get caught in a gravel slide."

The tree had grown from seed outside the boundary of the ten-acre plot. We left the pines and walked to the lone tree. It was the same ridgeline tree above the pit that Orla had chosen as a marker the day we found the calf. I handed Maggie the knife to let her do the carving.

Orla jumped in delight. "Do my name first!"

While Maggie was carving, I walked toward the edge of the pit, staying a good distance from the edge. The gravel bank to the floor dropped more than a hundred feet. The gravel was made up of all sizes of stones, but most of them were from baseball to basketball size. Some were smaller. I followed a path the deer and other wildlife had made when they traveled the steep path on the edge of the pit down to the river for a drink. The path rose steeply from the water's edge. Uncle Bill and Cooner had made such a big deal about the pit, that now, with some free time, I wanted to see more closely for myself.

In a short time, I was walking back to the tree. Maggie continued to carve.

She delicately peeled the bark, which was as soft as polished leather, and carefully cut each letter of Orla. Then she drew a line and cut almost the perfect shape of a heart. She lifted a narrow band of bark by following next to the line she had just cut. We stood quietly, watching her steady hand. While cutting the next letters, she wore a smirk, as if expecting a reaction. She was right. In the center of the heart, she carved:

Orla screamed, "You're not fair! Dusty is just as much my friend as he is yours!" She stomped toward the edge of the woods, picked up dirt left by the skidding of logs, and ran back to the tree, throwing the dirt at the heart.

Maggie just laughed. "Don't get so upset. It's only a heart with our names."

Orla didn't let up. She got some more dirt and rubbed it on the heart. The cuts, oozing thick, sticky pitch, mixed with the dirt. All the carved letters were filled with what looked like charcoal, and the surrounding space was a black gloss.

Orla's deep brown eyes took on a foreboding look. "See, Maggie, now the tree has a black heart. That means bad things will happen. If Dusty chooses the wrong girl, his life will be miserable."

"You're too superstitious. Nothing terrible will happen."

Orla held her all-knowing expression. "You wait. You'll be sorry."

When I was walking home in the late afternoon, the carving of the black heart wouldn't leave me. I didn't want to believe her, but Orla's creepy side convinced me that she might be right about having the ability to know things that none of us common kids did. Maggie wasn't worried. She turned toward Orla and mockingly laughed. "You're just trying to scare us."

Other than Orla's outburst, the day was great fun. However, the black heart frequently surfaced in my thoughts, resembling the shadow of a dead fly floating on the waves of my memory. As the years passed, the image didn't fade. I kept thinking I should go back, check if the weather and the seasons had erased what the girls had done. But I didn't, partly out of fear that the very thing I wanted eliminated would still be there.

Shaking my head to forget the past, I pump my bike hard, riding fast to where Orla's waiting. When I meet her, she's wearing a bathing suit with a bath towel slung around her neck. She jumps on the bike carrier, hugging my waist. In a short while, after passing by a cluster of houses, we're at the path leading to the trestle. I shove my bike into some bushes and we start walking. The path follows a ridge. On our left a large area of low swampland grows horsetail, skunk cabbage, and alders. New green grass has sprung up in the open spaces between the swamp plants. On our right, I can hear the Blue River, hidden by brush, quietly ripple past us. Alders, briars, and wild vines weave in a snarl over the shaded path. It reminds me of what walking through a jungle must be like, minus the squawking birds and poisonous snakes. We walk past bottles, cigarette butts, and trash strewn along the way. Orla leads with confident strides, eager to get to the swimming hole. I'm hanging back, taking in the surroundings, anxious over what might be ahead. Orla stops and flashes me a disgusted expression. "Come on, let's not take all day!"

She has me by the hand while I stumble along, thinking that this place is not for me. I should split—right now! She continues to yank on my arm.

After what seems like an endless walk, the path finally opens up, and we can hear yelling and splashing as we come to a flight of steps. Big slabs of marble, placed like steps, are used to hold up both ends of the railroad bridge called the trestle. We climb to the tracks where we can see the swimming hole below. It's loaded with kids splashing around in deep water. A large rope hangs from a big elm and it's in continual use as kids swing, plunging cannonball-style, spraying fans of water. I know most of the kids and feel some relief not seeing any strangers, such as gypsies.

On either side of the tracks are large smooth sections of marble. Girls in bathing suits are stretched out, soaking in the sun. Snaky is sitting on a rail, dragging on a cigarette, with his bare feet resting on marble. His girl is next to him. They pass his cigarette back and forth, inhaling and exhaling great puffs. Snaky checks out Orla and gives me a foxy grin. "Hey, the little dirt-eater's here."

I think about turning around and running for home while there's still a chance, but he doesn't move. He laughs. "I see you have the baby bomb with you."

Orla scowls and says nothing. She pulls on the towel covering her front. It's taut on the back of her neck from the pressure of the tug. Her brown eyes and set jaw convey an expression of confidence.

She looks at him with a steady gaze. Maybe she's envious of Snaky's girl. It's difficult for me to know. For sure, I'm showing my vulnerability by dumbly gawking at everyone and everything in this new place. I stiffen with fear, backed by Cooner's warning. He was right; I can't swim a stroke.

Snaky's girl ignores us and starts combing his jet black hair. She bends to kiss his cheek. He tips back, while the comb glides through straight channels of slickness. Abruptly, he sits erect and offers, "Sit down and take a load off your feet."

Orla, with no hesitation, takes a seat next to Snaky. He turns in her direction. "Geez, babe, you're all right."

Snaky's girl yanks him toward her.

Orla giggles. "Thanks."

I hesitantly sit with my knees bending like rusty pliers. Snaky picks his cigarettes up and says, "Here, have one."

His midsection is shaking in a snicker. I sit on the rail looking off onto the lowlands, thinking how I should say no to smoking. Orla whispers in my ear, "Smoking is what the big kids do."

Snaky's hand is steady as he holds the pack next to us with cigarettes sticking out. He urges with a firmer offer, "Take one." Orla draws one from the pack. I turn away, knowing that we should move on, but I want to show him I can handle the situation. Since Orla has accepted his offer, why not do the same? My fingers touch and cautiously pull the soft white stick as if it's dynamite about to explode in my hand. He drags, exhaling and blowing a gigantic white ball of smoke. He offers, "Here, put the end of it in your mouth. Draw and I'll light it for you." Orla fills her mouth with smoke with cheeks rounding out, looking like she is about to blow a bubble. She releases a big puff, showing she can handle smoking.

He holds the lighter, waiting for me. The teardrop flame flickers. Orla is on her second puff and acts okay.

He has a stupid grin. "Here, kid." I can see his stomach shake again. He's obviously trying to hold back his donkey laugh. "Draw and take a deep breath." Him having that jerky smile tells me that this is not good, but Orla seems to be doing just fine.

The flame wavers at the end of the cigarette—then his encouraging words, "It's okay, kid. Take a deep drag."

I recall Uncle Bill's comment: "Eddie's a good guy."

I decide to try. Maybe Snaky is being social. It goes through my mind to accept a favor, give him a chance. I draw deeply on the softness at the edge of my mouth. The flame collapses into the cigarette. In the next second, my whole body fills with smoke. It feels as though I have my mouth over a stovepipe sucking on the entire firebox. I cough and blow, cough and blow, as if I have an acute case of croup. Smoke comes out of my nose as well as my mouth. The river and lowlands below are all a blur. Everyone is laughing. I'm about to puke. Dropping the cigarette near the tracks, I sit on the rail with my head in my hands, hoping the sick feeling will pass. It sinks in my gut and creeps up my throat. My belly juices are fighting it out, rolling like a raging Blue in the height of a spring thaw. I stretch flat out beside the tracks. Orla's voice sounds from a distance. "You can't be that bad-off. Aren't you being a little dramatic?"

That's her new word. If a train came and cut off my leg and I was rolling in pain with blood spraying in all directions, she'd probably say, "Dusty, don't be so dramatic."

I can't stand the smell of smoke. I walk along the tracks and sit down again still feeling dizzy. Thankfully, my stomach starts to settle and the sickness passes. Although the place is crowded, I feel absolutely alone and want to go home. Cooner was right—this is no place for me. I walk down the bank from the tracks and watch the swimmers. Downstream, Orla is standing on a gravel bar timidly trying the water. I quickly change into my bathing suit behind some bushes, and walk under the bridge beside the marble buttress on the path leading to the gravel bar. Still feeling a little green with a bad taste in my mouth, I ask her, "How come that didn't bother you?"

She's up to her knees, bent over, lightly splashing the water with her hands. "I wasn't stupid enough to inhale."

I edge ankle deep and wait to get accustomed to the cool water. "I suppose you know all about smoking?"

"I've tried a few times, snitching from some guys at school."

"Yeah, you like hanging around that crowd."

"They like me." She tugs on the top of her suit.

I'm waist-deep in water and can feel the smooth gravel underfoot. I'm relieved to be by ourselves. We wade around for a while. Orla shows me some of the things she's learned from swimming lessons. She instructs, "Take a deep breath and put your head in the water, keep your fingers closed and paddle while kicking your feet."

I drop about a foot below the level of the water, only moving a few inches, coming up gasping for air. Since I haven't learned to swim, it's fun to have this chance to try doing the dead man's float while kicking my feet. I feel like I'm making real progress. It's the first time I remember appreciating Orla. She can see I'm having fun. We practice until we get cold. Then we take a break, sitting on the loose washed gravel with our feet in the water while the afternoon sun warms our backs.

She's running her hand over the pebbles on the gravel bar, watching the water ripple by. "Someday we can do a lot of things together. Maybe travel, visit foreign countries, live with nomadic tribes; you know, experience the world a little."

"Geez, Orla, I'll never do that!" I feel for a stone and throw it. "Nomadic tribes! I hope someday I can own the meadow and Grandpa Thad's place." I raise my voice to make sure she understands. "My dream is to be a farmer."

She slides her arm around my midsection and moves closer, trying to get my attention. "With me?" I notice the gold chain around her neck. The locket's under her bathing suit.

Feeling the side of her breast press against my arm, though warm, makes me uneasy. She looks like a grown woman and I'm still small, skinny, and not at all interested in having her in my life. "I think a lot about my future."

"But farming! What a turn-off!" She slaps the water. "I want to get out of Huntersville, Vermont, and see the world."

"Well, farming might sound like a turn-off to you, but it isn't for me."

She holds me tighter. "I want to be a Murray someday."

I sigh and watch the water trickle over the stones. "What's the big deal about being a Murray?"

She picks up another stone with her free hand and throws it with force—*splash*. "You don't get it, do you?"

"I guess not. My family is far from perfect: I never knew my parents, Uncle Bill is dying, and I don't speak to my grandpa. Thankfully, I have Cooner, Addie, and Maggie."

"Yeah, Maggie! How about me?"

"Well, she's—she's more like me."

"Right, I'm as dark as a roasted chicken."

"I don't mean that." Her arm and hand pulls on my waist. I push away and shift slightly, wanting some comfortable distance. "There're plenty of nice families in town. I don't see why you *have* to be a Murray."

"The Murray name means more to me than any I know: there's Murray's Flats, the Murray homestead, and of course, Murray's Meadow and the Marcus Murray pines." She slings another stone, only farther, and it makes a bigger *splash*. She raises her voice. "Gosh, don't you understand? I'm an outcast— a freak." Tears start filling her brown eyes. "All I've got going for myself is a big set of boobs and even that is an embarrassment sometimes." She gives the top of her bathing suit a tug.

"Embarrassment?" I pick up a fistful of loose gravel and plunk it in the water. "I wouldn't have known that's how you feel by the way you act around Snaky."

"He's a guy." She tugs again on her suit. "But Dusty, you're my *only* true friend. You're all I have."

"Well, you have that locket and can see things that the rest of us can't."

She slaps the water. "That's no big deal. The locket's just a part of me." She pulls it out from under her bathing suit and holds it. "It's helpful, letting me see things—showing what's ahead." She slides closer again and puts her hand on my shoulder. "Marcus and Orla Murray, doesn't that sound romantic? We'll have kids, and they'll all be Murrays."

"Kids! That's years away!"

"Next week you'll be fourteen." She bends to look into my face. "And I'll be your girl."

"Well—maybe my friend." Her declaration makes the goose bumps scamper up my back. "Remember the black heart? You said bad things would happen if I choose the wrong girl? How do I know you're the right one?"

Orla puts on her distant gaze. "My locket tells me we're a match!"

I study her expression. "Really? That locket doesn't talk."

"It doesn't need to." She purposely turns her head. I want to see her expression—her eyes. It's then that I wonder if she's telling lies to get her way; but I'm not sure. She jumps up and dives into the water. I don't move. It's too cold to swim. I know that locket gives her unexplained insight. And there's no doubt she has powers like no other.

Just last week, our English teacher Mrs. Naggy misplaced her handbag. She thought it might be in the lunch room, and she left our class to get it. She came back without it. Orla sat holding her locket. She said, "Mrs. Naggy, Sparky has it."

In seconds there was a tap at the door. Mrs. Naggy answered. We heard the voice of Sparky, our janitor. She walked back to her desk holding the handbag. A hush went over the room. I heard a kid say, "Mother-of-pearl, this is creepy."

Everyone stared at Orla as if they'd seen a ghost. Kids knew of her powers before that incident; however, it only reinforced anxious feelings toward her, and explains why she has no friends.

She carefully steps on smooth stones, leaving the water—again sitting next to me. I don't want to be mean and tell her that the black heart scares me, and that I think of her as bad news. On the other hand, Orla and I together would be a disaster. Tying the knot with her would be a lifelong prison sentence.

She's shivering, drying herself, wrapped in a bath towel. I continue, "Orla, I just don't think like you—at all. Sure I'm a Murray, but I'm not any great prize."

"You'll change."

I pick up a gray stone the size of a baseball and run my hand over its smoothness. "Yeah, dream on." I toss the stone toward another on the bank. I miss hitting it. "Why don't you go for stuck-up Silver? His grandfather, I'm told, owns the bank. Now, there's a name to tie onto."

"Yuck, he's a creep."

"Well, what about Snaky?"

Orla brightens and smiles. "He's just great to be with."

"Yeah, right!"

"You're just jealous."

"Jealous? No way!" With my arms crossed at my chest, I rub my hands over my chilliness. "I'm going home."

A train whistle makes us both jump. It sounds a long way off, but everyone gets out of the water, and the sunbathers run down the steps. Orla and I run along the path under the marble buttress. We head toward the open field where everyone else is standing. The train must be coming fast because the whistle blasts again, and it's about to cross the trestle. Snaky is standing in the middle of the long bridge with no railings. We all look up at him like you would if your favorite cat was stranded in a tree. Only difference is, he's no favorite of mine and he should have more brains than a cat. But at this point, I'm not sure. He doesn't have time to get off the tracks. It's too far to the other end of the trestle.

An older boy yells, "LaQuine, you're an idiot!"

He's standing, raising his arms, flexing his muscles, pushing with his hands, acting as though he's Superman about to stop the train. The whistle blows a constant blast. The huge engine and long line of freight cars shake the ground. I feel the earth tremble even though I'm two hundred feet from the tracks. I'm clutched in fear.

The continuous whistle is deafening. The wheels are sliding on the track, unable to hold back the enormous weight. Sparks are flying. The whole underside of the engine looks like a million Fourth of July sparklers. The train thunders toward the middle of the trestle. Snaky doesn't move. My breath is caught in my throat. The girls are hysterically screaming. I don't like Snaky, but I don't want to be eye witness to a bloodbath with body parts flying in all directions. In an instant and within feet before the train reaches him, he jumps. At that same time a large cauldron of steaming water is thrown out the engineer's window as punishment for the interruption of train traffic. Snaky and the boiling water descend through the air, but the reprimand doesn't gain on the brazen Snaky. He plunges into the river and is out of sight before the hot water hits the Blue in a momentary puff of steam.

I'm seething with a mixture of anger and hatred toward him, having fallen into his trap of trying to smoke. Now, his antics on the trestle prove that this guy is an absolute jerk.

He bounces out of the water with a champion-of-the-world grin—walking up the bank as his girl rushes to hug him, spouting a whimpering cry, "You're so brave!"

Pounding his chest, he acts as though he has some supernatural powers as he offhandedly replies, "Aw, it's nothin'."

I've had enough of swimming, enough of the trestle, and enough of Snaky. I change and start for home. Orla yells, "Wait for me!"

We both walk along the vine-covered path. The smell of damp earth and swamp grass from the lowlands fills the air. Riding home, we breeze through a small settlement outside the main village of Huntersville. We pass little white houses and yards that seem sleepy. Occasionally a lazy old dog raises his head and watches us pass. A guy is mowing his lawn; but other than that, the world seems caught in a Saturday afternoon nap.

We're heading down Murray's Flats, nearing Orla's place. She cries out excitedly, "My mother's car is here! She's home! Come in and meet her."

"Okay." I really want to get home, but I'm curious about her mother. I've only seen her at Uncle Bill's where she always acted cool, distant, and aloof.

When I walk through the back door of the house, the smell of cigarette smoke immediately makes me feel like gagging. When Orla isn't looking, I put my hand on my mouth and nose in an attempt to filter the odor. Her mother, Zelda O'Neil, is almost never around. This is the first time I've been invited to Orla's home. As far as I know, Orla was let loose to grow up on her own.

The house looks like no one lives in it. The walls are dark and bare: no curtains, no plants, no pets, no rugs. It's the last place I'd want to be, and I guess Orla must feel the same. I can hear a loud gravelly voice in the next room, talking on the phone.

"You tightwad, Marty, you always try to screw me. I'll switch suppliers if you don't ease your prices …that's a line of crap. Look, the show is coming to town tomorrow and I'm supplying a booth with red and yellow roses. I want two hundred dozen for the booth and my other stores …well, that's better. I'm still not making much. I've got to pay off that gypsy S-man before he'll let me on the midway … You know him, he heads the clan that puts on the show … the cocky lowlife … that was years ago … yeah, he was handsome all right and I was crazy for him…yeah, a long time…oh, I don't know… about fifteen years ago."

Orla's intently listening. I start to leave, but she grabs me and whispers, "I want you to meet my mother."

Zelda hangs up the phone. We walk into a makeshift office/den. She's a tall, dull blonde with a narrow gray face and a sharp chin. Her almond-shaped eyes squint through silver-rimmed glasses. Cigarette ash is peppered on the front of her black business suit. "Orla, what are you doing in here?" She snuffs out her cigarette in an overfilled ash try. "And who is this?" Her voice is demanding—not pleasant at all.

"Dusty Murray, he lives right down the road."

"Well—well, just barge in and make yourself at home. I'm sorry you—darn, Orla, why didn't you let me know you were here?"

"So we didn't have to hear you on the phone?" Orla flashes those dark eyes at her mother and asks in an accusatory tone, "Just who is this gypsy S-man you were crazy in love with some fifteen years ago?"

"Forget you heard anything!" While standing, she turns to look on the desk, fumbling for her pack of cigarettes.

Orla demands, "Well, I did hear. You were crazy for him?" She steps closer for an answer.

"He's some scumbag of a gypsy I have to deal with to sell at the carnival's midway."

"My father, a scumbag?"

Orla's mother throws the pack on the desk. "You're bold and right in front of your friend."

Orla fumes, "Be honest with me!"

"Shut up!" As she talks, the unlit cigarette wags between her pale lips.

"So, you got hooked by the S-man!"

Zelda O'Neil's face flushes. She lights her cigarette, dragging deeply and filling the little room with smoke.

I start to back up, wanting to leave. I realize for the first time that Maggie's father's a gypsy. I continue to step back staring at the bare walls, realizing she never knew her real father.

Orla follows me. "See you, Dusty. Oh, let's go to the trestle again and practice our swimming. During the week, all the big kids are working and we can have the place to ourselves."

"To the trestle?" I closely look at her and conclude that her dark coloring, black hair, deep brown eyes, and black eyebrows must come from her father, and Maggie's blond hair and blue eyes come from her mother.

"Yeah, after school, if we have a warm afternoon."

I comb my hair with spread fingers. "Well, I wish Maggie could come."

Orla stands on the back step with her hands on her hips. "Well, she can't! We can go alone without her!"

"We'll see if the weather's right and I don't have to work."

I push off on my bike, thinking I'm covered and probably won't go. But loading hay isn't anything great to look forward to either because of pea-brain LaQuine.

As I ride down Murray's Flats, the sun is low enough to bring in a rush of cool spring air. All I can think about is the fact that the girls have a scumbag for a father.

—— CHAPTER TEN ——

It's a hot day in late May. I agree to go to the trestle again, since I want to learn to swim. It seems okay because as Orla says, all the older kids will be working. We'll have the whole place to ourselves.

Although Cooner asked how my first time went, I didn't say much, only that it was a good swim. I also mentioned Snaky's antics with the train. In a nice way, Cooner loves to remind me that he's usually right. This time, I didn't want to give him the satisfaction. I'm getting old enough to handle tough situations on my own. At least, I hope so.

I'm riding my bike along the flats about to reach Orla, who is standing by the road. As I ride closer to her, I notice the locket resting on her bathing suit. She always wears it. In a way, it's a part of her—she claims it's the good part.

At that instant, I'm reminded of my father and mother. All Cooner knows is that my dad kept a flock of hens and peddled eggs door-to-door. And from what he's heard, Grandpa and he didn't get along. That's no surprise.

Apparently my mother ran the house, paid the bills, and peddled eggs with my father. That's how they got killed. A trailer truck rammed their pickup. They flew through the windshield, but I landed on the floor board. Cooner tells me that I was just a baby at the time.

The bike brakes squeak when I come to a stop.

"Hi, Dusty, what a great day to go swimming."

"Yeah, I hope no one's there."

"Don't worry." She swings her leg over the bike carrier and hangs on to my belt, while I stand to pump. In a short while we reach the path. It's hot. Due to a spell of warm weather, the leaves of the alders have burst from their covers. Dandelions and violets are scattered on the edge of the path that's littered with empty bottles, cigarette cartons, and parts of old clothing.

We walk along at a fast pace and quickly get to the trestle. We don't hear much noise. However, we're shocked when we start climbing the stairs leading to the tracks. The place is mobbed with strangers. Orla seems excited. "They're a bunch of gypsies from the carnival."

Women are washing clothes off the gravel bar where Orla and I sat. Men, women, and children are in the water scrubbing themselves with bars of soap. Suds are bubbling causing foam to float down the Blue, making the place look like a giant bathtub.

Plenty of folks are out of the water in the open field sitting on towels with small children; some are just sunning themselves. I want to leave, but Orla insists that we get a closer look. She's interested because she's one of them. We're on the stairs leading down from the tracks.

It's immediately obvious that the clan has a leader. He's a big guy with a wide chest and big arms like a TV wrestler. He's only wearing a skimpy bathing suit. He isn't relaxed, but struts around the field keeping watch over the activity, like a stallion would his mares.

He spots us and walks our way. Orla pulls my hand. "Let's meet this guy."

He says to Orla, "So, you have a scrawny little white guy with ya."

Then he lunges toward me and grabs my neck, lifting me off the ground. I'm kicking in midair looking straight at his chest. Under the left nipple of his bulging chest is tattooed *sweet* and under the right side *sour.* This must be the S-man. Suddenly, he throws me onto the ground, like I'm garbage. I jump to my feet and back away. His eyes remind me of Orla's, dark and deeply set.

He sneers at me. "You might swim here usual, but you ain't today! I like your little gypsy, but ya leave—ya hear?"

Orla speaks right up. "You know my mother Zelda O'Neil?"

"The flower witch? Oh! So you're her kid? I think you and me have connections." He scans her up and down and smiles in approval. "You should join the show." He grabs her by the forearm.

She tries to pull free. "I—I don't know. Maybe after school lets out."

"Forget school! We gypsies have our own." He yanks her, throwing his arm around her midsection.

"Let me go!" she yells.

He laughs. "I can use you on the midway." She continues to scream for help. "I need a cute kid like you to draw the crowd."

I wonder what I can do. Then I remember the stone I threw on the bank.

Her feistiness draws his attention away from me. I run toward the bank under the trestle while another guy is helping to hold her by her feet. She's flat on the ground. The gypsies have formed a circle around the struggle.

She's not giving in easily. No one notices me. The stone fits comfortably in my hand. I hurry back to Orla. The S-man is bent, holding her by the arms. I swing and hit him on the back of the head. His knees buckle like folding paper. I slug the stone at the guy holding her feet. It hits him in the neck. He grabs his throat and falls backward. The clan freezes in place in total surprise. Orla scrambles to her feet, and we run for the marble stairs.

We're puffing and breathing hard by the time we reach my bike. No one's trying to catch us. Orla remarks, "I wouldn't mind going with them, if that creep hadn't been so nasty."

"What?"

"It would be fun to get away from this dull world."

"I don't believe you!" I'm pumping my bike starting to gain some speed. She's more of a mystery to me than ever.

"I want to go back, since the S-man has been put out of commission."

Her arms are wrapped around my waist. I'm sitting, coasting into her drive. "If that's the way you feel, I'm sorry I risked my neck." We stop by her back door.

"I found out you think enough of me to help in a bad situation." She's standing by my bike with one hand on the handlebars.

"Well, I wasn't going to just walk off and leave you."

"Thanks." She climbs the stairs to her back door. "Stick with me. Remember what I said about the black heart."

"How can I forget?"

—— CHAPTER ELEVEN ——

After doing chores, I head toward the house. The peepers are singing their nightly song under a cloudless sky. The moon's just beginning to show a faint outline. The lilac bush by the backdoor is in full bloom, and the warm night air stirs a sweet scent from its purple blossoms.

When entering the kitchen, I'm surprised to see balloons hanging from the ceiling light. Addie's wearing her Sunday dress. "Hey, what's going on?"

She smiles; the back of her hand moves strays of gray hair away from her face. "Do you know what today is?"

"Yeah, my birthday. But you've never made a big deal over birthdays before."

"Well, I'm making this birthday special, since it's your fourteenth." She resumes peeling potatoes. "How about wearing some dress clothes?"

"It's a party?" I glance at the larger table with more than the usual three place settings.

"You'll see."

I wash up, wondering who might be coming. Upstairs while buttoning my shirt, I step toward the alcove of my room and watch Cooner leave in his truck. The lights flash by my bay window.

In the kitchen, Addie has the wood cook stove working hard. Pots and pans are steaming. She has a potholder in hand and opens the oven door to check on a roasting chicken. She glances up and smiles. "You look sharp tonight."

"Thanks, Addie. Thanks, too, for going to all this trouble."

She stands. With a pass of her hand, she again moves stray hair away from her face. "I'm havin' fun puttin' on a birthday party."

"Gee it's hot in here. I'll open the doors."

Afterward, I take a chair. There're two extra leaves in the table and extra place settings. Addie and Cooner's captain chairs are at both ends. Seeing them brings memories of Addie holding me as a kid, while humming a tune, acting as if she had all the time in the world. I miss the affection of childhood. But growing older is more exciting, especially tonight. A party should be fun. Inviting folks for a celebration is something Addie's never done.

I think the kitchen looks just about the way it did when Cooner and Addie moved in. Although the buildings look to be in good shape, Grandpa isn't one to spend money on decorating. And Addie's the kind that's perfectly satisfied with the way things are. Would Grandpa ever buy an electric stove for Addie? No, although it would make it nicer for her in the summer.

The floorboards sag as Addie nimbly slides her feet from her work space to the stove. Delicious smells roll from her cooking corner. I hear footsteps, and "Uh."

That's Grandpa. I guess his mind works slower than most because he almost never says a thing unless he begins with "Uh". He's standing ramrod straight at the kitchen door. At seventy-five, he's trim with a full head of snow-white hair and a wrinkled forehead. He moves with the ease of a thirty-year-old, but his pure white hair and face could be that of a man way beyond his years. Deep sparrow tracks are at the edge of his dull gray eyes, and, as always, he has a squinty scowl.

In recent times, as far as I can remember, he's never been at the farmhouse. He's early, probably thinking about the good food he knows Addie cooks.

She jerks to attention. She's spooning the sizzling juices over the brown roasting chicken. She shuts the oven door. The back of her hand rests on her forehead. "Come in, Thad. Take a seat. Cooner will be along."

Grandpa sits as if he has a poker up his back. He continues nervously clearing his throat and not saying a word. He always wears that ugly expression, with his jaws working the muscles on the sides of his face. The suit coat he's wearing is the only one he has. Cooner told me he bought it for his wedding.

He can't help but see the row of my school pictures pinned to the wall. Grandpa's staring, absorbing them, saying nothing. I wonder what he's thinking. I've never given him any pictures, because I'm quite sure he wouldn't have cared. He hasn't yet said a word to me, and I'll be darned if I'll say anything to him. We sit silently in a standoff of sorts.

Addie places special china bowls of steaming potatoes, beets, and onions on the table. She pinches the corners of her apron and pulls the cloth smooth. Her face is fixed in a serious expression, which isn't the Addie I know. Grandpa's making her nervous.

She's showing great courage in bringing us together, especially for a party—doing something common that's not common at all for my family. If Maggie is coming, I'm sure Addie is worried how Grandpa will accept her. I also know that Cooner and Addie want to give Maggie a home when Uncle Bill's no longer able. All these thoughts must be going through her head while she prepares the meal, wanting something to work that might not be workable, wanting Maggie's acceptance when she might not be acceptable.

When Cooner's old Chevy pickup swings into the yard, the lights from the truck momentarily flash across us. We sit like wooden soldiers at a funeral instead of a birthday party.

Two doors slam. Addie goes rigid. In moments, Maggie is framed in the doorway. "Hi everyone! Happy fourteenth, Dusty! How about that? We'll be in high school next fall."

She's especially pretty tonight with a blue satin ribbon pinned in her long wavy blond hair. She's wearing navy blue slacks and a long-sleeved white blouse.

I choke, "Ma-ggie!"

Although fourteen, she seems a lot older than me.

Grandpa's in her line of sight. He clears his throat. The wrinkles at the edge of his mouth deepen and his eyes squint. "Uh...who on earth is this—this—girl?"

"Bill's girl, Maggie," Cooner says, while pulling a chair out from the table, motioning for her to sit.

Of course Grandpa doesn't know her, since he isn't speaking to his brother, Bill. This is the first time she's been at our farm since the day years ago when she and Orla were sent home. But I think Maggie impresses him by her winning smile. Grandpa's expression noticeably mellows in her presence. Other than asking who she is, he remains speechless while continuing to stare at her.

Taking a few steps toward the chair, she says, "Isn't this fun?" Looking at Grandpa, she shrugs and lowers her voice, "Well, at least *I* think it's fun!" Holding a wrapped package in her hand, she quickly scans the room.

"Give it here," Cooner offers. He sets it on a shelf in back of the stove. Even he has changed for my party. He's parted with his bib-overalls and changed into dress pants and a white long-sleeved shirt.

Addie asks, "Where's Orla?"

"She wasn't home. She knew about the party." Maggie turns to me. "You were with her this afternoon."

"I was, but I'm not sure where she is now. We escaped the carnival gang at the trestle by the skin of our teeth. When I left her off at her house, she said she wanted to go back. Maybe she did. We met her father. Sorry, Maggie, but what a jerk."

"I don't care about him. *My* father is Papa."

Cooner announces with obvious pride, "Did you know Maggie's helpin' Zelda at her florist shop in town? Well, she came to see Maggie and asked if she'd like to learn the trade. She wanted to hire Maggie—someone that's eager to work."

"Really?" I ask. "You have a job?"

Maggie explains, "After I learn how to do things, she's promised to give me a good wage. Right now, I'm learning how to arrange flowers, make corsages, and fun stuff like that."

"How come you call her Zelda when she's your mother?"

"Well, I like her, but she's all business. She hasn't asked me to call her anything but Zelda. Anyway, I don't think of her as my mother."

Truck lights momentarily bathe the barn siding. A door slams. Rapid footsteps are coming through the entry. I glance toward the door. "Shirley!"

She stands in the doorway with her alert eyes and a broad smile, wearing a dressy beige blouse and slacks. Her arms are crossed over her chest, hiding a magazine. "I heard we have a young man here with a birthday." She laughs.

Cooner says, "Come in, Shirley, and take a chair."

I comment, "This is quite the party!" as I watch her sit, placing the magazine on her lap.

She turns toward Grandpa. "You're Thad Murray. I'm Shirley Iverson, Dusty's 4-H leader."

He growls, "Uh...4-H ain't never meant nothin' to me."

Shirley sits back in her chair, smiles, and winks at me from across the table. Then she looks again at Grandpa, raising her voice, "I'm proud to be a 4-H leader. It's a great bunch of kids, including your grandson."

"Uh...I ain't knowin' about that." He stares at her. "You up on Pine Mountain?"

"Yeah, my husband and I have lived and farmed there for some time on the Harold Tully place."

"Uh...years back I heard tell Tully weren't much of a farmer."

"He was a good man. That's how *I* remember him."

Addie places the roasted chicken on the table. "It looks like a delicious meal," Shirley remarks.

"Thanks." Addie nervously smiles. "We're ready to eat."

Cooner asks, "Shirley, would you return thanks?"

"Sure:

Lord, we're grateful for Dusty's birthday
as he begins his journey toward manhood.
We ask that he may reach his life's goal, and that
we adults will support him in any way we can.
Thank you for this food and for the hands that have
prepared it. Amen."

"Thanks, Shirley." Cooner pushes his chair away and stands. "I ain't done much carvin' at a party before, but I sure have skun a pile of coon."

Maggie and I laugh, but Grandpa scowls and sits stiffly and silent. I notice Addie. She continues to move her hands along the edges of her apron. Family time for my family is just plain painful. Grandpa acts as if he's just taken a swim in the icy waters of the Blue.

Cooner piles the chicken on my plate. "I'm servin' the birthday boy first."

Grandpa's mouth is closed, and the jaw muscle on the side of his face is working, moving in and out. He continues to stare at Maggie. Awkwardly, he asks her, "Uh... how—how's Bill?"

"Not very good. The doctor says he has cancer."

The word *cancer* causes Grandpa's mouth to pucker shut. Then he mumbles, "Uh...that so? I didn't know."

Maggie draws a deep breath. "He says he's got to sell the farm in order to pay the taxes, the mortgage, and set money aside for me." She directs her remarks toward Grandpa. "I told him he doesn't have to worry since I'm working for Zelda."

Grandpa's looking his usual grumpy self while starting to chew on his chicken. "Uh...sell the meadow? Why—why he can't do that! A Murray has always owned it." He pounds the table with his fork in hand. A chunk of chicken is stuck in the tines, pointing toward the shadows on the ceiling. He grumbles, "I'll tell you, young lady, by rights at least forty-five acres of that meadow belong to me!"

Maggie's not fazed by Grandpa's anger. "Here's your chance to own it. If you don't buy it, Buster Erickson might. He's made an offer, but Papa says it's not enough."

Grandpa has no further comment. I sense the thought of buying the meadow is overwhelming him, but he continues to stare at Maggie while eating. She senses his interest and returns a smile.

"This is a great meal, Addie," Shirley compliments.

"Thanks."

After some silence, Grandpa says, "Uh...I hate the idea of payin' for property that by rights should have been mine. I've always farmed little pieces of land here and there all over town. Now that I'm about to call it quits, somethin' I've wanted *all* my life comes up for sale."

Maggie adds, "That's what I was saying. You can buy it, and Dusty can have it for his farm someday."

I draw a deep breath and nod.

Grandpa grumbles, "Uh...well, if that don't beat all, me buying all that land I ain't needin' anyhow. If I owned the meadow we could milk more cows, but I don't know's I'm up for that at my age."

Cooner turns to Grandpa. "There ain't no tellin' what will happen if Buster Erickson gets his hands on it. Next year we might see the land plastered with buildin's."

I add, "Remember, corn's growing on some of the meadow."

"Uh… but there ain't no tellin' feedin' corn will make me more money. Twenty-five cows just ain't enough for a livin'. I might's well sell the herd."

Cooner quickly breaks in, "Maybe you should talk to Bill about the meadow."

Grandpa rears back in his chair, his fork clattering on the plate. "Bill! Uh…yes, well—well. That'd mean makin' amends."

Maggie smiles at Grandpa. "Papa would love to see you."

Grandpa's cross lines deepen again, running down to the bridge of his nose. "Uh… I—I 'spose maybe I should—then again—if I'd only known. Uh… if only it had been different."

I sit up and lean forward. "Different in what way?"

He scowls at me. "Uh…it—it ain't nothin' to talk about."

Addie, having eaten almost nothing, looks around the table at empty plates. Maggie jumps up and helps Addie clear the table then she takes her seat. There's a long pause of expectation while Addie, with her back turned, stands next to the kitchen counter. I hear a stick match strike. She's working over something in her cooking corner. She turns holding a cake with candles flickering. For the first time all of us do something as a family: we sing *Happy Birthday*. Forgetting who it's for, I'm singing, too. It sounds almost as good as our church choir. Everyone around the table is singing with force and joy in their voice. Even Grandpa mumbles a few notes. I draw a deep breath and blow out all fourteen candles. Everyone, except Grandpa, claps. While Addie cuts the cake and places pieces on special china saucers, Maggie reaches for Grandpa's hand. "Come and see Papa."

He doesn't say a word, only stares at her. Tension builds in every muscle of his clenched jaw. Maggie smiles, waiting for him to answer. The whole room is silent.

"Uh." He clears his throat. "Uh… I—I need to think on it. Then again I s'pose I need to find out what he's askin'."

Addie is cutting the cake while we all watch; it's providing a welcome distraction. Maybe Grandpa is letting the bar down on his fifty-year-old grudge. His jaw muscle continues to flex like a heartbeat. After a brief silence, he turns toward Maggie. "Uh…it just ain't right. I only got five acres of the meadow!"

Maggie reaches for his hand again. "Does it matter anymore?"

"Uh…well—well ain't you seein' my point?" His pleading voice begs for understanding.

"I don't know, Uncle Thad. That was years ago." She comments in a pleasant tone. "All I do know is that Papa would love to see you." She pulls her hand away.

Addie serves us the cake and we all quietly sit, enjoying the treat.

Shirley places the hidden magazine in the middle of the table. I wonder what it means. It has a picture of a beautiful black and white cow on the cover. Outlined in green is the title: *The New England Holstein Bulletin.* She compliments, "Yummy, a great cake!"

Grandpa glances at the magazine out of the corner of his eye and says with suspicion in his voice, "Uh…what's that?"

"It's for folks who own registered Holsteins."

"Uh…why did you bring it?"

"For Dusty, since he's interested in Holsteins." Shirley explains, "It's an old issue that was sent to my son, Steven."

Feeling a little stupid, I ask, "What's a registered Holstein?"

"Registered means a purebred," Shirley says. "An official certificate is issued by the Holstein Association showing who the calf's mother and father are."

Cooner starts looking through the magazine and reads some of the recent sales reported. "Reg'stered cattle are bringin' good money. Never realized there was such a difference between reg'stered and grades."

Shirley turns to Grandpa. "Probably someday Dusty will have a herd of his own."

Grandpa snorts, "Uh…maybe. Every reg'stered cow I ever seen weren't no better than a grade."

Cooner isn't listening to Grandpa. He likes what he sees and keeps flipping through the pages, reading the prices, and the sales of registered cattle.

"Gosh, Thad, see here," Cooner remarks. "Jim and Janice Iverson had a heifer sell in the state sale for $5,000. She was sired by Astronaut, the same bull we've used some. Only difference, you ain't ever gittin' prices like that because your cattle ain't reg'stered. You know, Thad, your herd is full as good as the Iversons'." He turns a few more pages. "Well, maybe not quite as good, since they have a big name in Holsteins."

"Uh…why should the boy start a herd without ownin' the meadow? Dang blast it, I'm seventy-five years old. Then again, a Murray should own that land. What a mess!"

"Well, he doesn't necessarily have to farm here," Shirley says.

"Uh…no. I s'pose not." He sets his jaw.

Shirley explains, "The 4-H dairy project requires record keeping, learning how much it costs to raise a calf. A growth chart is kept. A pedigree is required—all important information for a future in dairying."

"Uh…I ain't never sprung for the kinda money it takes to buy reg'stered."

Shirley remarks, "It's a lot, but from what Dusty tells me, he really likes cows."

"Uh…let me have that magazine."

Cooner passes it to Grandpa. I doubt he'll ever give me a calf, but the party has changed him. He seems more relaxed than when he came to the table. Maybe I've changed in how I see him—not as an old grumpy woodchuck who has crawled out of his hole, but an old man willing to sit up and think of folks other than himself.

Maggie glances at the shelf in back of the stove. "I want Dusty to open my present."

Cooner jumps up. "Golly, Maggie, we almost forgot." He passes the wrapped package to me. I'm in anticipation wondering what it could be as I tear the wrapping paper.

Maggie watches me pull the paper off the package. She's smiling, wide-eyed. The paper falls to the floor and I hold a silver box in my hands that seems to be a small radio but it isn't. "A portable tape recorder? Thanks, Maggie. Show me how it works?"

"I will. Zelda didn't have any use for it so she gave it to me. Here, Cooner, say something."

"Happy Birthday, Dusty."

Everyone quietly sits. Maggie presses a button for the rewind and a second button for the recording. "Happy Birthday, Dusty." We all laugh; even Grandpa breaks into a slight smile.

I leave with Shirley and go out the door. "Thanks for coming, and for bringing the magazine."

She jumps in her truck. "I had a good time."

"I think Maggie even might have warmed the old grump's heart."

"I agree, he's gruff, but with a kind streak too wide to cover," she says as she slams the door. "You should get to know him. Have you ever given him a chance?"

"He's difficult." My hand is resting on the door handle.

"Sometimes you have to meet people more than halfway."

"Yeah, that's true with Grandpa." I stand back.

Shirley waves and leaves the yard.

After the party, Maggie and Addie are doing the dishes. I'm sitting with Cooner. He's all smiles. "I think Thad likes you, Maggie."

"Yeah, it was great to meet him after all these years. I like him, too."

—— CHAPTER TWELVE ——

The next morning, I knock at Grandpa's door. This is a first, going to visit him. I've wrestled all night with Shirley's idea that I should get to know him.

"Yup?"

"This is Dusty."

"Come in."

The walls of his two-room apartment are unpainted and dingy with no curtains, plus there's a stale smell of woodsmoke in the little room. But the place is clean and orderly. The magazine Shirley gave us is opened on a stand next to his overstuffed chair.

"I'm in here."

Following the sound of his voice from an open door across the room, I come to his bedroom. He's lacing his boot, resting his foot on a stool by his bed. A faded red-checkered flannel shirt shows between the straps of his bib overalls. He doesn't lift his head, but continues concentrating, as he threads the eyelets. I rest my hand on his bedpost.

"Grandpa?"

"Yup." He remains bent. All I can see is white hair and his back.

"Cooner is worried."

"Uh…what's the problem?"

"You know—selling the cows and making him find another job."

He doesn't look at me. He throws his jacket across his back and humps to slide his hands into the sleeves. "Uh…is that your business?"

I raise my voice. "Yes! It is."

"Uh…you think you own those cows?" He heads for the door.

"No, but how would you like to have to find a job? Cooner's close to being your age."

He abruptly does an about-face with a thoughtful expression. I now realize that he really hasn't given Cooner much thought. "Uh... I'm sick of goin' to the barn mornin' and night and makin' no money. Cooner only sees the cows. I see the milk check." He stares off into emptiness and sits on the wooden stool by his bed. "We'd be fools to keep doin' somethin' that don't pay."

"It might pay if you farmed the meadow. Then we could grow more feed and milk more cows." I'm watching Grandpa's expression, waiting for him to react. My eyes wander over the bare walls of the little room. A six-over-six pane glass window is facing nothing but an over-grown bush which blocks the morning light. There's a nightstand on the opposite side of his bed. A small pile of six or eight *Hoard's Dairyman* are beside the lamp with the magazine edges bending off the stand. Under the magazines the fuzzy edge of a slate-gray folder is showing—just enough to reveal a frame. I wonder if there's a photograph inside. Why is it by his bed, and why isn't it opened for him to enjoy? It might be of my family, maybe one of my dad and mother or my grandmother.

Finally Grandpa responds, "Uh... I know we could keep farmin' if we had more cows."

I move to sit on the edge of his bed, turning my back to the window. "Why didn't Great-Grandpa leave more of the farm to you?"

He snaps to attention as if he'd been jabbed by a needle. He stands, wanting to leave. But he stops. His shoulders slump, and he gazes, speechless. He draws a deep breath. "Uh...I ain't ever said, but I might's well tell you." He sits back down on the stool. "Uh...since last night at the party, I realize that I ain't acted just right. I've always seen that meadow layin' before me, not bein' able to forget."

"Forget what?"

"What I lost and what I did. I was interested in the farm, Bill really wasn't. I worked hard. Bill didn't. He was a sharp-lookin' guy— the women loved him. He was spendin' a lot of time at Rosie O'Neil's house. Our old man told me often, 'You'll be a good farmer someday. I can see Bill ain't carin' about it.'" He gazes out the window. "My old man as much as told me he was leavin' the whole place to me."

"Uncle Bill must've liked Rosie O'Neil a lot."

"Uh… Yup! Well, he ended up marrying her!" He pauses, seeming angry for some reason. Then he continues. "Rosie was Zelda's older sister. Zelda is at least fifteen years younger than Rosie was. Bill and I grew up with them." His face flushes, and he turns toward the window again. He seems distracted, continuing in a distant whisper. "She was a beauty. Last night seein' Maggie, she come back to me."

"Well, what happened?"

"Uh… I was about to tell you before you interrupted. I was always readin' about new ways of farmin'. One winter I come across this article that said wood ashes was good for the land. My old man had a team of horses, born the same year I was, in 1895. They were beauties, Nip and Tuck. Just like family. He'd raised and trained them himself." He places a hand on his knee and rubs it. "Every farmer had horses, and some even had oxen in those days. 'Course there weren't no tractors. But no one I knew had as fancy a pair of work horses as Nip and Tuck.

"Uh…they were a team that people stopped and looked at. Much the way folks admire a good-lookin' cow. I drove them around town collectin' all the wood ashes I could find. That spring I spread the ashes on a part of the meadow that I wanted to seed to timothy and red clover. It was my project, but my old man went along with it, as he was interested in seein' what we'd get for a crop."

"Why wood ashes?"

"Uh…wood ash is potash. The soil needs potash to grow a good crop. We buy it now in a bag. Anyway, I plowed and spread the ashes and manure on this plot of land. I pushed the horses some to get it done in between rains. At the time, my old man warned me about workin' the horses too hard. I half listened. Come summer, I had a bumper crop of hay. Bill said, 'You'll never dry it.'"

"Well, did you?"

"Uh…let me finish . Anyway, by mid-July the new seedin' was ready to cut. There came a clear spell, so I mowed and worked that hay. My old man warned me a couple of times, 'You're wantin' to push Nip and Tuck too hard. It's hot, give 'em a rest now and then. If they were mules they'd know when to quit. Horses will work themselves to death'."

"He must have really liked Nip and Tuck."

"'Course he did. More than anythin' he owned." He turns my way. "That hay was hard to dry, but the hot weather did the trick. The raked hay was thick and heavy. I knew if it got wet, I'd never get it dry again. After mornin' chores, I looked west and could see the weather was changin', and by mid-mornin' it looked as if in a few hours we'd be havin' rain. I harnessed the team and asked Bill to help. We loaded a couple of loads. It was beautiful stuff and was I ever proud. But, the bad weather was comin' soon. As my old man left for an errand in town, he warned, 'It's hot. You've got to rest that team.'

"Uh…I didn't stop for dinner, bein' driven to prove my idea—my project. After my old man left, I went right back to the field and loaded the hay myself. The team was blowing hard, but they kept goin'. They were lathered white with sweat. Golly, they had heart. Too much. Bill wouldn't help. He said, 'You've gone crazy over that hay of yours. I'm going swimmin' with Rosie.'" He stops talking. Even in recall, Grandpa's jaw muscle starts working.

He continues. "Uh…I was steamin' inside over him leavin' me and goin' with Rosie. The black clouds were comin' fast, and the heavy hot air felt like it could rain any minute. I whipped Nip and Tuck to get home and under cover. They never made it. Nip fell to the ground right in front of the barn doors. The skies opened up and the raindrops seemed as big as marbles. Tuck died a while later.

"My old man came in the yard to see his horses lyin' dead. He was heartbroken. He spoke steady-like. 'Thad, you treated Nip and Tuck mean.' There were tears in his eyes. 'I'll tell you this: you ain't killin' another team on the meadow.'

"Uh…after that day, he weren't never the same to me. It was plain that he favored Bill. Bill stayed and I moved out. I came here and fixed up this house and barn on the end of the meadow. I weren't more than seventeen. I married a school friend, your grandmother. We both worked hand in hand, dawn to dusk. I was bound to show the cockeyed world that Thad Murray could make it on his own. Weren't needin' any help from my old man. My feelin's toward him and Bill festered. I was pigheaded, thinkin' it was me against the world. Then my old man turned sick. Bill came to tell me. I barely spoke to him. A few weeks later, my old man died. I didn't bother with the funeral."

"Did you ever tell him you were sorry for killing his horses?"

"No, I didn't. Lookin' back, I should have." Grandpa stands and leaves his bedroom. "That weren't my nature."

As he starts to leave his apartment, he sits on the arm of an overstuffed chair. His right hand holds the doorknob while he hangs his head. He draws a deep breath. "Uh…I read some in that magazine Shirley left. There ain't no reason for you to start off in farmin' like I did. From what she said, you can learn from havin' your own 4-H calf. You know, the kinda animal that's reg'stered, and a good one will cost a pile of money. I ain't used to spendin' money like that."

"I know."

"Uh…well… I'll tell you what. I'll give you five hundred. It ain't the whole amount to buy anythin' fancy." He walks toward his desk piled with papers and sits and writes in his checkbook. "But you dicker and see what you can do."

"Gee, thanks, Grandpa! I never thought—"

"I know. You never thought I'd do a thing like this. But I've watched you around the cattle. You'll be a good cowman someday."

"Tha-nks." Staring at him, I shove the check in my pocket—dumbfounded over the change in Grandpa.

"Uh…Cooner and you go to Shirley's place." For the first time ever he smiles at me as I stand in shock as stiff as a scarecrow. "Get her to help you buy the calf." He heads for the door. "If I sell the herd, you can keep the calf here." The door slams and he's gone.

Curiosity brings me back to Grandpa's bedside. I'd never seen a picture of any of my family before. I pull the fuzzy-edge folder out from under the magazines and open it. Inside is the picture of a beautiful young woman. She's maybe sixteen or seventeen, I'd guess. Although she's posed with a serious expression, her mouth has that slight slant and there's a twinkle in her eye. The picture interests me because she reminds me of Maggie. In the corner of the stiff-paper frame, I can barely make out the faded writing:

To Thad, with all my love, Rosie.

I leave, wondering about Rosie O'Neil and Grandpa.

—— CHAPTER THIRTEEN ——

Saturday, mid-morning, Cooner and I set out in search of my calf. It's near the end of May. The hardwoods are fully leaved, showing their variable shades of green. We travel the valley, following the winding Blue. North of town the road climbs enough for us to see farmland for some distance next to the river. The lush meadows are fresh with new growth seen only in late spring. Cornfields are alive with row upon row of seedlings poking through the ground, reaching for the morning sun. Flocks of crows scour the land feeding on bugs and bits of trash—hopefully not the corn. A lone deer is feeding belly-deep in alfalfa.

When I called Shirley to tell her the news about the calf, she asked us to come to her farm. Apparently there's a family meeting planned, and her son Steven would like to visit with Cooner.

Cooner says, "Steven wants more land. I'll bet they're wonderin' about Bill needin' to sell the meadow." He shifts into second gear as we are climbing a long grade. "This farm we're passin' at one time belonged to the Perkinses. That's where Steven Iverson wants to build a new barn. Addie heard at her Home Demonstration Club meetin' that Mildred Perkins left the whole place to Shirley." He turns my way.

"Up 'til Shirley was nine, she lived with the Perkins family. After Mildred's husband died, she changed the will, bypassing her own family and leavin' the farm to the one who cared for her the most. Late years, Shirley looked after Mildred, treatin' her as good as any daughter would a mother. She probably never thought she'd be given the farm; but when Mildred died this past year, that's what happened. Shirley didn't want to leave Pine Mountain. Steven was finished with school and wanted to farm so she gave him the place.

"Now the young fellow has a foothold in the valley and will probably end up farmin' most of it. He already rents the Durkee place, and he probably wants to farm the meadow, too."

"Well, he doesn't have any right to the meadow *yet*."

"No, he don't. But there's no tellin' what might happen."

"Yeah, I know."

"Shirley was a state kid—never had any parents. She surprised the whole town when a girl with nothin' up and married Joe Iverson, our county agent. He's a real nice guy. He's just been appointed to head a town committee to help write development rules. Yup, folks think a lot of Joe."

We're crossing a covered bridge over the Blue. The truck cab darkens. I can hear the bridge's planking rumble beneath the truck. Off the bridge, we travel a road that follows a branch of the Blue. We pass several places that were once small farms. The houses look to be in okay repair, but the deserted barns are falling in. They all sag with rotted boards, and some have missing roofs. It looks like a heavy snow or a good blow could flatten them. Cooner turns right onto a lesser traveled road.

"Years ago Bill and I came up here coon huntin'. Soon as we got to the farm the dogs sniffed out a hot trail and started barkin'. The place looked deserted. There were no lights. Harold Tully, the codger who owned the mountain, came out of the house. We could see moonlight reflectin' off the barrel of a gun. He said somethin' like, 'What in all thunder are you fellas doin'? You act like you own the place.'

"'Well', I says, 'sounds like our dogs just treed a coon.' 'Course I was talkin' in the dark. Couldn't even see his face.

"'Yup, out back of the barn,' Harold said. 'Let's see.' We walked through a cow pasture to a single maple. The dogs were jumping up the trunk, barking their lungs out. Harold took charge. 'Shine your light, and we'll catch his eyes.'

"The beam of light searched the yellow leaves that clung to the tree. Harold acted sorta excited. 'There he is, a big one!' He aimed his shotgun toward the pair of reflecting beads and fired. The coon fell to the ground. It *was* a big one. Must have weighed a good thirty pounds. He carried his catch toward the house—coon in one hand, gun in the other. 'Now, you fellas can leave, since you took care of what you come for.'

71

"We laughed all the way down the mountain. Because of our dogs, Harold Tully had just walked off with a twenty-five-dollar pelt. We never went back."

Cooner takes another turn to the right onto an even lesser road. We pass a rotted thing that seems like it was once a platform. I ask, "What's that?"

"An old milk can stand. When farmers shipped their milk in cans, they had to bring them to a place for pickup." Cooner shifts gears and we begin to climb. "Most of those stands around town are long gone."

The truck groans around a steep hairpin turn. At my right, down an almost vertical bank, there's a huge maple tree in the middle of a waterless island of fresh ferns. It has two central leaders that bend in a curve and grow high into the sky. I've never seen a tree just like it. The truck transmission whines as we climb what seem like endless hills. The road is well graveled with water bars built in several places and culverts to direct run-off.

I ask, "Does a bulk milk truck come all the way up here?"

"It used to until Steven took the herd down to his place. I'm told Shirley just keeps heifers now. Her hired man, Willy, ain't able to work like he did in the past. He's a little off in the head."

We finally reach the farmstead. All the buildings are neatly painted. The white farmhouse sits on high ground overlooking the valley below. A group of huge pine trees are in back of the house. We leave the truck and turn to admire the view of mountain ranges. Cooner says, "I think we're lookin' way off into New York State at the Adirondack Mountains." Several heifers are coming in from pasture. A short, slight man drives them into the barn. "That's Willy."

A car and two fairly new Ford trucks are parked in the yard. High as we are, a constant breeze filters through the pine needles, causing the trees to play an undulating *whoosh*. We climb the knoll to the back entry. Shirley meets us with her usual warm smile. She's wearing a red checkered flannel shirt and blue jeans. "Hi, come on in. What good news! Your grandpa wants you to own a calf."

"Yeah, I can't believe he wrote me a check."

"I'm a little surprised, myself." She leads us toward the house. "Come in and meet my family."

I glance past her, seeing two people who probably want to ask questions about the meadow. A tall, middle-aged man stands near Shirley. She places a hand on his arm. "Meet my husband, Joe."

Cooner replies, "I know Joe, our county agent." They shake hands.

Shirley introduces me. "This is Dusty, Thad Murray's grandson."

Joe, in an easy pleasant manner, reaches for my hand. "Hi, Dusty, have a seat."

Cooner comments, "I hope we ain't interruptin' you folks."

"No, not at all," Shirley says. "Steven has some big plans for a dairy."

We walk into a modern kitchen similar to those seen in one of Addie's Home Dem. pamphlets. A small Franklin stove heats the large kitchen. I quickly look over the room: rich wood cabinets, black marble counters, a refrigerator/freezer, a double oven and double sink surround the kitchen. Joe and Shirley lead us toward the center of the room. Shirley says, "Dusty and Cooner, I'd like you to meet our son Steven." We shake hands. Shirley motions and urges, "Pull up a chair."

It's obvious to me that the reason for our visit is more about the meadow than finding a calf. I sit next to Cooner at a wooden table. Shirley and Joe are across from us.

Steven sits at the head of the table. His hair is dark, curly, and neatly combed. He has a lean face with a broad chin, and bushy eyebrows which are his most outstanding feature. He seems to me to be in his early twenties. For his age and situation, he acts confident. "Dusty, it's good timing that you came looking to buy a calf, since I'm looking for more cropland. Mother told me about your party last night. Apparently the meadow is for sale."

"I hope Grandpa can buy it. I want to farm my grandfather's place."

"Really!" Steven says. "That's a few years away, isn't it?"

"No, not that many. I want to start right out of high school. In fact, the calf we hope to buy can be the beginning of my herd."

Steven, seemingly unfazed, asks, "How big a herd do you plan?"

"I'm not sure. Grandpa says it has to be more than twenty-five— at least fifty cows."

"You two should work together," Joe suggests. "Steven can plant and harvest your corn in exchange for the use of fifty acres. What acreage your grandfather uses now, plus half of the meadow, should support fifty cows."

Cooner adds, "As Dusty said, Thad might be buyin' the land."

"Keep me informed," Steven says. "In the future, maybe we can work together in some way. You really ought to come to work for me after school. It would be good experience for you."

"Thanks, but Grandpa and Cooner really depend on me."

"Well, it's an open offer. Keep it in mind." He stands and pushes his chair back.

Joe and Steven leave to probably discuss Steven's future plans. Shirley turns her attention toward us. "Well, let's go and see if we can buy that calf." She gets up from the table. "How much did your grandpa give you?"

"Five hundred. He said I was to make up the rest by dickering."

"Oh! This might be a problem. We'll see. I know exactly where we can find a calf—but to buy it may be a different matter."

Leaving the house, she leads the way. "Let's go see my brother-in-law Jimmy Iverson. Iverson Holsteins are usually worth big money; but since it's for a young fellow in town, Jimmy might part with one for a reasonable price." As we near the truck, Shirley says, "He runs the place. His aunt Janice and her husband do all the work."

We meet Joe in the yard. Shirley raises her voice, "We're going over to your brother's to see if we can buy a good calf for this young man."

Joe comments, "He doesn't usually part with his best."

"Exactly, that's why I want to go along. I'll meet you later at your office." We get in the truck. She rolls down her window.

Joe heads toward his truck. "Good luck!"

Shirley waves. "We'll need it."

We ride a bit in silence. On the hill just before the hairpin turn, it seems like we're headed directly into the huge tree I noticed on the way to the farm. "Wow, what a tree!" The truck brakes are screeching, having been used plenty on the hills.

"Isn't it, though? One of our town's natural wonders."

I can feel myself moving forward in my seat as we slow for the turn.

She continues, "We call the tree Mary Maple. She's given me a lot of comfort over the years. Some days I come down here and just sit at the edge of the road soaking in her beauty. It's relaxing, helping me to forget my worries."

"Really? I can't imagine that tree could help me with any of my problems."

"Like?"

"You know. What's going on with the meadow."

"I understand," We ride in silence for a while until she says, "We're almost there. Buying a calf for five hundred dollars won't be easy."

We pull into a beautifully kept farmyard. Huge maples line the drive. A large sign picturing a Holstein cow hangs near the edge of the road. Below the cow is printed:

J-J Iverson Registered Holsteins

Cooner calls the barn an underground stable, meaning that one side is below ground level. The gravel road runs level with the haymow. We step out into the farmyard. Shirley leads the way. Entering the milk house, we follow stone steps down into the cow barn and meet an older woman. Her wavy, salt-and-pepper hair shows at the edges of a faded blue cap. "Shirley! Great to see you!"

Shirley's face brightens. "Janice, you know Cooner who's on the Thad Murray farm?"

"Cooner, gosh, it's been years since I've seen you. You should still be hunting coons. Golly, they did a lot of damage in our corn last year." She leans on the handle of her fork.

"Yup. I've heard that from other folks. The pelts ain't worth much." He pauses. "Besides, my huntin' partner is ailin'."

"I know. I'll bet the vultures are circling wanting to grab that meadow."

Shirley nods. "That's for sure." She places a hand on my shoulder. "I'd like you to meet Dusty Murray, Thad's grandson."

"Are you in Shirley's 4-H Club? Her 4-H'ers are the luckiest kids in town. She watches over them like a mother hen."

"Janice, that's a little overboard." They laugh. "This young man wants to buy a calf for his 4-H project. He's planning to start his herd with a good foundation animal."

"Well, you've come to the right place, but to separate Jimmy from one of our best might be difficult. He's not feeling too good today. Go to the office but beware."

We follow Shirley in back of a line of cows, all of which totally amaze me. They are tall, deep-bodied cattle with beautiful udders. Someone is throwing hay from the mow, stirring the air with the sweet smell of alfalfa. Yet the air is fresh, being moved by huge fans at the end of the barn. We squeeze into a small room located off the main stable. A slender, older man sits at a desk with one elbow and hand supporting his head. "Who ta hell is this crowd? Oh, it's Shirley. What a bad way to start my day."

This Jimmy guy seems older than Janice, but he's Shirley's brother-in-law—Janice's nephew. His unshaven bristles are gray and, under that dullness, a network of hair-sized blood vessels weaves into a pale, gaunt face. His pointed nose is red and runny. Wiping it frequently with a blue-checkered handkerchief, he limply holds the cloth in an open hand.

The wall space of the little room is crammed with dusty pictures of beautiful cows with this guy, at a much younger age, at the halters. Faded rosettes of blue ribbons hang from most of the pictures. Certificates of herd achievements fill any remaining space. Cooner has told me that Jimmy Iverson is known far and wide as an expert showman. This character with sagging jowls and a caved chest, who seems to be presently sinking into his chair, is supposed to be the last word as a breeder of Holsteins.

Shirley steps toward the desk. "Jimmy, I'd like you to meet Dusty Murray, Thad Murray's grandson. He wants to buy a calf for his 4-H project and a future herd."

"Sorry, there ain't none for sale. You've done it before. Brought in wimpy little Billy Stark wantin' a calf. I go to his place weeks later to check on that *special* calf only to find a half-fed bony runt with turdballs stuck to her tail. It made me sick. No, *n-o*, I ain't sellin' to no kid." He pulls out the bottom desk drawer and reaches for a large mug. He places it on the desk, pours coffee from a flask, grabs a bottle of liquor and adds a generous amount. "You're interruptin' my coffee break."

Cooner and I stand motionless. Shirley nudges her silver barrette and hops to sit on the desk. Her legs dangle off the edge. With her foot, she pushes the swivel chair. It pivots—he's facing her. She's looking down at him. "Jimmy, you're out of it and can't think. This young man is Thad Murray's grandson. Thad knows his cattle. With Cooner's help, they'll do a great job raising one of your calves."

"Huh, Thad, the old coot. I ain't seen him in years." He swings the chair back and reaches for his drink. "It was some time ago, he said somethin' like, 'What ya doin' wastin' your time playin' around with these show cattle? You're just on a big head trip instead of tendin' to business at home.' I felt like flattenin' the old grump." He takes a swallow from his mug.

"So, he hurt your pride a little. You aren't dealing with Thad. This is Dusty. I know, and you know, that any calf going to that farm will be grown right."

"You act as though I might give in to ya."

"Jimmy." She swings the chair again and reaches, pushing his head and shoulders back. "Look at me! Listen! You've done a great job in the past with the J-J Iverson name, but recently you've had to give up showing. Dusty is the new generation. He can be the one person who will continue your good name in cattle."

I feel a little scared as Shirley makes this bold promise, and I don't know a thing about showing a calf. But she continues trying to bend his will her way. Cooner and I watch in silence.

"Yup, in late years my arthur-i-tis has been nippin' at my heels."

"Yeah, and your liver isn't too happy either." She holds his attention by raising her voice. "Give this boy a chance and he'll make you proud."

That was another bold statement, but her reputation for getting results from her 4-H'ers makes me realize that I'll have to produce. And one thing is for sure, she isn't budging from her seat on the desk until she gets her way with this Jimmy character.

"I do have a fancy senior calf that I was aimin' to show this next fall. She's a beauty—out of our best cow family sired by Paclamar Astronaut."

She jumps off the desk and puts her hand under his arm. "Here, let me help you stand. Let's take a look."

He throws his head back and roars, revealing a mouth full of broken teeth with several missing. "Gosh, woman, you're determined! You think I'm sellin' the best show calf in the barn?" He stands, wincing in pain. "Where's my cane?"

"Well, Jimmy, *you* can't show her! You can't even get out of your chair." Her arm holds him on one side while the cane supports him on the other. He scuffs his feet toward the back of the barn. A large number of calves stand in a row of pens—all clean and bedded with fresh sawdust.

We reach the last pen and Jimmy says, "Here she is, J-J Iverson Astronaut's Pride."

She's taller than the other calves and smooth over her top with a slender neck and legs placed wide on her front end. She has a white patch in the center of her head, white in her tail, plus white on each of her four legs; but other than that, she's entirely black.

Cooner comments, "Wow, what a beauty!"

"Yup, born the first of September. She'll take her class at most shows, I'll bet."

I ask, "How much is she worth?"

"Two grand at the least, but I ain't sellin'." Jimmy humps over the edge of the pen. He offers the flat of his hand to the calf while she licks it.

"Oh." I step back, realizing Grandpa's check can't even come close to buying the best.

"Come on, Jimmy. Dusty's just a young fellow. Give him a chance. You were treated royally at his age." Shirley glances at him while he hangs on the gate admiring his calf. "It looks to me as though the curtain is closing on you. Have one last thrill, watching a J-J Iverson animal take her class at the county show."

Jimmy pauses. "Yeah, the Grim Reaper is climbing up my back." He strokes the calf's head, no doubt remembering the day when he could have led this calf into first place. But those days are gone, and he knows his next ride may be in the back of a hearse. "I'll tell you what I'll do. I'll sell her for less, but if she don't finish in the top five, I'll take her back."

Shirley asks, "How much less is less?"

"Oh, a thousand."

"How about five hundred?"

"What?"

"You heard me!"

"I can't do that."

"You can if you realize this kid is the only one you know in town that can show a J-J Iverson Holstein." Shirley leans over the gate to gain eye contact. "Isn't that right?"

He lifts himself from the gate, and looks at me. We stand in silence. He's thinking. Finally he says, "Well, kid, a thousand is cheap for this calf. You're lucky to have Shirley on your side, because there ain't nobody else that could talk me into sellin' her even for a thousand."

"Come on, Jimmy. You know Dusty can't come up with that kind of money."

"Boy—you go home, and talk to your old tightwad of a grandfather. Tell him you've located about the nicest calf you've ever seen. The calf will be yours on the condition you do a good job of showing her at the fair. You screw up and she comes back to my place!"

"Five hundred more?" I look at Pride. "She's sure a beauty, but, gosh, five hundred more?"

He straightens as much as he can and turns to Shirley. "Help me back to my office."

Shirley grabs his arm and yanks him to attention. "Jimmy, let Dusty take the calf today with the understanding he'll pay the five hundred this fall."

He scuffs toward his office not saying a word. Shirley's alertly looking at him for an answer. Cooner and I follow. I'm thinking how can I ever earn that much money. I doubt it will come from Grandpa.

Surprisingly, he says, "Load the calf. You have a check by fair time or I'm taking her home with me."

Shirley glances toward me. "I guess half a loaf is better than none at all."

"Geez." I look toward Cooner. "I don't know."

Cooner reaches for his tobacco. "I've known Thad for over forty years. He don't spend money easy."

Shirley set her jaw in an expression of determination. "Load the calf. We'll work out the details." She turns toward Jimmy who is about to fall if he isn't helped to his office. "Transfer the registration paper to Marcus Murray. We'll see you this fall."

"I ain't transferring nothin' until I get paid." He moves toward the office door. "Get me to my chair!"

Shirley raises her voice, "You transfer that calf. Dusty needs the paper in order to show her as his 4-H project."

"Yup, and I'm out my five hundred."

"You'll be paid," Shirley promises. "You have my word."

"Geez, I don't know. Grandpa's never paid me for working. "

Shirley bluntly says, "Have faith, you'll do it. It will be good for you to figure a way to buy this calf."

I can already feel the weight of debt and I'm only fourteen. Agreeing on the second payment is a joke—an empty promise. Grandpa will probably throw a fit. He's never bought anything by installments in his life. When I glance at Shirley, she gives me a look of determination. I'm sort of in a state of shock, full of hesitation. But Shirley motions for me to say yes. So I do. "Okay, some way or another I'll have the five hundred by this fall."

"That's the spirit." She smiles. "What a generous guy you are, Jimmy." She finishes her sentence with a chuckle.

He glances toward her. "You always were a real wiseacre."

"No, really—thanks, Jimmy, for giving Dusty a chance."

I pass Jimmy the endorsed check.

He takes it and grimaces. "I must be outta my mind."

Jimmy loans us a calf blanket before we load my new calf. He's left his chair. Shirley helps him to the barn door. He leans on the casing.

I quickly run my hand through my hair. "Thanks, Mr. Iverson, for giving me a chance. I promise I'll take great care of her and do my best."

"You better, or I'll load her and bring her home."

"I'll sure try to complete my end of the bargain." I don't know whether I will or won't, but I have to act halfway confident.

Shirley holds Jimmy by the arm, and they take baby steps back toward his office.

He mumbles, "I can't believe you got me to sell my best."

With all of us in the truck, we pull away from the barn. I'm sitting in the middle. I turn to see if Pride's okay. She seems fine. "Gee, Shirley, you were a big help."

She laughs, "We caught him in the right mood."

Cooner scratches his forehead. "Golly. I didn't think you'd pull this deal off. He seemed as set against selling as if you tried to pull a cat backward by the tail."

Shirley remarks, "I wondered myself. There's a lot of history between us two. I lived and worked as a state kid at that farm when I was in high school. He was a handsome guy then, and full of himself—too much so. I left and eventually ended up on Pine Mountain with Steven."

Cooner says, "I remember when Tully died and left you the farm. No one in town could believe it."

"His death was the saddest day of my life." She breathes a sigh, and rests her hand on her knee. "I'll stop by soon and give you the records you need to keep."

"Okay, but five hundred dollars, geez!"

"Don't worry. You'll figure a way. " She rests her hand on my shoulder. "You know the things you worry about the most never happen."

"Maybe." *She* isn't facing my challenge.

The truck enters the main street of town. We stop to let her off. "I'll see you soon."

"Thanks again."

After leaving Shirley in town, we travel the road next to the Blue, down in the valley where the view always seems peaceful. I again check on Pride. She's riding well. My excitement to have her is shaded by the hard cold fact: I could lose what's been given me.

—— CHAPTER FOURTEEN ——

After putting Pride in a pen, I head for the house. On the way, I stop to pet Slue as sort of a distraction from my heavy thoughts. She tightens her chain, and wags her tail, loving the attention. Since Cooner gets upset seeing her run free, I leave her chained. It's nearly noon. Addie is busy preparing the meal, humming a tune. I sprawl in my chair, and place my elbows on the table. My hands slide up my face with eight spread fingers raking my hair. "Geez."

The humming stops. "You didn't find your calf?" She pulls up a chair and sits with me.

"Well, yeah, sort of."

"Sorta, like what?"

"Well, she's a beauty, but I only own half of her. I've got to come up with five hundred bucks by fair time."

"Oh, no!"

"Yeah, that's what I think."

"Have you told your grandfather?"

"No, I don't dare." My hands are flat on the table. I'm staring off into open space, in shock.

"A deal like that with cattle?" Addie says, "Never heard of such a thing. It's best to buy what you can pay for."

"Shirley encouraged me to take the calf."

"That's Shirley. She's bolder and braver than most. And that's not all bad." Addie places her puffy hand on mine and gently shakes it.

"Dusty, you need to face this problem head-on. Tell your grandfather the whole story. He'll be here shortly. I've invited him for dinner."

"Where is he? I thought he'd be at the barn when we unloaded my calf. Well, kind of my calf."

"He's gone to the woods to dig some wild onions. He claims he needs a good spring tonic." Cooner comes from the bathroom, takes a seat, and is uncharacteristically quiet.

Moments later, Grandpa walks through the door, carrying a brown bag overflowing with wild onions. "Uh…here you go, Addie."

"Goodness, I guess so. I'll have these washed and cooked in no time." She takes the bag and turns toward the sink.

Grandpa sits at the table. "Uh…when I came by the barn, I took a look at that calf. She's sure a nice one for five hundred dollars. I told you Shirley could get the job done."

Cooner rubs his forehead and clears his throat. He fumbles for his tobacco.

I sit up straight in my chair. "Well, Shirley didn't get the whole job done."

"Uh…what'd you say?" He stiffens and glances at me with his eyes squinted and cross lines running onto the bridge of his nose.

"I…I've got to earn some money somehow." I try and act brave, but I can feel my insides tighten.

"Uh…how much?"

"Five—five hundred."

"Uh…you mean you only own half of the calf?" Grandpa's getting more upset as reality strikes.

"Yeah."

He pounds the table with his clenched fist. "You ain't gittin' no more money outta me!" His jaw muscles start working. "This 4-H stuff has gone too far. Yup, too far. Landin' yourself in debt over a confounded calf."

"She's Iverson's best—sired by Astronaut, and out of a cow that's scored 'Excellent' with outstanding milk records." There's a pause. I'm trying to think of what to say next. Grandpa continues to glare, but then I remember. "Maybe I'll go to work for Steven Iverson."

"Uh…what?"

I didn't mean to sound threatening, but it completely catches Grandpa off guard. I can see he's deep in thought. I continue, "Sure, he'd pay me well; there're no other farm kids in town. I could help him a lot."

Grandpa has both fists clenched. He turns to me. "Go ahead. Work for Iverson, but you're on your own. I ain't payin' for the keep of you."

Addie breaks the tension. "This talk has gone far enough." She slides a dish of steaming wild onions on the table. "Thad, a feed of greens will be good for what ails you!"

The meal is quiet. Grandpa shovels in the greens. Cooner and I take a few. They have a strong onion taste, but I say nothing. Addie eats little. She appears glum and upset.

Grandpa finishes and leaves the table. He stomps toward the door. "Uh… you're such a young whippersnapper; knowin' all there is about farmin', you can start milkin' night *and* morning." He slams the door.

The three of us sit in silence.

I leave the barn after night chores and glance toward Grandpa's apartment. Remembering what Addie said concerning the importance of facing problems, I feel the need to finish the discussion we had earlier in the day. I knock at his door.

"Yup." He's in his easy-chair. "Come in." He's holding *The New England Holstein Bulletin*. "Uh…what's up?" He slides his reading glasses down his nose.

I'm standing by the door. "Well, milking full-time, I was wondering what you had in mind?"

"Uh…to see if you have what it takes to be a farmer. You can stable a fancy calf, show her, and stuff like that; but milkin' twice a day is another matter."

"If I prove I can?"

His expression softens. "Uh…we'll settle up for the calf at fair time."

I take a seat. "Thanks, Grandpa."

"Uh…well, it makes sense to start off farmin' with good stock. From looking at the heifer, and knowin' her pedigree, it looks like you got a good deal. But I also want to see if you can earn it." He puts the magazine on the stand beside his chair.

"I've got to do well showing her at the fair or Jimmy says he'll take her back."

"Uh…you didn't tell me that!"

"Well, Shirley says not to worry about it. I'll do just fine."

"Ain't you got yourself out on a limb with this calf?"

"I don't think so, especially since you've promised to pay me by fair time."

"Uh…well, I'll tell you one thing, he ain't takin' the calf back if I have a thousand bucks into her."

"I'll work hard, and try the very best I can to make sure that won't happen."

"You'd better." He sits in silence for a moment. Then he says, "Uh…tomorrow afternoon I'm seein' Bill. You can come. Maggie asked. It's the least I can do for the girl."

"Sure."

Grandpa continues to stare, probably wondering how his visit will go—his first in fifty years. He lies back in his chair and softly says, "I want to see him before his lights go out and ask about the meadow." He's talking to the ceiling, seeming to forget that I'm in the room.

I stand and open the door. "We'll see you, Grandpa."

"Yup."

Sunday afternoon we're both in front of the lean-to garage at the back end of the house. We swing open the wooden doors. Grandpa's dark blue '41 Plymouth is gray from dust. We wipe the windows—pathways of clear glass follow the swipe of the rag. "Uh…I come in here from time to time and start her up to keep the bat'try alive, and to keep the engine from lockin' up."

I swing the car door open. A rotten stink hits me. There's a shriveled dead mouse lying on the passenger-side floor. I pick it up by the tail and throw it outside and slide in onto the fuzzy seat. Grandpa pushes the starter. The car fires and in moments the engine is running smoothly. He backs out and heads for Murray's Flats. To ride in his car is a first for me. I can't ever remember him leaving the farm.

Grandpa grinds some gears—the car bucks and spits, but soon we're gliding along. He's not talking but thinking. His mouth is clamped shut and that jaw muscle is working overtime. He's probably mulling over what to say to Uncle Bill.

We drive into the yard and jerk to a stop. Grandpa gazes at the old barns—speechless, maybe remembering the spot where Nip and Tuck dropped dead. We leave the car. "Uh… you knock. I'll follow." We climb the rickety back steps.

Maggie comes to the door. "Dusty! Uncle Thad!" She welcomes us with her usual smile. "Come in!"

Uncle Bill is sitting at the table wearing a threadbare robe. He's been failing since the last time I saw him and is much thinner. He presses with his hands on the table to steady himself to stand. His face flushes. He offers his hand. "Dusty! Thad!"

"Uh…Bill."

"How are you, Thad?" His eyes water—he wipes them with a Kleenex. "Have a seat."

"Uh…you—you ain't feelin' up to snuff?"

Uncle Bill drops into his chair, and shakily passes the tissue across his nose. "No, I'm at the end of the line."

Maggie slides a cup of coffee to Grandpa and a glass of milk to me with a plate of Oreos. "Thanks, Maggie."

Grandpa only nods, but he watches her when she takes a seat at the old table. Maggie looks as if she could cry as she looks toward her papa. He lifts his coffee cup to take a sip—some runs down his chin. She quickly passes him a napkin.

"I've been thinkin'." Grandpa reaches for Maggie's hand. "You might's well have a room at the farm when it's time."

Maggie smiles, "Gee, I'd like that."

Uncle Bill nods in approval. "Thanks, Thad; that will give her a good home—I appreciate the offer."

"Well, that's the least I can do."

Since it's such a sad visit, I hide the joy I feel knowing Maggie at some point will be living with us. I know Cooner and Addie will be happy to hear the news.

Uncle Bill continues, "Maggie and I have been talking about plans. It isn't easy." Tears run to the edge of his eyes. "I've got to sell. This cancer has broken me in the pocketbook." He wipes his eyes again. "Erickson wants to buy, but he isn't offering enough. Before I pass on, I want the mortgage, taxes, and bills paid. I also need to set money aside for Maggie."

"Papa, don't worry about me. I told you, I can take care of myself." She's continually rubbing a tight fist in her open hand. The cheerful expression has been washed from her face.

"Yes, well at least I want to leave with a good name. I need to pay my taxes."

"Uh…what are you askin' for the place?"

"Two hundred thousand. That's a deal for this place." Uncle Bill's head rests against the back of his chair. His eyes close.

"Uh…how 'bout to family?"

"Oh, a hundred …" He slumps forward.

Maggie and I jump up and each take an arm. Uncle Bill rallies. "Help me to bed."

We support him as he scuffs across the floor. I can't believe this is my uncle Bill —soon to be gone out of my life.

We help him get in bed. Maggie explains, "I think it's the pain pills he's taking."

On returning to the kitchen, Grandpa continues to sit, seemingly stunned. "Uh…Maggie, show me the tax bill?"

"Okay." She leaves for the front room and returns. "Here." She passes it to Grandpa.

"Uh…tell Bill I'll have a check this next week for his taxes; but I sure ain't got enough to buy the whole place."

Maggie sits at the table and starts sobbing. In moments she stops and wipes her face with a Kleenex. "This is terrible. I'm going to miss Papa so much."

I don't know what to say. "I wish I could do something."

"There's nothing. Death is the end," she cries.

Grandpa reaches toward her. His knobby hand holds her slender fingers. "Uh…Maggie…I'm sorry."

"Thanks, and thanks, too, for your offer to stay at your place. It means a lot to Papa and of course to me, too."

"Uh…well—in the past, I ain't done right."

"You came today. That's what matters."

—— CHAPTER FIFTEEN ——

After returning home, and before I get the cows from pasture for night milking, I run in the house. Cooner and Addie are seated at the table having a cup of coffee. "Guess what? Grandpa has asked Maggie to live with us after—"

Cooner breaks in, "I had a feelin' he might when he got to know her."

Addie adds. "It's the only proper thing to do." They look at each other and both nod in agreement.

That night, I lie in bed wondering about Orla. Maggie hasn't mentioned her since the day of my party. Maybe Zelda has heard, but I sense there is a general lack of interest as to her whereabouts. Although she's no longer in my life, she's left me the memory of the black heart.

For the next two weeks, I train Pride to lead. I hold her head high with the halter just as Shirley said, in order to make her look her best. The most fun, though, is teaching her to follow as I put grain in my hand and hold it behind my back. She walks behind me around the barn, taking a nibble, acting as though the bits of grain are tiny candied apples.

In a short time, a certificate arrives. It's Pride's registration paper. *Marcus Murray, Owner* is printed in a space at the bottom. I frame and hang it on the wall in my bedroom—pleased to see my name in print.

On a late Sunday afternoon, I'm working with Pride and decide to lead her in the yard. The nearby car races have just ended. It's the first race of the season, drawing a big crowd. The road by the farm is crammed with traffic.

Near chore time, the door to the house slams. Cooner's come to watch. He instructs, "Keep her head high. Don't walk too fast. Now stop. Hold her head higher—good job! Okay, start and walk slowly and smoothly, both of you movin' together. Good, I like what I see. By gosh, Dusty, I think you have a winner."

"Hey, Cooner, look at this." I slip the leather halter off her head. "See how she follows me!"

"Well, ain't that somethin'. You've done a good job trainin' her." He walks toward the barn. "I'll get milkin' started for you."

"Okay."

There's a warm spring mist working hard to turn to a light rain. Cars continue moving slowly. Steam is rising off the hot cement, warmed by a few hours of sun. The slow rolling tires on the wet pavement sound like sausage frying in Addie's skillet.

Pride helps me forget the races. I accept the fact that Cooner is dead set against them. Anyway, I don't care about car races now. I only hear the background music of passing cars.

Even with the halter off, Pride continues to follow me with a little coaxing. I reach in my pocket for grain and walk with my hand open and wrist bent behind my back. I can feel her warm tongue licking those little molasses-coated bits as we slowly walk. Tiny drops of rain are rolling off her hide. The raindrops look like Maggie's fake pearls set against Pride's oily black coat.

Taking her back to the barn, I don't bother to put her halter on. I'm near the barn door. Suddenly, the blast of the milker-pump being started drowns out the music of rolling tires. The pump sounds like a lawn mower with no muffler. The noise scares Pride and she rears backward. I laugh at first and try to put on her halter, but she turns charging toward the road. I lunge to grab her, but my running is no match for her gallop. It's useless trying to catch her. I yell in desperation, "Pride—Pride—stop!"

I hold my breath—putting my hands to my face. If she doesn't stop, I know she'll be killed or break a leg. Jimmy Iverson will be ripping mad. I know Grandpa won't pay for a dead heifer, and if she breaks a leg, she might as well be dead. It flashes through my mind—I can't imagine seeing her sprawled on the highway.

It seems the more she runs, the faster she flies. Her four legs are just a blur. She bolts under the maple tree not slowing her speed one bit, heading right onto the pavement and into the line of traffic.

Diving headlong between two cars, she stops at the guardrail and spins around. The driver of an oncoming car slams on his brakes. To my amazement, she heads back, just as fast as she left, galloping right to me. I can't believe it! She isn't even hurt! I quickly slip on her halter.

The car didn't even come close to hitting her. However, the jamming of brakes, and quick stopping, causes a whole bunch of cars to skid into each other. Car parts are flying in all directions. The racket of smashing glass sounds like the shakedown of a hundred china cabinets like Addie's.

I run toward the barn and put Pride in her pen. I can't believe what I see out the window. All those wrecked cars: one, two, three, four, five, six, seven. Grandpa's in the road trying to help. Cooner stops milking and rushes out the barn door.

I let out a whimpering, "Oh, no!" Snaky's car is third in the line-up. His hot Ford is wrecked in the front and back making it look like a metal accordion. He's screaming at Grandpa and Cooner, pointing at the barn. Men are shaking their fists. Kids are crying, and folks are mad; but it doesn't look as though anyone's hurt.

Grandpa backs away from the mess with his hand on his forehead, no doubt thinking he's going to have to pay for fixing up seven cars. I cry, feeling badly for all those people, knowing it's my entire fault.

No one can help me. I'm all alone. After I have time to think, I head toward Uncle Bill's; I need to see a friendly face even though he's awfully sick. He'll be someone I can talk to. I'll finish chores when I return.

Two police cars race down the flats with their sirens screaming. My tears roll faster as the shivers jump up my back when two wreckers come speeding toward me. It's like throwing gas on my burning guilt. I'm all out of breath and blubbering when I reach the old homestead. I climb the back rickety steps and pound on the door. Maggie comes. Her special one-dimple smile washes over me. I hug her, which is something I've never done before.

"What's wrong, Dusty?"

She hears what happened and immediately her cheery expression vanishes. A hand slides down her face, and her mouth opens in shock. "Oh, no! Snaky's car!"

We go in to see Uncle Bill. The dark shabby bedroom, with the faded wallpaper and gray curtains, does little to help the way he looks—nothing but a skeleton. He has a slight smile and strength to sit on the edge of his old iron bed. It sags enough for his feet to rest on the floor. His bony right arm lifts to shake hands. Fingers like sticks fill my hand. The motion is weak. His hand releases and drops with a thud against the mattress. A bedstand holds a lamp, a couple of books, an empty glass, and a framed picture. The frame's turned so I can't see who it is.

After I tell him the bad news, he reacts sounding confident. "That accident wasn't the calf's fault or your fault. I know you feel badly, but people who drive cars are supposed to have them under control. You say your calf was never hit?"

"Yeah, that's right."

"Bumper-to-bumper traffic, wet pavement, and maybe some drivers having too much to drink was an accident waiting to happen. Your calf only sprung the trap."

I add, "Snaky's was the third car. It looked to me to be a total wreck. When I left, he was yelling at Grandpa."

Uncle Bill doesn't smile as he heaves a deep breath and musters all his energy to lift his legs and lie back on his bed. His head sinks into the pillow. "Eddie's a hothead, but he'll calm down. For all we know, the police will give him a ticket for having that illegal muffler. And knowing Eddie, he probably had too much to drink."

I leave Uncle Bill's, worrying myself over Snaky and what he might do for a payback but feeling better knowing it wasn't my fault. I walk down Murray's Flats, toward the scene of the accident, and decide that I'm not going to run. Instead, I go to the state trooper to see if Uncle Bill's right. All the wrecked cars are gone and a highway worker is sweeping broken glass off the pavement. The evening sun has just broken through the clouds causing the glass to look like diamonds being flicked into the late afternoon light. A state trooper is measuring with a tape. "Hey, son, hold the end of this, will you?"

He's wearing black sunglasses and towers over me. His pistol, held in place by a black leather holster, is just below my eye level. His face and square jaw barely move as he talks. "You the kid that let the calf go?" He passes me the end of the tape and walks away as if he doesn't care to hear the answer. He writes in a small black loose-leaf notebook, slips it into his shirt pocket, and begins rolling the tape. His thumb and forefinger are whipping on the rewind. "I didn't hear you."

I gulp. A lump comes so big in my throat that I almost can't speak. "Yes—I—I lost control of my calf."

"How long was the calf in the road?" Pulling the book from his pocket, he's ready to write the answer.

"About two seconds."

He points with his pencil toward the edge of the road. "I see what looks like hoof marks here. Is this where the calf came into the line of traffic?"

"Yes."

"Was the calf hit or hurt in any way?"

"No."

"Okay, son, thanks for your help. Your name's Marcus Murray?"

It takes a split second for me to think. Nobody has ever called me that before. Finally I stutter, "Yeah—uh, uh, yes, but everyone calls me Dusty."

The trooper smiles for the first time while still writing. "I wondered. You look smart enough to know your own name."

We both laugh.

"Officer, I feel awful that this happened—the calf getting loose on me, but do you think all this mess was my fault?"

"I just report accidents, but the law reads a driver must have control of their car at all times."

"Really! Thanks."

He slaps his book shut and leaves. The sound of his boots rings off the pavement. I've been right next to the law, and not having it grab me wipes away my worry. Uncle Bill is right: the accident wasn't my fault.

Grandpa's coming from the barn. He asks gruffly, "Uh…how come your calf got loose?"

"I didn't have a halter on her." Tears are coming again. My voice wavers. "I—I'm awful sorry for all those people—and Snaky— darn."

"Uh…well, it sure was a mess, but I ain't havin' to pay for it." He rests his hand on my shoulder. "See's it ain't happenin' again."

"Oh, don't worry, it won't." The weight of Grandpa's hand calms me. I feel better—forgiven.

In the barn, I sit on a milk stool tipping it up against the alley wall opposite Cooner. I put my elbows on my knees and hide my face.

He's squatting by a cow, pulling down on the milking machine, working for the last drop while chewing tobacco. He spits in the gutter. "You're lucky that calf didn't get hurt." He removes the machine and carries the milker pail to the aisle. "When I went out there, folks were mighty upset."

"I'm sorry; I feel awful."

He grabs a hoe. With the end of the handle, he begins drawing a line in the inch-thick sawdust that covers the cement alley. "Now you watch. See those bits of sawdust move? Some of them ain't bein' touched by the end of the hoe handle, but they're movin'. That's like Pride runnin' into the road. She wasn't even touched, yet she caused a big pile-up." He looks me in the eye to see if I understand.

"Yeah."

"Legally, the smash-up ain't your fault. But her doin' that has caused grief for a lot of people. Limpy LaQuine's wife was yellin' at him that he was goin' to sleep down cellar until he learned to pay attention when he's drivin'. 'Course, Snaky was followin' his brother and it looked to me as though his car was totaled. He'll have to handle a lot of hay to pay for it. The cops threw the book at him for operating a car with an illegal muffler and for bein' half drunk." He steps between two cows to continue milking. "He deserved what he got."

"Eupha Smith was crying that she would have to put off buying her kids' clothes in order to get her car fixed. You see, if you move one little part in life, other parts fall to take its place, and what happens might not end up bein' a good picture."

"I won't do that again. I just hope Snaky doesn't come after me."

Cooner nods. "I hope not, too." He walks up the aisle. "I've got to start feedin'."

—— CHAPTER SIXTEEN ——

It's June. The yellow dandelion blossoms of May have turned to fluffy white seeds ready to take flight with the slightest breeze. The purple flowers on the lilac bush by the back door have faded away.

I've yet to hear from Snaky. His possible motives to do me in are scary: his pride and joy was turned into a mangled piece of tin, plus he had to pay a fine, and he lost his license. I know he'll blame it all on me.

As if worries about Snaky aren't enough, I have to be honest with myself and admit that the black heart continues to haunt me. Orla's gone, but the question remains: does she have the power to cast a spell of bad luck? I wonder. Whatever the case, the odds of a Snaky revenge are almost absolute. My day of reckoning will be soon.

I worry something awful, too, about my size—being reminded every day while standing next to kids in my class that I'm not growing. Of course, any encounter with Snaky will be a disaster. I can hardly fight my way out of a wet paper bag, and he has muscles as hard as cement. Knowing him, my final resting place will be six feet under and I'll be looking at grass roots by fall. Upstairs in my bedroom at night, I sit in my captain's chair in a gut-wrenching fear. It's important to keep an eye on Pride, making sure no one walks in the barn and takes her, especially Snaky.

Night after night, I fall asleep and wake with a start in a sweat over the same nightmare: a gigantic Snaky chasing me. I jump out of the chair to look out my bay window. No cars are coming across the flats. No cars are in the yard. Then I hold my breath to listen for sounds. Hearing none, I flop on my bed but still worry. Cooner tries to help me by making a joke out of my sleepless nights. "You ought to take a bale of hay to bed to feed your night*mare.*"

I force a laugh, but it doesn't help. I begin spending more of my nighttime sitting in my old captain's chair in front of the bay window. Since the window's big, I can see everything, on guard for imminent danger. Way in the distance, a faint light glows in the kitchen of the old homestead. It reminds me of a firefly in the blackest of nights.

Sitting and watching at the window gives me time to think. I recall sitting in my homeroom admiring the big picture of Napoleon Bonaparte. Mr. Carron, our teacher, visited France and had way too much to say about French history. Most kids groaned, "How boring!"

However, I was fascinated by the picture. Napoleon was brave and had courage as he defeated armies in Italy, Austria, and Russia, controlling much of Europe. He built excellent schools, a banking system, and wrote the Napoleonic laws. He was a bold, brilliant man. I liked that.

Actually, I liked reading French history. I studied a painting of him in a book, riding that same white horse as in the picture on the wall. He was on his way to conquer Russia. Against the background and the grayness of marching men, he's riding an all-white horse. Napoleon was fearless. It occurred to me there was no reason why I couldn't have courage even though I didn't have a white horse.

A while later, Cooner and I are on a trip to the town dump. We're bringing mostly tin cans, bottles, and things that won't burn. Grandpa never throws anything away unless it's totally worthless. At the entrance, we meet a new shiny Volvo pulling a trailer. The trailer's carrying a big white overstuffed chair. The white is what catches my eye. "Hey Cooner, is that guy going to throw out that chair?"

"That guy is Hiram Silver, past-president and owner of the Huntersville Bank. He's probably the richest man in town."

"So that's Hiram Silver, the grandfather of that stuck-up kid in school."

We watch him as he backs the trailer up to a pile of trash. Cooner and I get out of the truck and watch. A brown, short-haired dog the size of a cat starts barking from inside the car. It jumps on the back of the seat and stands with its nose pressed to the window yapping its lungs out. Mr. Silver is trying to calm his pet as he opens the door. "Now, Petey, be nice. I'll be right back."

His Saturday work clothes look like he has just walked off the page of a Sears Catalogue.

Cooner asks, "You aimin' to throw that chair?"

Mr. Silver walks to the back of the trailer as if he hasn't heard. He struts, acting mad at us for getting his Petey upset. He looks straight ahead, flopping down the tailgate.

I move closer. "If you're going to throw that away, I'd like it."

He's about to push the white chair into black, burned tin cans and trash. "You don't want this!"

I step even closer and firmly say, "I do!"

His face gets red. "My Petey had an accident on it."

The seat cushion has the irregular outline of yellow, reminding me of the world map hanging in front of our classroom. The accident is about the size and shape of Australia minus a few sharp points of land.

I casually say, "That's okay, I'll turn the cushion over."

He fidgets some, still wanting to shove the chair, and draws a deep breath. He turns his head acting as though he wishes we weren't watching him. Finally, he takes his hands off the chair, stretches his neck, and nervously clears his throat. "Petey has had more than one accident."

He hesitantly turns the seat cushion over, showing another yellow spot.

Cooner laughs and says, "Looks like a little dried Petey pee to me. That don't hurt nothin'."

Mr. Silver reluctantly gives me the chair. When we get home, Cooner and I show it to Addie. She comments, "It's a nice chair, but it's all white. I'm willing to make a cover for it."

"A cover? I want it *all* white."

Addie leaves and comes back with a pillow case. "Here, this will cover the spot."

That night, I sink into my chair feeling the smooth arms as soft and warm as cat's fur. It's right in front of my bay window. Now, I can look out over my empire—much the way I imagine Napoleon viewed his vast holdings while sitting on his horse. The only difference is that my white horse doesn't eat hay. I know, too, it's a lot more comfortable.

Resting in the chair and remembering Napoleon's courage, I'm not as anxious about my worries. I just have to keep watching for

Snaky, reminding myself not to get so shook up. In my lookout, I always check on the little light at the Murray Homestead.

My mind drifts to Uncle Bill. He's going to die. It's just a matter of time. Life will change, but who will end up owning his farm? Grandpa's right: without the meadow there will be no farm and no future for me, at least at the Thad Murray place. Dairy farming has changed. It takes a lot more cows to make a living— and more cows means more land. Steven Iverson's offer to share the meadow might work, but I wonder if he and Grandpa as partners would have enough money to buy the whole place.

The next night, Grandpa asks me to go with him to Uncle Bill's to give him the check for his taxes. We ride in his car to the old homestead and park behind what looks like a brand-new Cadillac. "Uh…whose car?"

"I don't know for sure, but I'll bet it's Buster Erickson's. Maggie told me he drives a Cadillac." The man is faceless to me; however, I've heard about him all of my life. Cooner told me, "He's as crooked as an apple tree limb, as sharp as a porcupine quill, and as mean as the north wind in January."

I've never met a through-and-through crafty swindler before, but the thought of doing so reminds me of courage, and it helps having Grandpa at my side. Also, being in Maggie and Uncle Bill's house will be comforting. A sign, as seen from house lights, on the steel gray Cadillac door reads:

Buster Erickson
Dealer in Hay and Land
Huntersville, Vermont

The back steps sway slightly underfoot as we both go to the door. I knock and Maggie answers. Surprised to see us, she doesn't have her usual smile but seems worried. "Come in. Papa isn't good tonight." She's nervously talking in a high-pitched voice. "He didn't even leave his bed today, and that horrible Buster Erickson is in his room trying to get him to sign over the farm. Of course, the crook stopped buying our hay. I'm sure he owes for some hay he's already taken, but he won't admit it. He's saying, 'Sign this sales agreement and I'll pay your taxes.' Poor Papa isn't up to dealing with him. He just lies in bed with his eyes closed."

I follow Maggie and Grandpa into Uncle Bill's room. A dim light hangs from the ceiling casting shadows over the dingy bedroom. Buster Erickson seems surprised when we enter. He abruptly stands while removing his gray fedora. He towers over Grandpa. He's heavy with a big belly. The tips of several cellophane wrapped cigars show in the pocket of his white silk shirt. His voice booms as he bends to wildly shake Grandpa's hand. The cigars jiggle and almost drop to the floor. "Pleased to see you again, Thad. It's been a while. I wish it wasn't over such trying circumstances."

Grandpa nods. "Uh…this here's my grandson, Dusty."

"Well, well, the next generation. Pleased to meet you."

Erickson shows his broken, tobacco-stained teeth as his big mouth opens. The guy's a fake. The tone of his voice tells me he's wishing we hadn't come interrupting his scheme to buy a farm for next to nothing. He passes his hand over his cigars, pushing them back in place and lets out a gust of air while settling into the chair. Fingers dance on the rim of the fedora before it rests on a knee that fills the hat to capacity.

As sick as he looks, Uncle Bill opens his eyes and smiles my way. The edge of a frayed blanket lies across his chest. His face has a yellow appearance and his breathing seems shallow. He makes no effort to lift his head from the pillow but does motion for my hand. I go to the other side of the bed. His arm slides across the bedding. I grasp his hand. There's no grip—it's cold. He's shut his eyes, but his welcome gives me confidence.

At the moment, Maggie isn't the Maggie I know. With arms crossed, she's tightly hugging herself. Her attention is on her papa, no doubt sensing his grave condition. Intermittently she shoots a glance of disapproval at Erickson.

I decide to face up to the man who's on the other side of the bed. If I'm going to save my kingdom, courage right now is badly needed. Drawing a deep breath, I momentarily scan the room. A picture in a silver frame rests on the stand by Uncle Bill's bed. It's the one I couldn't see from where I stood in the room the day Pride triggered the crash. In the picture a young-looking Uncle Bill is standing in back of a woman who's seated. She's holding a baby, probably Maggie. His wife is beautiful, similar in looks to Maggie, slender and tall. It occurs to me that I've seen a picture of her before at Grandpa's. It's Rosie O'Neil.

The last thing I notice before I confront Erickson is a placard hanging on the wall: *One Day At A Time.* My spread fingers comb through my blond hair. Taking a deep breath, I firmly say, "Uncle Bill, we've come with money to pay your taxes."

Erickson springs from the chair with his voice booming, glaring at me. He's holding a legal-looking paper and rattles it in my face. He fumbles for a pen, slapping the paper on the bed. "No need for you folks to meddle in my affairs! I'm paying the taxes! Bill needs to sign this agreement!"

I rivet my eyes on him. Mustering up all my bravery, I forcefully say, "Since we're Murrays, the farm is very much our affair. Our family will never sell it!"

"You're a cocky little runt! Don't be so sure of yourself!" Erickson's size and his loud voice bear down on me. "Trans-World Trucking is wantin' to own that meadow. You folks don't have a chance."

"Uh… how much are you offering?" Grandpa's jaws start working.

"A hundred grand."

"Uh…it ain't enough. Bill wants twice that."

"Well, he ain't gettin' it!" Erickson barks.

Grandpa points toward the door. "Leave! The boy told you. I'm payin' the taxes."

Uncle Bill opens his eyes and motions for Maggie. She goes to his side and bends down to listen. "Papa wants everyone to leave the room."

We glance at each other in surprise, but follow his wishes. The three of us stand in the kitchen. Erickson says, "What's this all about?"

Grandpa shrugs.

The best I can offer is: "I don't know."

Maggie motions for us to come back to the room. She's trying to hold back tears. She says to Erickson, "You can have the farm for one hundred and fifty thousand, but you've got to pay the taxes in cash.

"Cash? Okay, but of course you'll take a check." Erickson smiles, obviously happy he's closing in on the kill even at fifty thousand more than he offered.

Uncle Bill motions *no.*

I can't understand him. Maybe he's not thinking right. He told us he'd sell it to family for a hundred. Maybe he's figured a hundred thousand isn't enough to cover his debts.

Grandpa's shoulders slump—defeated. He has a right to feel that way, because how can a twenty-five-cow farmer fight the likes of a trucking outfit? Uncle Bill turns his head toward me and weakly squeezes my hand. He falls into a deep sleep. Maggie leaves the room, returning with a piece of paper and handing it to Erickson. She says, "Pay us in *cash* for the amount of the tax bill. Papa will sign your sales agreement in the morning when you come back with a legal witness."

He turns toward Uncle Bill, seemingly insensitive to the man's grave condition. "I'll do that, but Thad can sign as a witness right now." He whips around to Grandpa.

Grandpa holds a distracted gaze at the foot of the bed and says nothing.

"Can't you talk?" Erickson asks.

Grandpa's stunned at the thought of losing the meadow.

I blurt, "He won't sign!"

Grandpa motions *no.*

"This ain't your business, kid!"

I lean toward the bed feeling bigger and taller than I am. "It is! Grandpa would be stupid to sign a paper putting us out of farming."

Erickson points with his pen at the appropriate line and lowers his voice as if coaxing a chicken toward the chopping block. "Thad, you'll sign? Right here."

I grab the paper and throw it across the bed. "Don't do it!" Grandpa backs away from the bed shaking his head.

"Shut up, kid!"

"Grandpa won't sign!"

"Look! Keep out of this!"

That cold stone feeling comes to my gut and a big lump is building in my throat, but I try to sound as steady as possible. "I won't!"

Hearing loud voices, Uncle Bill opens his eyes. His head turns my way again, and I detect a slight smile of approval.

Erickson offers, "I'll pay by check."

Uncle Bill again moves his head slightly, motioning *no*.

Erickson draws a deep breath, takes the document, and edges toward Grandpa. His forcefulness causes Grandpa to back up. Buster disgustedly says, "Okay, it's against my better judgment to pay by cash; but, Bill, you'll sign in the morning when I bring a witness." He feels for his wallet from his back pocket. Uncle Bill again falls into a deep sleep. Erickson counts the money for the taxes into Maggie's open hand.

Grandpa offers, "Cooner will take the money to the Town Clerk's in the morning, if you'd like."

"Okay." She passes the cash to Grandpa.

Erickson stomps out of the room. I can feel the floorboards give from his weight. They creak as he walks into the kitchen. "I'll be here first thing in the morning with a witness." He thunders toward the door, then blares, "Thad, that kid needs his backend kicked!"

The door slams, causing *One Day At A Time* to clatter against the plaster wall. Maggie presses her papa's hand in hers. No doubt noting its cold, clammy feeling, she pulls an additional blanket over him.

Grandpa and I leave the old homestead. My bravery in front of Erickson got me nowhere. It's the first time I realize the power of money.

"Uh…Erickson's goin' to change this place; but it ain't the right change."

"Yeah, it looks like Murray's Meadow and the pines are gone forever." Again, I feel that lump. I clear my throat, but the feeling won't go away.

—— CHAPTER SEVENTEEN ——

Upstairs in my bedroom, I crash into my white chair. I know how Napoleon must have felt after marching deep into Russia toward Moscow. Thousands of his men were starving or had frozen to death. When he arrived, the city was deserted and burned down. The Russians were gone. Nothing was left—no food or shelter. Napoleon was a defeated emperor.

I, too, feel defeated. I don't want to join the army, or be an emperor. All I want is to be able to drop seeds in soft black soil and watch them grow. But it's no use; the Murray farm is history.

Uncle Bill is also on my mind as I look out my window at the far light. He was trying to tell me something with the squeeze of my hand and his smile. I know it was a smile telling me that what I was saying was okay. I think he liked the way I stood up to Erickson. Just the same, I know this much: Grandpa and I are the losers. By morning, legal papers will be signed.

I sit wrapped in my blanket. Passing car lights shine through a downpour. The new leaves on the maple droop from the burden of windblown rain. The outside howl sends a low whistling groan through a slight crack in my window, singing one long sad song.

From my high perch, I make a mental note of my frequent night watchman's duties. It's my Snaky watch: Slue isn't barking—check. No strange cars in the yard—check. No lights in the barn—check. No spooky noises in the house—hold my breath—check.

Now, absolutely sure that everything is okay, I fall asleep in my chair. Sometime later in the night, I wake. It's stopped raining and the night is clear. I look off in the distance at the old homestead. The place is ablaze with lights. A set of headlights has just turned into the yard. I hurry to dress and run downstairs to Cooner and Addie's bedroom. He groggily wakes. "What's up?"

"Something's going on at Uncle Bill's—the place is all lit up."

Cooner slips on his bib overalls and boots. "Oh, dear—oh, dear."

We chug along the flats toward a new chapter in our lives—one we don't care to read. We know what's ahead. Neither of us says a word because neither of us wants to share the obvious.

We enter the yard. A black hearse is parked near the back door. Choking from grief, Cooner shuts off the truck, flopping his head on his hands that grip the steering wheel. I leave him and start toward the house to find Maggie. She's standing in the doorway. Two men are carrying a stretcher with a white sheet covering Uncle Bill. They slide it into the back of the hearse.

From ground level, it appears as if Maggie's a statue. I climb the back steps. She pulls me to her with her long strong arms. Her body is shaking, pressed against my slender frame. We both mourn and cry as if we are one person. After a moment she draws a deep breath. "Poor Papa, he was so sick. I'll miss him!" She continues to cry as we watch the hearse leave.

"I'll miss him, too." I choke, "Why don't you come with us?"

"I think I will." Maggie shuts off the house lights and we go to the truck. Cooner and Maggie hug, quietly crying. After a while, he pulls himself together enough to drive us back to the farm. I decide not to tell Grandpa until morning.

We both go upstairs. Maggie continues to sob, but I feel sort of guilty that I'm happy to have her in the next room. She's better than my white chair. For the first time since Snaky's car was wrecked, I can completely relax because Maggie has always been my protector.

In the morning at breakfast, Maggie reports to Grandpa in a broken voice, "Papa died last night." She breaks down and sobs.

He reaches for her hand, speechless, but with a sympathetic expression. "Uh... the funeral—I—I ain't no good at stuff like that."

"I'll call Zelda. She'll help."

"Uh... go see the probate judge."

Maggie questions, "Probate judge?"

"Uh...he tends to all the legal stuff. You not bein' of age—it's all needed."

Cooner comes from the barn. His face is white. Tired circles make his eyes droop more than usual. We did chores, but we both went through the motions without talking much. After chores, in the house, Cooner says, "Dusty, you and I should go to the old homestead, close up the place, drain the water in the pipes, and shut off the electric'ty. It'll be months before anything is settled."

"Okay."

"You can't lock the doors," Maggie says, "because the keys are lost or the locks are broken."

We leave and go to Cooner's old Chevy, get in, and sit. He starts telling of all the good times Bill and he had while hunting and fishing. He pauses, gazing through the bug-spattered windshield. "He and I were drinkers, you know. It got way out of control. After Rosie died, he started up, and I did, too, to keep him company. Coon huntin' and drinkin' went hand in hand. Thad and Addie put up with a lot, with me hung over most of the time. Bill's farm was hurtin' 'cause of it."

After a while, he starts the truck and we leave the yard. The old truck's motor is groaning so loudly that it's hard to hear him. It really doesn't matter because he's mostly talking to himself. We travel through a cold, damp June rain before driving into the old homestead yard. When the motor is turned off, I ask, "Did you ever know Uncle Bill's wife, Rosie?"

Cooner turns toward me with a searching glance. "Why are you askin'?"

"I just wondered."

"Rosie O'Neil was a looker. She had a smile for everyone. She and Zelda, her kid sister, grew up in the house across the road." He pauses. "As young fellows, Thad seemed to be the one that was goin' to make somethin' of himself, more so than Bill. Bill was more into havin' a good time." He stops talking while collecting his thoughts. "When I was just a kid, I remember seein' Thad and Rosie at dances. They were a handsome couple. But as it turned out, Thad was into doin' his own thing, not payin' enough attention to Rosie." He pauses. "I guess. Bill saw the opening and took his brother's place."

"Maybe Grandpa's been grumpy all of his life over losing more than the meadow."

"Yup, maybe so. Bill got it all, and your Grandpa ended up with a convenient marriage, old buildin's, and five acres. Don't get me wrong, your grandmother was a good woman, and good for Thad; but she wasn't class as Rosie was, and maybe that's just as well."

We leave the truck. Cooner carries his toolbox to the house. Once inside, the place feels damp and lifeless. The friendly faces I've always connected with the place are gone.

Cooner says, "I'll pull the water pipes apart down cellar. After all these years, they'll be rusty. When I give a yell, you turn on the faucets. I'll watch to see if the water drains back to the cellar."

Apparently the pipes are hard to separate, because I wait quite a while, listening to Cooner's loud hammering. I stand by the kitchen sink and look out the window. The haymow door hangs open. Spring grass has covered the tracks where weeks earlier we loaded hay. The farm buildings are shabby and deserted.

Finally I hear, "Turn the faucets; I've shut off the water and separated the pipes."

After following Cooner's directions, I look through the window over the sink and see a gray Cadillac drive in the yard. It raises dust as hot white mist blows from the muffler. I gulp, seeing Buster Erickson and Snaky leave the car. Buster tugs on the brim of his fedora as they come toward the house.

I yell, "Buster Erickson and Snaky are here." Cooner clomps up the cellar stairs. I don't answer the knock at the door but wait for Cooner, who's holding a pipe wrench. I step to his side.

"What are you doing here?" Erickson asks with paperwork in hand. "Where's Bill?" He glances toward the bedroom. "I've come to have him sign this purchase and sales agreement." He glares at Cooner. "Where's Bill?"

Cooner hesitates. "Ain't—ain't you heard?"

"No! Heard what?"

"He—he died in the night."

Snaky's bottom lip draws tightly, worry lines build on his forehead, and his eyes squint shut. He hangs his head and backs up against the kitchen sink. That's a surprise to me. I didn't think he cared about anyone but himself.

Erickson roars, "I paid his taxes in cash. That's why he wouldn't take a check. He knew I'd stop payment at the bank. I've been robbed. He knew he was going to die. All I needed was his signature."

"Wait a minute," Cooner says, "no one knows when they're goin' to die."

"He did! The kid and he had it all worked out."

Cooner's anger flares. He points the handle of the pipe wrench toward Erickson. "Hog-wash. Dusty had no part in Bill's death!"

Erickson dramatically yanks on the brim of his fedora. "No one messes with Buster. I'm owning the Murray farm if it's the last thing I do."

Cooner yells, while continuing to point the wrench at Erickson, "You ain't buyin' it from a dead man!"

Buster stomps out of the house. Snaky is white and shaken, saying to the both of us, "Bill was a good guy. I'll miss him."

As we watch the Cadillac race out of the drive, Cooner laughs for the first time. "Ain't that somethin'. The way Bill handled Erickson. I know your uncle realized he stopped buying hay to force a sale, but instead, the whole scheme backfired." He mumbles as he gathers his tools, "Maybe Bill did know he was going to die before morning— who knows?" He opens his truck door and slides in his seat. He's in deep thought, then smiles. "As the old sayin' goes, Bill sure showed Erickson where the bear laid in the wheat."

"I guess." That statement doesn't make sense, but I don't ask what it means.

Cooner and I buy some *No Trespassing* signs to tack on the old homestead and on the barns because there is no way we can lock the place. Maggie and Zelda stop by on their way back from town and tell us the probate court is now in charge of the homestead and farm. The judge said it would take a few months before the property is sold and the estate is settled.

We all go to Uncle Bill's funeral. The church overflows with friends. Even Grandpa goes. He and I sit with Maggie and Zelda. To my surprise, Snaky is among those chosen to carry Uncle Bill's casket. Cooner, Mr. Silver, Joe, and Steven Iverson are also pallbearers. I don't recognize the other man.

Uncle Bill must have planned his funeral, because I know Maggie wouldn't have chosen Snaky. I figure he wanted folks to know that he was a friend to everyone.

That afternoon, after the funeral, Cooner, Maggie, and I are loading Maggie's clothes, some furniture, dishes, and valuable items she wants to store at Grandpa's. She points out the kitchen window. "Someone has been loading hay. Look at the truck tracks and the hay chaff on the ground by the mow door."

"Yup, I guess so." Cooner nods. "The tracks are fresh."

Maggie says, "This needs to be reported to the probate judge."

— CHAPTER EIGHTEEN —

Although I'm happy to have Maggie in the room down the hall, she continues to be quiet and sad over the loss of her papa. Most nights she comes to my room and just cries, saying, "I miss my papa so much."

There's no way I can help, except to listen and feel sorry for her. After a few days she begins to mourn less and less and starts talking about girl things such as, cute guys in high school, dancing, and the latest hit records. I come to realize how different we are, because I'm thinking about Buster Erickson, Snaky, Pride, and, of course, the meadow.

We're physically different, too, in that she, of course, is a girl and I'm a boy; but also because she looks sixteen and I look twelve. One night, I stand with my back to her back and feel my head press against her neck. She quickly turns around. "Dusty, what are you doing?"

"I want to see how much I have to grow to catch up with you."

She doesn't laugh, but instead looks very serious. "Don't worry about that; I like you just the way you are."

Those words feel great. I give her a big hug, thinking I've just been given the biggest gift ever.

Since school has let out, milking morning and night is easy for me. I can feel myself getting stronger handling the heavy milk pails. Grandpa comes to the barn at irregular times to see how Cooner and I are doing, but he never says much.

Maggie is able to work nearly full time at the greenhouse. She has learned enough to be left in charge when Zelda is gone. The money she's earning allows her to buy a radio, a record player and records, teen magazines, lipstick, powder, and other make-up stuff, and, of course, clothes.

After supper Cooner and I usually play cards or checkers. Maggie, after helping Addie, listens to her records and sings her favorite songs.

This particular Friday night, I'm at the kitchen table making Pride's sign to put over her pen. Cooner told me I should so that people would know all about the most beautiful animal in our barn. Besides, Shirley is coming soon to check on my progress. On a piece of white cardboard, I carefully letter Pride's full name, birth date, her sire, and dam. I'm copying the information from her registration paper.

Grandpa is eating with us more often. He seems to like having Maggie live with us. She breezes around the kitchen helping Addie. She smiles and laughs, brightening her space, especially today. A powder blue ribbon holds her wavy hair in place. A work shirt with tails drape over her blue jeans.

We've finished our meal, and the table's been cleared. The dishes have been washed. Addie goes to her room and Maggie stands by Grandpa, resting her hand on his shoulder. "How would you guys like a cup of coffee?" She bends to face him. "Uncle Thad?"

"Uh...sure."

"Cooner?"

"Yup, sure thing."

I'm concentrating on the sign. "No thanks, I'm full."

Grandpa watches me. "Uh... golly, Pride's lookin' fancy. I hope she milks as good as she looks." He turns to Cooner. "Uh...we got to get to hayin'. We're late. It's getting' ripe." He pauses. "Since we're in this dry spell, we should start."

"Yup," Cooner agrees. "I noticed this mornin' the sparrows were flying high and there were a bunch of cobwebs on the grass. I'll mow the Hubble place late mornin'. Dusty, you free to run the conditioner?"

"Yeah, okay."

"Zelda is home this week. I can help," Maggie remarks as she reaches on a cupboard shelf for coffee mugs.

Grandpa watches her as her head tips back and her hair spreads across her back. "Uh...you'll get hayseed in that pretty hair. Reminds me of Rosie's."

"My hair's no problem."

"Yup," Cooner adds. "Rosie, she never had to worry about hayseed—never touched a bale. She never set foot in the cow barn, neither."

"Really!" Maggie places the cups on the table. "So Rosie never helped my papa?"

"Not a scat. She was beautiful to look at, but beauty wears thin when you're tryin' to run a farm from dawn to dusk and your wife's in the house prancin' around in high-heeled shoes and a fancy dress."

Maggie places the coffee mugs on the table. "Huh, that's something I never knew, although she did act as my adoptive mother for a short time."

Cooner nods his head. " 'Acted' is a good word. Bill is the one who wanted you. But as it happened, Addie and I had you most of the time—you, Orla, and Dusty."

"Uh… let's stop talkin' about folks that have left us." Grandpa takes a swallow of coffee. "This feels good goin' down." He says to Cooner, "Uh…you might's well mow the Duffy place, too, long's we got all this good help."

"Yup, I'll do that before night chores."

I ask, "How come you talk about the Hubble place, the Duffy place, the Adams place, the Thorne place? All these people are gone. I never knew any of them."

Grandpa explains, "Uh…those were the folks that farmed when your grandmother and I were young."

Cooner adds, "I remember. Most of them had a few cows, layin' hens, a couple of pigs, and a big garden. They all hayed with horses, helped each other out—went to church, Grange meetin's and Saturday night dances. They worked together—good farmers who were sprung from the earth."

I comment, "That must have been neat, living back then."

Cooner continues, "It was, but not long after the war, in the fifties, down-country folks bought these little places, and most tore down the barns. Now you'd never know of all the farmin' that went on."

Grandpa grumbles, "Uh…now, you can't even make a livin' on twenty-five cows."

—— CHAPTER NINETEEN ——

Late Saturday morning, after the dew has dried, Cooner leaves the yard driving Grandpa's Massey-Ferguson "50" tractor with a mowing machine hitched behind. He heads west on the flats for a half mile toward the four-acre Hubble lot. I follow with a Ferguson "35" pulling the Cunningham hay conditioner. I've been running this hunk of metal for two or three years. Today, I'm happy with myself because I had strength enough to lift the steel pole and hook it up to the tractor—a first.

Cooner starts mowing, while I wait beside the road for him to circle the small lot a couple of times. He's slowly following the hedgerow, watching the cutter bar and where he's going at the same time. The cut grass leaves a mown path. Grass pollen and dandelion seeds follow the cutter bar, filling the air with a dusty haze. I start the hay conditioner with the rolls, spinning like a wringer washer—only faster. They clatter a deafening sound until I head into the first swath. The whirling rolls suck in the grass, leaving the crushed stems lifted from the ground, seeming like a million miniature teepees. Cooner says conditioning cuts the drying time, and the cows love the softer hay. Tomorrow at midday, I'll have to stir the hay with Grandpa's old tedder. But it's in good condition like all of his equipment.

Tuesday, mid-morning, Cooner rakes the hay, and by afternoon, Grandpa's baling. He follows the windrows with the reel on the baler devouring the loose hay like a bunch of hungry cows. The plunger on the baler pumps out firm, square bales that are tied with two strings. Cooner drives the tractor and wagon while I pick up the bales and Maggie stacks them. I'm surprised I can handle the thirty-five pound bales with no effort. I smile inside—it's great to be fourteen and getting stronger. Just lately, I've also noticed that my shirt sleeves and pants are shorter. I'm finally growing. When Maggie turns around to put a bale in place, I stretch as tall as possible and flex my arms. When she's ready for the next bale, I pass it to her.

After we load the wagon, she and I ride on the back with our legs dangling. I slip off my T-shirt and wipe the sweat from my face and arms. She takes the back of my shirt and wipes her face and neck. "Wow, it's hot today. We should take a dip in the pool behind the barn."

"Maybe we'll have to wade," I remind her. "The Blue's pretty low."

"Anything to get wet. We had a lot of fun there once."

"Yeah, until Orla pulled down my trunks."

Maggie laughs. "Zelda heard Orla's been traveling with a carnival show and hates it. I guess her father's real mean and treats her like a prisoner."

"I'm not surprised."

Cooner drives the hay wagon beside the hay elevator at the barn. I climb the tubular metal conveyor to the mow. Cooner leaves to find an extension cord to reach an outlet for the elevator motor.

From the mow door, I have a good view of the meadow. Except for the corn patch, it's showing mostly dead June grass. I'm sure there's other stuff growing, too, such as ferns, goldenrod, and paintbrush; but all I can see from the mow is a huge field of brown—like the amber waves of grain in *America The Beautiful.* Up close, it sure isn't grain, and it sure isn't beautiful. Of course, no one has heard from the court; so the land lies idle, not grazed, hayed or even mowed. What's growing has been living on a starvation diet for years. Many are wondering what will happen to all this open space right next to town. Since the court is taking its own sweet time making decisions, there're probably others wanting in on a chance to buy—Steven Iverson for one. I've seen a few out-of-state cars parked on the flats: folks probably looking and drooling over all that open space.

Cooner yells up to me, "All set, I'm plugging her in." The elevator starts and the carrier chain clanks until the first bale takes a ride to the haymow. I'm stacking the bales in the mow above the cow stable. Cooner passes them to Maggie. She places the hay on the elevator at a reasonable rate. Not like Snaky, loading the conveyor with end-to-end bales. I could never possibly handle them fast enough. He'd let out his donkey laugh, "How you doing up there?" He knew I was buried in hay.

Now as I stack the bales in the stuffy mow, I'm getting really hot. Maggie's idea of a dip in the Blue seems great, but we have a few more loads before that can happen. Besides, haying will run right into chore time. A break will have to wait.

After we finish, having handled about five hundred bales, Cooner looks and acts tired. Maggie and I offer to do the night chores.

"We put up a big jag of hay," Cooner says as he leaves.

"Uh…you kids make a good team," Grandpa mumbles as he leaves for his apartment.

'A good team' circles in my head while I'm getting ready to milk.

Maggie helps me tie up the cattle. She feeds hay and grain to the cows and tends to the calves while I milk.

A little after seven, we let the herd out to pasture for the night. Finished for the day, we partly wash up in the milk room. Maggie says, "I'm nasty dirty, but let's go swimming after supper."

"Swimming?"

"Well, wading."

As we walk in the house, Addie says, "My, my, you kids have put in quite the day." She places a plate of sandwiches on the table. "Look at you! It's time you both washed up."

Maggie announces, "Later we're splashing around in the Blue."

Addie offers, "You kids go along after supper. I'll do the dishes."

My shirt's spattered and limp from sweat. I slip it off before we sit. Maggie runs upstairs and changes into a yellow halter top and shorts. She takes her usual seat. We're enjoying some sandwiches and iced tea.

Addie says, "My goodness, this heat has drained the life right out of me."

Cooner agrees, "I guess." His bib-overalls hang by his side. White chest hair shows from the edge of his undershirt. His forearms and biceps are pasty white. "Maggie and Dusty have the right idea. This hot spell sure makes you want to shed your clothes."

Grandpa looks tired and says nothing. He munches on an egg sandwich.

We sit in silence. All we hear is the *purr* of a fan. After eating, I ask Maggie, "Can you get some towels and my bathing suit? I'll change in the barn. I've got to check on a cow. She might be calving." When

I'm at the barn door, Slue starts whining. I unsnap her chain. She's all excited, wagging her tail and slapping it against my leg. "You want a little freedom, don't you?" She whines as if trying hard to answer, and follows me into the barn.

Dusk closes in as the sun slowly fades behind the trees. Entering the barn, I turn on the lights, and walk to the back corner pen. Nothing is happening with the cow. In passing, I glance at Pride. She's lying down, chewing her cud.

Maggie's at the barn door, wearing her bathing suit and sandals, and carrying towels over her shoulder. She passes me my suit. I change in the milk room, and in seconds we're walking toward the river. "Thanks for your help today. It's lots of fun when we work together."

"Yeah, I agree." She pulls me by the hand. "Let's follow the cow path over the bridge."

The night is cooling, but it's still warm. The air seems filled with crickets as thousands sing their nightly song. The cows are resting under the willows. The ground is scorched dry. Grasses and thistles have withered to brown. Our sneakers stir the dust. We walk beside the Blue and can barely hear a trickle. We reach the pool, made by a three-foot stone dam that Cooner built. The water feels quite warm because of the shallow flow and hot weather. It's only about two feet deep at the base of the dam. I duck my head under for a second and then sit on bedrock, scrubbing myself with the flat of my hand. Water mixes with the sweat and pours over my head to my mouth. I spit the salty taste and duck again, scrubbing my head.

Maggie is beside me doing the same. We sit side by side on a flat stone. I put my arm over her shoulder, pinching a lock of her dripping hair with my thumb and index finger. It slips gently taut full length to the end. The straight hair reaches down her back. She turns and throws her arms around my neck, pushing me back into the water. I catch us from going under by my arm and hand bracing against a stone.

"You like pulling my hair?"

"Yeah, it's sorta fun." We laugh, and move to sit on the towels lying on the bank by the river. Slue rests near me, since she's already sniffed out everything close by.

Maggie says, "We need to plan more days together; not work necessarily, but just fun stuff like long walks. Maybe climb a mountain or swim at a lake."

"That sounds great, maybe visit the pines someday this summer if you can find the time. Do you think you'll spend your whole summer working?"

"Probably, I like it, and Zelda has been good to me." Maggie hesitates. "She—she's mentioned meeting you."

"Yeah, we met the day Orla and I came home from swimming." I wanted to say I wasn't too impressed but held my tongue.

"Instead of you being a farmer, she thinks you ought to go on to college and really make something of yourself."

"Yeah, that's her opinion. I would like to go to agricultural college, but I don't know how I'd ever get the money to go. You know as well as anyone that farming's my dream. Someday, if I breed outstanding cattle, this place will pay. The farm with the meadow, the pines, and the Blue—I can't imagine leaving it." I throw a short stick up-river. "But I know Erickson or others might have a different idea."

She places her hand on mine, which is resting on my knee. "Well, I love what I'm doing, too, or at least until I have a family."

I pull my hand away. "A family! You haven't even finished school yet!"

She slides her hand over my shoulder. She gives a determined look while drawing my head close to hers. "Someday."

Clouds have moved in. The night turns black as if we were under a blanket. "I hope we're in for a weather change. Our corn sure needs a drink."

Maggie laughs. "The farm again. It's always on your mind."

"Yeah, I guess so."

Suddenly, a sharp, long-extended howl opens up on the ridge, followed by *yip, yip, yip*. "That's a coyote and her pups. They sure sound eerie." Slue lifts her head and whines, sliding closer.

"I hope they don't run down here and eat us alive."

I laugh. "Really, Maggie! Coyotes are cowards. They feed on animals that can't defend themselves and dead stuff. Tonight I feel very much alive."

"Well, if you say so. I'm far from dead myself." We both laugh.

We lie quietly side by side. Her hand rests in mine. My thumb follows the long smoothness of her index finger, rubbing her soft knuckle, liking the tender feel. It thrills me to hold her hand, which seems crazy to say, but it does.

Maggie whispers, "It's so warm. Let's sleep here tonight."

"Sure."

Maggie's breathing and Slue's deep sleep make for a pleasing rhythm of sound as water slowly trickles through the stones of the dam. The crickets continue singing, and the cicadas join in the chorus of easy listening. The night air is filled with lightning bugs putting on their silent fireworks show.

With no warning, Slue jumps to her feet. Her head's in the air, sniffing. She charges along the bank into darkness and opens into a long piercing bark. In seconds, we hear snarling. The sharp chatter of a coon echoes in the valley. Up-river, splashing, growling, snarling, and yelping drowns out the peaceful sounds of the night. A life and death struggle between animals is frightening to hear. Slue lets out another piercing yelp. I'm helpless: no light, no gun, no possible way to come to Slue's rescue. Cooner has told me a big coon's more than a dog can handle, especially in water. Slue lets out a piercing yelp of pain.

The noise brings Cooner out of the house with a light and a gun. He's on the run. Maggie and I follow. Thankfully, the battle's in shallow water—too shallow for the coon to drown Slue. They're in a rolling death grip—soaked with water. Slue intermittently gasps for air, trying to get a strangling hold on the coon's throat. But the animal dodges and bites back. The water's red with blood. Slue's exhausted, panting, wobbling on her legs. The coon finally breaks away, running toward deeper water. Cooner yells, "Hold the light."

Slue's instincts won't allow her to give in. She follows the coon. The end is inevitable. The gun fires: *bang*. The twelve-gauge recoils. Slue charges, growls, and pulls the dying coon into shallow water.

Cooner says, "Whew, that was close!" He checks Slue for injuries. "She'll be okay." He angrily turns and stomps toward the house, grumbling, "Lettin' Slue free at night without you havin' a gun— might's well push her off a cliff."

Maggie says, "I'm sure Dusty didn't realize."

"Well, he does now!"

"I'm sorry," We start for home. "That was scary! I've never seen anything like it."

"'Course you ain't! You ain't a coon hunter!" He continues toward the house.

I put Slue on her chain. She flops down, and begins licking her wounds. Maggie has the towels and clothes in hand. We say, "Goodnight," and go to our rooms. I can hear rain beginning to sprinkle on the tin roof. Before going to sleep, I shiver at the thought of pushing Slue off a cliff. Then I turn to a more pleasant memory—feeling Maggie's hand in mine. She's changed and I know I have, also. Fourteen's more than okay—it's exciting.

CHAPTER TWENTY

Near the end of July, we've had enough rain to grow a nice second cutting of hay. The flock of Canada geese that hang close to the river has increased in numbers. The spring goslings are almost full grown. It's hard to tell the difference between the adults and their young. Daily, they take practice flights over the meadow, honking in a broken V formation.

Maggie shares a letter sent to her from the probate court. It announces that Zelda O'Neil has been appointed Maggie's guardian, with the Huntersville Bank as executor of Uncle Bill's estate. The court sets Thursday, October 15, 1970, for the opening of bids on the real estate, which will include all personal property; an appraisal of the value of items left in the estate didn't warrant holding an auction. All bids are to be submitted by October 9 to Emily Ann Gray, president of the Huntersville National Bank and executrix of the estate. The hay is being sold for mulch to a down-country buyer. It will be stored in the barn until May 30, 1971.

We're seated around the table for our noon dinner. Maggie passes the letter to Grandpa. He reaches for his reading glasses and studies it. We all sit quietly waiting for a remark. The portable fan on the kitchen counter sends a slight breeze toward the table, filling the air with the sweet smell of Addie's berry pies she's just taken from the oven.

Grandpa clears his throat. "Uh...Bill's gone, and that meadow should by rights stay in the family. I hate to, but I'm bidding forty thousand for the land." He glances at the letter. "Uh...It probably ain't enough, but that's as high as I can go. We already know Erickson's willin' to pay a hundred and fifty for the whole place. I need to find a partner."

"Great!" Maggie adds, "Zelda said she'd like the house, and would use the barn as storage for her florist business. She also told me that if she ever owned it, she'd build a new shop at the end of the meadow.

She also needs about five acres of the meadow for green houses and gardens."

"Uh…sounds good to me." He glances at Maggie. "Zelda and I can be partners." He folds the letter and passes it to Maggie. "Uh… 'Course I hardly know the woman. If we win the bid, we'll put the heifers in the old chicken house and milk more cows." He takes a sip from his glass of iced tea. "If we don't win, they're goin'."

I could have jumped up from the table with a big cheer. "Maybe the meadow can be saved!"

"Don't count your chickens yet," Cooner reminds me. "There are others that want that land as much as you do."

"Yeah, I know."

The next night at chore time, I'm tacking my sign over Pride's pen. She's stuck her head and neck over the gate, lapping my shirt. "Pride, you're being a pest." She has my shirttail in her mouth and is yanking hard enough so the collar is cutting into my neck. Tacks are in my mouth, and I'm holding one with my thumb and index finger. The edge of my hand holds the sign in place while I stand on a milk stool. Reaching with a hammer, I try to hit the first tack.

Grandpa happens to be in the barn. "Uh…you needin' some help?"

I'm surprised to hear his voice, so much so that I swing too far backward. The three-legged stool kicks out from under me and I fall in a heap, losing the tacks on the sawdust-covered concrete. As I fall, my shirttail slips from Pride's mouth. I jump up, pick up the hammer, search and find the tacks in the sawdust, and set the stool upright.

Grandpa hurries to help, throwing Pride some grain to keep her busy for a while. "Uh…here, let me hold the tacks, and I'll steady you."

I can feel his big hand firmly holding the cloth of my pants as it tightens around my knee. This is the first time Grandpa's helped me with anything. I swing the hammer with my right hand as I hold the tacks with my left, driving them into place. I step down. "Thanks." We both look at the sign and I comment, "Now people will know who she is."

Slowly he casts a glance at Pride from head to tail. "She's a fancy one."

"Yeah, she's grown a lot since she's been here."

"Uh… yup, I think she has."

On Friday, I'm in the shed helping Cooner repair a hay wagon when Shirley's truck pulls in the yard.

I leave to meet her. "Hi, what's going on?"

She opens the truck door and steps out, holding a manila folder. "How's the calf doing?"

"Just fine. See what you think."

While walking toward the barn, she says, "Golly, you were lucky Pride didn't get hurt in that accident. I hate to think what could have happened."

"Yeah, I know, but I'm worried that Snaky's waiting for a payback."

"Oh, forget him."

I open the barn door. We walk toward Pride. She's standing, her ears alert, with her head and neck hanging over the edge of the pen. She watches us come toward her. Shirley says, "Wow, she's a beauty. And the sign!"

I smile. "I thought you'd like it."

I easily slip on Pride's halter. She follows me down the alley and out into the yard. I've brushed her every day, eliminating her dead hair. Her coat's short, black and shiny, especially in the bright midday light. I lift her head and lead her in a clockwise direction.

Shirley, standing several feet away, watches us. "You two are looking good together." She becomes totally absorbed in observing me. "Now stop, and set her up. Remember, from a side view the hind leg, facing the judge, has to be in a backward position. I'll go to the other side. Now, make Pride change that rear leg."

"I didn't know." I'm pulling on her, trying to get that hind leg in the proper position; but she's looking awkward by moving her hind leg too far forward.

"You've got plenty of time until the end of August to teach her, but that leg change has to be done at the halter by moving forward." Shirley continues to watch me critically. "Your halter strap is practically dragging on the ground. Loop the extra length through the grommet on the chain, and hold it in your free hand."

Shirley's firmness with me shows she's all business. That's a side of her I've never seen, but I know it's for my benefit. After taking Pride back to her pen, we go to the house and sit at the kitchen table.

The manila folder she's holding includes a calf-raising record that I have to keep: pedigree information, purchase cost, feed cost, health information, growth rate in pounds, and a graph comparing her growth and height with the average Holstein her age.

"Gosh, there's a lot to this!"

"You're a smart kid. It shouldn't be a problem, but do a good job. There's a committee that will check your eligibility to show."

"Really!"

She slips on her jacket and opens the door.

"Thanks for coming."

She smiles. "It's fun working with an interested kid." She jumps in her truck. "Oh, by the way, Joe's been asked to help in appraising the meadow. I told him you might like walking the land. Zelda O'Neil wants to come, too."

"Yeah, sure, but why her?"

"Zelda has some big ideas."

The day after Shirley's visit, a truck pulls in the yard. Cooner and I are still working on the hay wagon in the shed. Cooner says, "That looks like Joe Iverson's rig. He ain't never visited this place."

"Probably because of Grandpa."

"Yup. Thad ain't one to take advice from a county agent."

"Shirley told me Joe was coming to check out the meadow with Zelda O'Neil." I go to meet him. "Hi, Joe."

The truck door slams. He's walking toward me wearing a crisp clean cap, a beige work shirt and pants. "How are you doing?" He's carrying a long tube-like thing.

"Fine."

"Shirley says you'd be interested in walking the meadow with me. Zelda O'Neil is coming, too. She'll be right along."

"Why?" I already know, but he might give me more information.

"Representatives from I-vest Engineering out of Boston are here today. We're meeting with them and Zelda to discuss the use and value of your Uncle Bill's property."

"What's that you're carrying?"

"A soil probe. We can check soil types and top soil depth."

"Oh."

I know Zelda O'Neil doesn't think much of me farming for a career. Maybe she doesn't think much of farming, period. I sure want Grandpa to have some ownership in Uncle Bill's farm. He will see things my way. The meadow, the Blue, and the pines are a part of us; something that most people don't understand.

Mr. Carron in history class told us once that, when meeting a person, the impression you get in the first eleven seconds is fairly accurate. Well, to be honest, Zelda O'Neil didn't pass the test for me. Maggie likes her, but I'm not sure I do. She's too pushy, and she sort of gave me the cold shoulder the last time I saw her. So on our jaunt, I plan to be quiet and stay in the background. I don't want to hinder her bid with Grandpa.

She pulls in the yard, driving a sleek black sports car. A cigarette's hanging from her mouth when she opens the door and steps out. She's wearing a business suit with leather boots that run halfway to her knee. Her graying blonde hair's in a bun with some of it hanging at loose ends against a face that has a smoker's shadow. In the sunlight, her almond-shaped eyes squint through her silver-rim glasses. She crushes the butt in our drive, while gushing toward Joe, "Hi, handsome." Her voice has that gravelly tone I remember. "What a nice day to romp through the meadow with just *you!*" She does a short skip and bows in front of Joe.

Joe stiffens, but shakes her hand. "You've met Dusty Murray?"

She glances my way. "Yeah, this spring. He and that daughter of mine were at the house. Unannounced!"

I'm standing a distance from them. Her attention is entirely on Joe. I know she wishes I was out of the picture, but her actions toward him seem fake. I have the feeling she doesn't know how to act around a man.

Joe says, "Dusty's coming with us."

"Oh!" She throws me off with the jerk of her head and the lift of an eyebrow.

After we cross the fence in back of the barn, we start walking in the meadow. The dead June grass doesn't reach my knee. Goldenrod is scattered throughout the meadow, but isn't in blossom yet. Little short broadleaf ferns are also noticeable in patches. The sky is clear, and the late-morning sun is getting hot.

Zelda, coughing now and then, begins to breathe hard to keep up with Joe. Sweat is beading on her wrinkled forehead. She fumbles in her pockets for a Kleenex. She stops and dabs at her face. "This sun!" She continues between each deep breath, "This is just a flat piece of land. . .that's good for nothing. No wonder Bill. . . almost starved on the place."

"Oh, on the contrary," Joe says. He pushes his three-foot-long probe into the ground, pulls it out, and shows us the circular core that lies in the instrument. "This soil is the best." He spreads some into the palm of his hand. "It's classified as Huntersville deep sandy loam." He throws the soil and rubs his hands. "If limed, fertilized and rotated, it will grow a huge crop." He turns her way. "Bill never took care of the land; of course it looks worthless. It's like trying to travel to Boston on a gallon of gas. The land has lost its fertility."

We pass Cooner's and my patch of corn that's tasseled and about eight feet tall. "Great corn!" Joe comments. "Zelda, see what some cow manure can do for the soil."

"I guess." Disinterested, she glances away and coughs.

Joe heads toward the Blue, and we follow. I'm trailing, but can hear the conversation.

She's a few feet in back of Joe. "If it's such great land, the whole field could be stripped of its topsoil and trucked down country for landscaping."

He stops in his tracks and abruptly faces her. "You aren't serious? That would be a crime!"

"If I bid on the property, I want to figure ways to recoup my investment." She shrugs, and lights a cigarette. "That was just an idea."

We reach the edge of the Blue, and Joe says, "This land has an endless potential for all kinds of crops. There's even a possibility of irrigating in a dry year."

She glances at the willows that line the river bank. "These trees should be cut so future residents can get a better view of the water."

Joe gulps. "Those trees are important to the river. They hold the banks in times of high water."

She shrugs again. "Just a thought."

He glances up toward the ridge. "I'm told by our forester that the pine stand we're looking at is one of the best in the county."

Zeldz squints toward the ridge. "They'd make a great timber sale."

Joe scowls and turns his back on the river to view the nearly hundred-acre spread. "Most farmers would give anything to own this land."

"Farming, huh! What a poor choice." She drags deeply on the cigarette and blows a cloud of smoke.

"I thought you were a florist, wanting greenhouses, and a place for gardens."

"I am and I do, but not a hundred acres."

We hear the buzz of a small plane flying over the meadow, making several passes, circling, gaining altitude, and traveling over the ridge and pines. Zelda says, "That's the I-vest Engineering plane."

"What are they doing?" I ask, holding my hand above my forehead, watching the silver aircraft.

"Taking aerial photos to draw up plans for possible future development. They'll make a proposal to your grandfather and me."

Although the plane's at a distance, I feel it's in my space. It's an intruder—circling like a turkey vulture, quiet, but menacing with intent to claw and tear up my dream. I feel overwhelmed: First Erickson, then Iverson and Zelda, and now with I-vest Engineering all wanting to take control. What chance do I have?

Joe adds, "Any such plan would have to be approved by the town."

"The town!" Zelda says, "That's no problem."

Joe says, "Huntersville has interim zoning. I'm on a committee that's writing zoning laws to be voted on in March."

Zelda throws her cigarette and crushes the butt with the sole of her boot. "The development I'm imagining would be a huge benefit to Huntersville."

Joe looks away. "Maybe."

Being with Zelda O'Neil is discouraging. She has such wacky ideas. I comment, "I never thought that Uncle Bill's whole farm could be turned into a small town." I frown. "I don't know what's worse; a trucking place or a bunch of houses."

She says, "You wouldn't know, just being a *kid*."

Her tone of voice is filled with sarcasm. I'm ready to explode, and I know she doesn't like me. Maybe it's because I don't live and breathe dollar signs. She obviously doesn't care for the ground she stands on, Great Grandpa's pines, the willows, or the sun. She even coughs up the air she breathes. But I keep my thoughts to myself. I'm comforted knowing Grandpa won't approve of her. He can flatten her far-flung ideas after they've signed on the dotted line; however, she and Grandpa might not even win the bid. I cringe at the thought.

— CHAPTER TWENTY-ONE —

On a warm day in late August, Maggie wants to walk to the Marcus Murray pines. I like the idea of visiting a place that's special. After leaving the house, we head toward the Blue in back of the barn. We stop on the bridge and face upstream. The shallow water moves toward us, curling lazily around all sizes and shapes of brown and gray boulders.

As we stand, we're almost touching—close enough for me to smell the fragrance of her hair. Maggie's hand lies limp by her side. I drop my arm to almost touch hers. Do I dare reach and show my feelings toward her like I did the night after haying when we washed in the river? Hand holding then was almost by accident, but this would be obvious, showing I really like her. My heart's in my throat. My clenched fist is damp. We continue to watch the river flowing in our direction.

In a fun loving way, Maggie chuckles. "You were almost getting romantic the night we splashed around in the river." She bumps my hip with hers. "Let's go to the pines." She reaches for my hand. "We can just sit and talk."

Her light hearted mood puts me at ease. I draw a deep breath, relax, and follow.

We stir dust as we walk off the bridge. The thistles growing along the cow path have gone to seed; white fuzz shows in place of pink blossoms.

We slip through the gated barway, leave the pasture, and follow an old logging skid path. It sweeps across the slope in a slight incline toward the ridge. Maggie leads the way through Uncle Bill's old heifer pasture. Saplings of a number of hardwoods, plus spruce, fir, and pine are rapidly filling in the open spaces. We follow the old fence line along the stone wall. Here and there, weathered posts lean in all directions with strands of age-old wire sagging like limp rope from rusty staple to rusty staple. Frost and tree roots have caused what was once a straight wall to be crooked, with stones being moved over time through decades of seasons.

We walk quietly. Suddenly Maggie throws up her hand, motioning for me to stop. Up ahead, three baby foxes are playing on the wall. They're the size of house cats. All have healthy rich red fur, with fluffy tails and pointed noses. They spot us and dive for their den on the back side of the wall. We laugh. Maggie says, "Aren't they precious?"

"Yeah, they look almost like stuffed animals." We pass their den, with the path on an incline below the wall. We can see sets of eyes peering through geometrical openings. They crouch in their cubicles, checking on us intruders. Light reflects off their glassy eyes and off their noses that are similar to black corks.

The stray white pine grows below the direction we are headed, at least five hundred feet from where we walk. We both notice it. Maggie asks, "Remember the heart I cut in that tree?"

"Yeah, the black heart. I'm enjoying the walk. We don't need to check it out, and let a bad omen ruin our fun."

"You still think about that?"

"Sometimes. Maybe there's something to the strange powers Orla has in that locket of hers. Do you think because you put your name next to mine in the heart, and she covered it with black dirt, that the future may be miserable?"

She continues to walk. "Of course not; that heart means nothing."

"I wonder." I watch her stride in front of me. The white daisy on her blue shirt pulls taut across her square shoulders as her arms swing. We have almost reached the ridge. The pines are a few hundred feet ahead of us. We leave the skid path and follow another one that's been traveled by wildlife, mostly deer. In soft spots, cloven hoofmarks are evident, a telling sign of a path recently traveled, leading to the cover of pines.

Maggie stops. She turns to face the valley. "Come on, slowpoke."

Breathing hard, I reach her, and pull a handkerchief from my pocket to wipe the sweat from my face. "Whew, that's a climb!"

She tucks loose hair under her bandanna and pins it. "I think the pines will be cooler." She reaches for my hand and squeezes it.

My flushed face covers my blush. Maybe she's blushing too, but I can't tell. In a glance, her dimpled cheek is brighter than her red face. I look at the three white daisies with yellow centers evenly placed on the front of her T-shirt, and tell her, "You have a bug crawling across one of your daisies."

She pinches her shirt, pulling it outward, then brushes it off. She looks up and says, "You have one in your hair." I tip my head toward her. She pushes her fingers through my short hair. "Stand still." She holds her hand in place. "I want to show you this bug when it crawls on top of my finger. It's a ladybug."

While she holds it in her hand, we watch the orange and black shelled insect crawl to the tip of her slender index finger. "The horticultural guy that stops at the greenhouse calls this bug 'a beneficial.' It helps control damaging insects."

"Really!"

Our eyes meet. We're within inches of each other. We embarrassingly laugh, and back away. I quickly turn and press up against her back-to-back. I feel her head against mine. "Hey, I'm almost as tall as you."

Maggie says, "I've noticed. It's all that cow manure you've been standing in." We laugh.

On the ridge, we enjoy the view. The brown grass in the meadow is in sharp contrast to the deep green corn patch. "I can't imagine what the valley will look like if Zelda O'Neil gets her way. Do you like her?"

"Yeah, well, she's my mother." She glances my way. "You don't?"

"Not really. She wants to ruin all that I've grown to love, just for a few dollars."

"She's been good to me."

"How come you still call her Zelda?"

"I've always called her that. She's never been a mother to me. We only talk florist business, and not personal things. Papa was more of a real parent than Zelda is or ever can be."

"That's for sure. She's never been there for Orla."

"Orla's not a worker." Maggie rechecks the bandanna covering her hair. "Zelda has this love-hate feeling toward her. Especially when Orla calls, asking for money."

"After being with the woman on our walk through the meadow, I feel sorry for Orla, but I must admit that feeling sorry has its limits."

"Orla isn't bad. She's just difficult."

"Yeah, spoiled, always wanting her way."

The light breeze feels good while we rest, standing on the ridge watching several cows drinking from the river, while others are grazing, and a few lie in the shade of the willows. I ask, "Do you think our family will ever own the entire valley?"

"Maybe someday; time will tell. Orla wants to come home. If she does, she might be a factor in the future."

"Do you ever hear from her?"

"No, but just lately Zelda has. Orla doesn't like the carnival. I don't think she'll ever be content, regardless of where she is. Zelda told me that Orla wants her to own Papa's place."

"What?" I look off at the calm sleepy Blue, like a crescent moon winding its way around the meadow "I'll bet she figures it'll be a way to torment me."

"Oh, Dusty, that can't be the reason. She probably wants to sell it and make a small fortune."

"Yeah, maybe."

We move on, cross the old remnants of a fence, and enter the pines. An instant quietness surrounds us. The darkened cover is cool. Only the slight breeze and *swish* of the treetops can be heard. We notice the white flags of deer tails as they quietly leave, darting over a bed of pine needles and stirring an odor of the dank ground cover. We're the only souls hidden in this secluded place; just the two of us, free to enjoy some solitude and to explore each other's dreams. "This is like a grand cathedral, dark, cool, and calm," Maggie says, "similar to one I visited with Zelda."

We walk toward the interior of the grove—find a rise at the base of a tree and sit. Maggie bends her legs and pulls them toward her body with her hand grasping a wrist, pressing her knees against her daisy shirt.

I'm lying flat on my back next to her, looking up into the tops of the towering trees. "I feel odd being here, visiting this awesome place—with hours of free time."

"Yes, but it's important. It'll give us time to talk." She stretches her legs, removes the bandanna, places it in her lap, folds the cloth, and puts it in the basket. Two bobby pins stick from the edge of her mouth.

"Talk about what?"

"You know—about us. I want to hear what you think." She gently nudges my arm with the toe of her sneaker while clipping the bobby pins in place. "You've never said because you're always full of business about the farm, and I'm almost never around to be with you."

"Well—well, I think you're—a good friend."

"Golly, Marcus Murray, don't go overboard. You're just like Uncle Thad. I can't imagine he could ever tell a woman he loved her either." She laughs and pushes the toe of her sneaker into my ribs.

I grab her shoe with both hands and pull it off, throwing it a few feet from us. She takes a handful of pine needles, straddles me with her knees on either side of my midsection, and shoves the scratchy stuff down the front of my shirt. I push a handful up her back. She sits on my stomach, lifts her shirt to the edge of her breasts to free the itchiness, and follows through, throwing pine needles in my face. I spit and wipe them away.

Next, with arms clutched, we roll over the accumulated ground cover. I'm thinking at the moment that it would be fun to see if I am strong enough to pin her to the ground. She's apparently thinking the same. We continue to roll, laughing at our effort, but end up at a stand-off. We stop, our noses almost touching; we're inches from each other. We pause. We kiss. I'm almost dizzy from the feel of her lips. "I love you, Maggie. There, now are you satisfied?"

She kisses again. "I love you, too, Dusty."

I cautiously move my hand up her back over her smooth warm skin. She does the same to me. We are tight together as our hearts beat rapidly, engulfed in each other's aura of sweetness—breathless for a mini-second, then each of us exhale together. We cling to this new-found excitement and to each other.

Finally we separate. I pick up her sneaker and kneel at her foot, brushing the needles away, and slip on her shoe. "I feel like the guy who put the glass slipper on Cinderella."

"Yeah, well I'm no Cinderella and that sneaker is no glass slipper."

We both laugh. Her heels are buried in needles with her toes pointing skyward.

I continue to kneel with each hand on a toe of a sneaker. "Remember the time we came here as kids?"

"Sure, that's the time I carved the heart."

"Well, for a few minutes you and Orla were with Cooner while I ran in here. I stood quiet-like, gazing way up into the treetops. The wind picked up. It was then that I swear somehow I felt the trees were whispering to me."

"Really!"

"I never told anyone."

"Well, maybe they were."

"Yeah, maybe. Zelda's idea of cutting all these trees scares me."

"Oh, you worry too much." Maggie begins to brush her hair. She tips her head toward me. "Are there more pine needles that I've missed?"

Dark bits and pieces contrast with her honey-blonde hair. I pick out what I can see. "This stuff looks like bedbugs to me."

"Stop, you're teasing!"

By late afternoon, I feel the time has passed by too quickly. We stand at the edge of the pines, hand in hand, facing west under the cover of a low sun. The cows are ambling toward the barn, crossing the bridge in single file. Cooner is behind, using his leverwood stick for a walking cane. Maggie squeezes my hand. "This was a fun day"

"Yeah, one to remember. Let's go home a different way, follow the path to the Blue."

"You mean down that steep bank by the edge of the pit?"

"Yeah, let's try that way."

"Dusty, walking near that bank is dangerous. I don't want to." She pokes me. "You're such a guy, doing scary things."

I laugh, having felt a moment of bravery. "Okay, we'll go home the way we came."

─── CHAPTER TWENTY-TWO ───

By the end of August, goldenrod and asters have blossomed. I pass a wild apple tree on the way to get the cows. The scabby green apples are so hard and sour the cows don't even reach for them. Evening shadows have grown longer, and the cool breezes remind me of fall. Summer's surely drawing to a close.

It's time for the Huntersville County Fair. Although Grandpa hasn't mentioned the money I owe Jimmy Iverson, I've done all the milking for the entire summer.

Pride is fully trained for the show ring. The calf record Shirley gave me is completed; I'm feeling good about my 4-H responsibilities. Shirley continues to tell me I'll do just fine in the show ring. Since I've never been to a fair, say nothing about showing, I'm a little in wonderment over the whole event. However, Shirley gives me enough confidence that I almost forget about Jimmy Iverson's threat of taking Pride back if I don't do well.

Thursday night while milking, I hear the barn door slam. Grandpa walks up the aisle, looking over the herd. I'm squatting between cows, ready to take the machine off. He stops. "Uh…you've done right well this summer, doin' all the milkin'."

"Thanks, I've tried." I'm surprised to hear his compliment.

"Uh…here's the check for the calf." He passes it to me.

"Thanks. Grandpa." I fold the check and slip it in my pocket. "Are you up for doing chores with Cooner while I'm at the fair?"

"Uh…yup."

Friday morning we load Pride in Cooner's truck and head north for the fairgrounds. Entering by the back gate, we wait in line for the cattle unloading ramp. Big trucks with farm names lettered on the doors, loaded with show cattle, are in front of us. The sheer numbers make my insides go cold. This is a big deal. Shirley meets us at the unloading ramp and instructs me to take Pride to the wash area. She'll help me.

I tie Pride at the wash rack and watch. Several showmen are spraying their cattle with power washers. The cattle hump and shake from the cold water that thoroughly soaks and rinses them. Brushes are used to clean hooves. Wet tails are dropped into a Clorox solution to make stained white switches whiter.

I have no equipment—only Pride, some hay and grain, and a sleeping bag. I've worked myself into a frenzy of inadequacy. Thankfully, Shirley knows the right people to give me a hand. A friendly fellow, Charlie Dobs, who's the leader of his 4-H club, says, "Dusty, I'll loan you my washer as soon as I've finished with our own cattle." Club members are busy scrubbing their animal after he sprays them. He hands me a pail and brush. "Go to work on her feet while you wait."

Although shaking from the cold, Pride comes away from the wash rack looking spotless. The same guy lends me a blanket to cover her until she's dried. Shirley reserved a place for me to tie Pride with the calves from Charlie's club. His members have Jerseys and Ayshires. Pride looks a little out of place, standing alone as a Holstein; but I'm feeling a little more relaxed because everybody is friendly and willing to help. I see kids with electric cow clippers preparing their animals for the show. Again, a shrinking confidence attack strikes me.

Shirley enters the barn with Jimmy Iverson who is traveling in an electric wheelchair. She's carrying a clothes hanger with a white shirt and pants. She also has a set of clippers.

Shirley says, "Here are some whites. Hang them on that nail, so they'll look fresh for tomorrow. Jimmy's going to show you how to clip your calf."

He judiciously examines Pride. "This calf, at first glance, is a winner if she's handled right." She stands in a bed of clean straw. "Take the blanket off, I want a closer look." I remove the piece of flannel. "She's about as fancy a calf as I've ever bred."

I pull the check from my pocket. "Here's my payment for Pride."

He grabs it and stuffs it into his shirt pocket. "Just do a good job of showin' her."

He continues observing Pride, reminding us both that *he's* the breeder. "Astronaut as a sire was a right good choice."

Shirley thrusts the clippers toward Jimmy. "Show Dusty how to clip her."

He turns away. "I ain't lettin' him use them now! If you'd asked me this summer, I would have; but, hell, it's too late."

Shirley's voice rises. "You're helping Dusty, now!"

"I ain't." He reaches for a flask and takes a few swallows. "It's being taken care of tonight around seven by a professional."

"That's against the rules. Kids in the showmanship class are supposed to clip their own animals."

The young showmen around us who've been using their clippers shut off the chattering noise. I notice they're listening to the conversation.

"Screw the rules. I'm handling it my way. If the judge asks you if you've clipped your heifer tell him, 'Yes'." He glances at Shirley. "You've got to lie a little to get ahead in this business."

Her mouth draws tightly. "That's terrible."

He yells, "I ain't havin' a half-baked job done with my heifer being nicked to hell, lookin' like some hack job."

Shirley explodes, "I would've asked you this summer, but you were in the hospital—remember?"

He ignores Shirley. "Hey, kid, most animals have an identification card hangin' over them. Do the same for your heifer. I want folks to see the J-J Iverson prefix." He pushes a lever on his chair and leaves.

Shirley's holding the clippers. "I don't dare have someone else show you how to do this because of the deal with Jimmy. A bad clip-job can make a difference how she places." She pauses. "If the judge asks if you fit your own animal, just tell him the truth. The truth usually gets you further than lying, even in the show ring." She turns to go. "Feed and water your calf, and then come to the 4-H Exhibit Hall."

Outside the cattle barn, on my way to the 4-H building, I notice the midway: the Ferris wheel, the merry-go-round playing accordion-like music, pony rides, and a rollercoaster with people screaming as if they're about to die. Miniature airplanes attached to long arms whirl in circles. There are all sorts of chance games, too, with barkers urging folks to play.

Two little kids holding candied apples run past me, their lips and faces smeared with sticky red. A little girl licks a cotton candy ball bigger than her head. The puffy pink fuzz blocks her view. She nearly bumps into me. Her mother warns, "Watch where you're going, Honey!" She grimaces and glances my way.

I return a smile.

A crowd of guys are watching Snaky swing a wooden maul. He's trying to ring a bell by driving a steel clapper fifteen feet in the air. The clapper slides skyward in its groove almost touching the bell, but fails. A guy yells, "Come on, Snaky, show us your peach."

I hurry by.

The building with the big green 4-H clover on the front is up ahead. Inside the building, there are long lines of exhibits with kids and leaders preparing them. Maggie, other kids, and Shirley are busy working on the Huntersville Hustlers' exhibit. Cornstalks, pumpkins, sunflowers, zinnias and mums are attractively arranged. Clothing, foods, gardening, examples of horsemanship, sheep, goats, poultry, and my dairy record are tucked in the array of projects representing our members' activities. At the center of the display on a table, a dozen day-old chicks scurry, scratching, and pecking at bits of grain under the silver dome of a heat lamp. Shirley steps back and remarks, "Kids, this is great!"

I hang around for a while, then I tell Shirley, "I've got to go back and check on Pride."

"After you check on your heifer," Shirley suggests, "why don't you and Maggie have some fun on the midway?" She pulls her wallet from her handbag and hands me a ten. "Here, just be back by seven to clip your calf. I'll be here by then to bring Maggie home."

"Gee, thanks anyway, but I want to stay with Pride."

"Hey, enjoy the fair a little," Shirley urges. "You've never been before."

Maggie agrees. "Come on, loosen up a little."

"Charlie Dobs plans to be around," Shirley says. "Just tell him you'll be gone for a bit."

With ten dollars in my hand, what can I say? "Okay."

Maggie comments, "Gee, I wish I'd brought my own money."

135

Shirley, standing between us, nudges with both hands. "Go, enjoy yourselves."

After I talk with Charlie, we head for the midway. Music from the merry-go-round sends me into a carefree mood. It's great being with Maggie. The sky is dark, though, and it starts to rain with the air turning damp and cold. People are hurrying to leave the fairgrounds. A vendor runs out from under his awning and grabs my arm. "Come over here and throw a ball in the basket and win a prize for your sweetheart."

Maggie and I run for the canvas cover. She urges, "Let's play the game."

Before I agree, he breaks in, "Three balls for fifty cents. All you need to do is make one ball stay in the basket, and you win a stuffed animal."

We face a line-up of bushel baskets that are tipped toward us. They seem only about fifteen feet away. Miniature stuffed animals fill a shelf above the baskets: elephants, cats, dogs, cows, horses, pigs and others.

Maggie jumps with excitement. "I want to win that fuzzy white kitty with the pink nose."

I hand the guy the ten and stuff the change in my pocket. With three baseballs in hand, I aim and throw the first. It hits the bottom of the basket and bounces out. The guy instructs, "Throw it easier—easy now."

I lean over a wooden counter in front of the booth and toss the second lightly. The ball doesn't even reach the basket. "Here, Maggie, you try the third."

"Okay." She starts to giggle. The baseball flies from her hand and hits the shelf above the baskets. *Bong.*

I comment, "This looks so simple; we should be able to make at least one ball stay in the basket." I hand the guy my half-dollar. We both try and miss. The guy senses our discouragement. "Since you're just learning, I'll give you four balls for fifty cents."

Maggie says, "We can do this."

I pass the money to the guy. "Okay, here, we'll split the four balls. You go first." We are both laughing at ourselves not being able to win what seems like a ridiculously easy game. She throws the ball perfectly, but it rolls out onto the floor, as does the second try. I throw my first ball.

In the process, I notice that although the guy is leaning on the counter, he's moving his feet when I throw the ball. When the ball hits the bottom of the basket, it seems to bounce back too quickly. "You're cheating!" I accuse. "The ball should stay in the basket."

He gets nervous. "Hey, kid, that's just your imagination, but I'll tell you what. I'll give you a choice of my stuffed animals."

Maggie steps forward. "Give me the white kitty, unless *you* want one, Dusty?"

"Heck, no. Take the kitty and let's go."

She rubs the white fluff on her face. "This will be my special memento of the night you took on midway corruption." She chuckles.

The rain has stopped, but a slight breeze blows in cold air. The grounds are deserted except for the vendors who wait in their tacky booths, hoping for a late-night crowd. We're beside a stand that advertises fried dough. I ask, "Fried dough? I've never tasted it."

"Me neither. Let's buy some."

The woman in the booth is sitting practically asleep. She's wearing a grubby white apron with a funky white cap and hair net. I step to the counter. "We'll take two fried dough." She hands me two paper plates with round, sugared dough that look like small pizzas with no topping.

I'm chewing on a piece. "Mmm ...this is good."

"Yuk." Maggie pulls something from the dough on her plate. "Look, a long gray hair." Sure enough, the hair reaches from the plate to the bite she's about to put in her mouth. Maggie says, "I guess her hairnet didn't do the job." She turns to a trash barrel. "I'm throwing this stuff."

"No, don't. I'll eat it. I'm hungry." I place it under my plate.

"Gosh, you must be. What I've seen of this midway so far, is crumby." Maggie looks around. "Probably it's like the one Orla travels with."

"Yeah, well, you do have a white kitty."

She again rubs the fluff against both sides of her face. "It's cute, and right now it feels good."

I gobble the fried dough, which tastes good; however, I have more than a full feeling when finished. We walk the grounds, checking out all the games and rides. In spite of the setting, I'm having fun being with Maggie.

In passing, I notice a booth selling tinware necklaces, rings, and pins of all sorts and colors. "Hey, Maggie, I want to buy you a necklace."

"Gosh, this stuff looks cheap, and it is cheap." She sorts through a long counter displaying hanging necklaces. She says, "Here's one—a silver colored heart." She slips the chain over her neck. "It's junk jewelry, but I like it."

The booth attendant holds an electric needle. "I'll engrave your names for fifty cents."

"The necklace and engraving for three-fifty?"

"Yup."

"Okay, write 'Maggie' and below it 'Dusty'." I hand him the money, and Maggie removes the necklace, passing it to the vendor. The tool buzzes as he prints our names.

"This is so special!" She hugs me and slips the chain back over her neck.

I examine it closely—then let the heart rest against her blue turtleneck sweater. "It's a little bigger than a quarter, but it's sure nicer than the black heart with our names cut in that tree."

"Gosh, not that again. You can't forget it?"

"Well, almost, since Orla's gone." I shove my hands in my pockets and feel the money we have left. "Let's see if we can buy a ride for two dollars."

"Sure."

"Which ride would you like?"

She shrugs. "I don't care." Maggie stops by the entrance to the airplane ride. "Let's take this one."

"Okay." I zip my jacket to its limit. "I'm getting cold."

We're at the booth to buy tickets. The lady attendant is reading *Soap Opera News*, and doesn't look up. After I clear my throat, *a-hum*, the attendant lifts her head. "Two tickets, please." I slide two dollars toward her.

"Can't you read the sign? It's three bucks."

"We've only got two."

"Go ride the merry-go-round." She starts to refocus on her reading. "It looks more your speed." She sits, filling the ticket booth with large arms and puffy hands resting on the counter. Black grease or dirt is under every long fingernail.

"Don't insult us!" I turn and look back at the empty fairgrounds. "Hey, lady, nobody's here tonight. This will be your last sale."

The woman in the booth scratches under her arm and sends me a whiff of her body odor. "Okay, you whiner, here's two." She tears off the tickets from a roll and shoves them at me.

"Now that we have the tickets, I'm not sure I want to sit in that thing." I squint into blackness at the furthest plane. "It's cold. Maybe we should go back to the barn."

Maggie checks the time. "We've got a half-hour. This will be fun." She grabs my hand. "Come on."

The operator's on a stool, wearing a yellow rain jacket with the hood practically covering his face. He's asleep, in a trance or something, making no effort to move as we walk toward him. A gas engine, turning a big pulley, idles at his right.

I lift the edge of his hood. I guess the guy must be deaf. "Hey, you've got two riders."

He groans to stand and opens the tin door on the little plane. "Get in." A tall lever is at his left where he's resting one hand. He's waiting to pull it to send the plane in motion.

Maggie says, "I'll get in first. You steer."

"Okay."

The plane is held in place by a roof attachment at the end of a long steel arm. Maggie slides in and sits in a hump with open hands pressed between her knees. I get in and squeeze beside her. There's no extra space. As it is, when I raise my head, it almost hits the tin roof. We both stare out of dirty windows. I can feel the cold tin sucking the heat right out of me.

The plane lurches ahead. We begin to gain altitude. I can hear the engine's governor kick in as the little plane goes to its limit of height. The operator looks to be the size of an ant. I turn the wheel to the left. The plane tips and glides to the spot where we started. Maggie leans into me. We start to gain altitude again. I turn the wheel to the right and the plane levels until we reach the highest point. Because of the speed that we're traveling, a stiff breeze blows in and out of the side openings.

Maggie's long hair flies in my face. She asks, "Are you having fun?"

"Well, let's say it's okay." I don't like the breeze.

She presses the kitty against her face to shield the wind. "My fluffy prize is coming in handy."

The engine again kicks in to raise us to the highest point. The plane continues to circle. After about the fifth revolution, I notice the operator's walking away with the ticket woman.

They enter an old half-bubble-looking camper nearby. The dim light that glowed from the front window is shut off. My heart sinks. "The operator has turned in for the night." I grab Maggie's wrist to look at her watch. "I've got to be at the barn in ten minutes."

"Sorry, we can't do a thing about it." Her hair continues to fly in several directions. "My ribbon!" I think it just went out the window."

"I don't mind your hair." I grab her wrist again to check the time. "When is this thing going to stop?"

"Probably when it runs out of gas." Tension builds in her expression. "Especially if that guy's gone to bed with his honey." She places the kitty on my chest, runs her arms under my jacket, and presses her head against her stuffed toy. "I'm getting cold."

A wave of sickness strikes me. "I feel like puking." I sit up straight. "All I'm doing is burping fried dough." The circular motion continues. There's no sign of the engine quitting.

"You're really that sick?" She lifts her head and looks at me in the dim light. "You're pale."

I rest my head against the sheet metal in back of the seat. "We're supposed to meet Shirley at seven. Will we ever get out of this thing?" I view the empty fairgrounds. "I've got to meet the guy clipping my calf!"

She's looking worried. "Well, let's try to relax and keep warm." She places the kitty on my chest again and rests her head.

The engine keeps purring and kicks in for more power as we climb in the revolution.

"This could be cozy."

"Cozy! I want out!" I grab her wrist again. "It's way past seven. Geez!"

"Forget it. We're caught." She sits up. "How do you feel?"

"If I keep the plane level, and keep burping, I'll be okay. But the time! And that jerk just walked away."

She adjusts the kitty on my shoulder, and snuggles tighter. "This is awful. This ride was a bad idea!"

"I'm going to lose Pride!" The engine again throttles up its power. "This is terrible!"

"I know. Put your arms around me, shut your eyes, and relax. Let's try and keep warm."

"Okay." After a couple of revolutions, I open my eyes and notice the operator walking toward us. "Hey, look at this, we're going to be saved." She sits up. The engine speeds up lifting us to the very top. The guy is below shutting off the machine. The plane jerks to a stop. The lights that line the arms blink off. He starts walking toward the trailer. I yell, "Hey. mister, we're up here!" He's looking around. I'm waving my arm out the window, but it's too dark to be seen. "Up here!" He still hasn't gotten the direction of my voice. The guy must be stone deaf. "Look up, you flaming idiot! Up here!" The guy's at his trailer door. I scream, "I'm going to beat the crap out of you!"

Maggie laughs. "Gosh, you sound brave for a prisoner in a tin can."

In the far distance down by the 4-H building, I notice a truck coming our way. "It's Shirley! It's Shirley's truck! Yeah, I hope she keeps coming!" She's slowly driving in the lane between the booths. She's closer now. I start yelling, "Shirley! Shirley! Up here!" The truck speeds up, coming closer. "Shirley, up here!"

She jumps out. "What in the world are you doing way up there?"

"The operator left us on the ride. He's in that little camper trailer."

She struts to the door, knocks and knocks, waits and knocks. "Anybody in there?"

"What in hell are ya disturbin' the peace fer?" comes a shouting voice at the door.

Shirley points toward us. "Two kids are caught up there."

"Oh my god, lady, sorry! I'll be fired for this!" He runs in his long underwear and bare feet toward the engine.

"Forget about being fired. Just get those kids down here!"

The engine starts and in seconds we're free. "Geez, thanks, Shirley! What a relief!" I want to hug her. "I was so worried!"

"You were? What about me? I knew you were responsible enough to come back by seven. Your calf is clipped. She looks beautiful!"

"I'm just sorry I wasn't there to at least watch."

We ride to the barn.

"I'm sorry, too." Shirley stops the truck. "Get a good night's sleep. We'll handle the situation in the morning."

I wonder: will I lie?

—— CHAPTER TWENTY-THREE ——

My first time staying overnight at the fair is awful. Apparently talk has gone through the barns that folks should stop and take a look at the J-J Iverson heifer. Poor Pride can't bed down and rest at all. Guys stop by and make her stand to take a look. I hear comments such as: "She could show in pretty fast company…an Astronaut…That Jimmy knows how to breed fancy cattle…I'll bet she'd place well at the state show."

These comments make me feel proud to own her; but at the same time, I'm nervous, wondering about the next day. Jimmy said to lie about the clipping, but Shirley made it clear that I shouldn't. What will it mean if I tell the truth? Would it disqualify me? From the comments I'm hearing, I realize Pride is worth a lot more than a thousand dollars. I also know Jimmy will make good on his terms if I screw up and she doesn't place well.

I roll out my sleeping bag a few feet from Pride in a bed of straw. I'm warm and comfortable. Most of the lights have been turned off, but a few stay on, giving just enough light to find my way around. I plan to go right to sleep, but no way. Somewhere in the barn there's a party going on. There's a lot of loud talk and laughter. It sounds as if in the next aisle over a cow is calving. Her groans and strained bellowing echo throughout the place. I'm a wreck over the thought of losing Pride.

The lighted clock on the wall shows it's way past midnight. I haven't even dozed off. I feel terrible having been caught in that plane. I wouldn't dare tell Jimmy why I didn't show for the guy clipping my calf. I know he'd think I was lying. Geez, what a mess I'm in. Maggie would say, "Just relax." Yeah, right! Pride isn't her calf.

Two guys walk by and stop. They obviously are partying. My eyes are open just enough so I can see both of them through stems of straw that surround me. I know they don't see me. Their faces are flushed. They share a bottle, while standing in back of Pride. They drunkenly

143

laugh, over what, I have no idea—and I wonder if *they* know. They boot Pride in the rear to make her stand.

"Hey, Paul, this here's a hell of a heifer."

I'm immediately filled with rage, and jump out of my sleeping bag, grab a pitchfork and yell, "You bum!" I fly at him with the tines of the fork aiming for his mid-section. He doubles over, backing away. Then they turn and stagger off. "Whoa, that kid wanted to kill me!"

I sure did. I never realized there was that much rage in me. The barn lights flick on. It's four o'clock. Cows are being taken to be milked. Everyone is ready to start the day. My day never ended.

Shirley told me I'd have to wash Pride in the morning. I notice kids are starting to do just that. Jimmy brought one of his blankets. I use it after washing Pride. She's standing in her stall eating a bucket of feed. Shirley arrives at five-thirty with food—pancakes, maple syrup, scrambled eggs, and orange juice.

I'm sitting on a bale of straw, devouring my breakfast which tastes a heck of a lot better than fried dough. Shirley walks toward me and places her hand on my arm. "How are you this morning? You seem miserable."

"Tortured!" I munch down on a mouthful of pancakes. "Everyone will see me make a fool of myself." I feel like crying and I must look it.

Shirley sits on the bale with me. She puts her arm around me. "Hey, everything will be fine."

"But what if I get disqualified because I didn't clip Pride?" I drop my head in my hands.

"That will be okay. Jimmy wants her to place well in her conformation class. In the fitting and showing class, it won't matter to him."

"Really?"

"Yes, really." She hands me a Kleenex. "Pride should be dry now. I'll show you how to work the top line with this hair spray."

With the spray, scissors, and a brush, we're able to train and cut the top-line hair, making it perfectly level.

The loudspeaker blares: "Intermediate showmen, prepare your animals for the ring." Pride has just flopped down in some fresh manure. "Oh, geez." I panic. When she stands, I notice specks imbedded on her flank. "Wouldn't you know!"

"Just relax," Shirley urges. "This isn't the end of the world." She hands me a wet brush to wipe her clean.

Cooner has just come. He comments, "She's lookin' great, Dusty. You'll do just fine."

On entering the all-breed class of intermediate showmen, we walk in sawdust. People are either seated or standing, watching the cattle circling. Pride leads like always. I've worked with her enough so she's learned the correct placement of her legs. While circling, I notice kids that don't have control of their animals. Some have dirty hooves and manure stains. Other entries are poorly clipped. I'm feeling okay.

The judge is a young, bright-appearing guy with a pleasant personality. He motions for us to keep moving. After all entries have come to the ring, we continue leading our animals clockwise in a circle. The judge is in the center, concentrating on each participant until he's viewed us all. He picks me first to ask questions. "When was your calf born, son?"

"September 1, 1969."

"You sure of that?" He smiles.

"No, but that's the date on her registration paper." Since Jimmy filled out the application, she probably *wasn't* born September 1st, but I have no way to know. He might have fudged on the date, making Pride one of the biggest calves in her class, which she is.

"Did you clip your calf?" He walks to the back end of Pride, and motions for me to move forward.

I draw a deep breath. I notice Jimmy and Shirley at ringside. I tense—to lie or not to lie. For me, telling the truth seems the logical way to go. "No, I didn't."

"You probably helped?"

He's now on her left side, backing away, continuing to view her. I move her ahead again. She places that rear leg perfectly. I want to say I was stuck in an airplane, but that would sound ridiculous. "No, I didn't."

His eyebrows lift, and he actually acts disappointed, as he moves to the next calf. What did his reaction mean?

The judge completes the circle and starts selecting kids to be placed. He skips over me and eventually puts me dead last. The kid next to me has an animal that looks like he's just brought her in from pasture. He can't control her as she continuously moves out of position. First place goes to a girl who handles her Jersey heifer perfectly. I probably could have done just as well. The judge did say, "The heifer in last place is beautifully trained and clipped." He pauses. "I think it's admirable that the boy admitted he didn't clip his animal; however, the whole purpose of this class is to recognize the ability of the youngster to prepare and present their animals. In the intermediate division, showmen should be able to clip their own animals."

I'm tying Pride in her stall when Jimmy arrives. Is he ever mad. "I felt like crap seein' my heifer in last place! I know all those kids in that class ain't clipped their calf. I'm tellin' the bastard that, too."

Shirley is standing by. "Just let it go. The judge explained his reasons, and I think they're valid. If you *do* say anything, wait until after the show. I think he liked Pride, and he liked Dusty's honesty. It just might affect how she places in the conformation class."

Jimmy, grumbling, leaves in his wheelchair. I relax, taking time to watch the senior class of showmen.

A while later, after watching the Ayshire, Brown Swiss, Gurensey, and younger Holstein classes, I hear the announcement blare over the loudspeaker: "All senior Holstein calves be ready to enter the ring."

Jimmy wheels by. "This is it, kid. You screw up in this class and that calf is mine."

"I know." His comment doesn't scare me one bit. From hearing earlier remarks, I'm sure Pride will do well. There are about ten Holstein calves in the class. We circle as before. The judge views each from his center position checking each individually. He reconfigures the order of the circling heifers, placing Pride first, and readjusts the order some while we move. He motions for me to remain in first place as we line up in the order of his placing. He has the microphone in his hand. "What a fine group of senior Holstein calves we have here this morning. The lad in first place takes this class easily, placing over the heifer in second place for her size, smoothness throughout, dairy quality, plus her depth and spring of rib. Second over third ..." He continues giving reasons.

I'm given a blue ribbon and slowly move Pride toward the exit. In a way, I think Jimmy was hoping I would place down the line so he could reclaim her. I didn't see him for a while after her class. Shirley is waiting with Cooner to congratulate me. Shirley reminds me, "You'll have to be ready to bring Pride back in the ring for the award of the champion and reserve champion of the junior Holstein show."

"Oh, I have to do that?"

"Yes, and the open show will follow. That's when the adults show with the youth. And that's when we find out how good Pride really is."

In about a half-hour's time, I'm leading Pride in the ring for the selection of the champion and reserve champion of the junior Holstein show. The judge motions for an older cow to stand as grand champion, and to my surprise, he chooses Pride for the reserve champion. The judge comments, "The aged cow has to be the grand champion of this show. She exhibits a beautiful udder as well as outstanding feet and legs. And I really like this senior calf for reserve champion. All in all a fine show for your young people."

I head for the exit with a smile, leading Pride and carrying a silver bowl with the inscription: Reserve Champion of the Huntersville County Junior Holstein Show.

There's an announcement: "After a short break, the open show will begin. All juniors are invited to enter."

Shirley again meets me with her congratulations. "You realize in the next class there will be twice the calves and much stiffer competition." She turns to leave. "I won't be here for the senior show. I've got other club members to help."

I also know that Cooner has to leave for home to bale some second-cutting hay.

She continues, "The open show will be all on you. I'll see you afterward."

"Okay, I'm fine." I'm relieved that my worries over the loss of Pride seem a dead issue. She should place well in the open show—a miracle for Dusty.

I've got at least a half-hour for the Jersey junior classes to be shown, so I crash on my sleeping bag and re-read the inscription on my trophy. I feel relaxed and sleepy, but I fight the feeling and sit up.

I lie back down and stretch—admiring my trophy again. I'm out in a flash.

I wake to the sound of a crash. A beer can hits my trophy with a *clank*. "Hey, kid! Are you goin' to sleep through the most important part of the show?" It's Jimmy. "The senior-calf class is complete and you're here sleepin' like a baby."

I untie Pride, slip on her halter, and try to get her to stand. She's pooped but eventually comes to her feet and allows me to drag her toward the ring. There's no time to take her to the water tub. She has straw dust on her back and pieces stuck to her flanks. I continue dragging her to the ring and enter, but she's uncooperative. I'm trying to hold her head high but she wants to lie down. In fact, she does so right in the circle that's in procession. The judge helps me make her stand. "You're late. I thought you might be bypassing this class."

"I'm sorry. And sorry, too, that I'm not more ready." Darn! I was stupid to fall asleep. Jimmy's ripped!

Everything I've learned about the proper presentation of a show calf isn't working. All she wants to do is bed down. She's apparently exhausted. I try in vain to hold her head high. My arm is tiring as we circle. Her top line sags and she noticeably breaks in the shoulders. Basically her body parts are falling apart. I glance with alarm to notice that my halter strap is dragging. I know we both look a wreck.

The judge follows the same routine, but only glances briefly at Pride. He changes the position of the circling heifers in the order of his preference. Pride is fourth in line. She continues to balk. Her hooves seem stuck in cement. As I pull on her halter, her neck stretches to the limit before she'll move her feet. She doesn't feel right for some reason.

Finally, I'm wide awake, and start to correct what I can of our rumpled appearance. While the judge concentrates elsewhere in the ring, I fold my lead strap and with the flat of my hand wipe Pride clean of dust and straw. I gently jerk with pressure on the halter. The quick tug momentarily enlivens her. I circle out around the lineup to bring her back into a more correct position. She catches the judge's eye as he walks down the line for a final examination of his placing. He motions for me to stand at third instead of fourth. I'm relieved because I know this will satisfy Jimmy. The judge gives his reasons over the microphone: "The heifer in third place is not showing her best this afternoon. It looks like the calf and her leadsman need a good rest."

After the class, when I offer Pride water, she's really thirsty. Maybe that was her problem. Jimmy is approaching in his wheelchair. "You almost blew that, boy. If you'd done it right, she'd have taken her class."

Steven Iverson comes by to see me. "I thought you were out of the running in that class. You did well to place third."

"Thanks. I learned one thing: don't fall asleep."

He laughs. "Mom has a picnic for us. I'll see you a little later."

In the evening, we are all gathered outside the show barn at a picnic table. It's the first time in a while I've felt relaxed and not worried about a thing. My trophy is being passed around for everyone's inspection. Steven and I sit on a bench together while Shirley, Maggie and others prepare our plates: sandwiches, potato salad, pickles, and chips. We have more food than I can possibly eat.

Steven asks, "How much are your grandfather and Zelda bidding on the Murray property?" While asking, he continually glances at Maggie.

"I have no idea." He's an intense guy, wanting more information. I shrug. "I guess it depends on the I-vest plan."

"The town will never accept it." Steven's eyes are still on Maggie.

She's embarrassed and leaves to serve us more drink.

I remark to Steven, "No one has seen the plan yet."

"Yeah, that's right." He gets up and walks away.

I leave my seat to say goodbye to Maggie. She gives me a big hug. "You were so handsome in your whites."

"Thanks, that's why I did so well." We both laugh.

Shirley smiles. "Pretty good day, don't you think?"

"Yeah, it sure was!" With my trophy in hand, I head for my bedroll and collapse. Cooner will take us home tomorrow after the cattle are released by the fair's superintendant.

—— CHAPTER TWENTY-FOUR ——

Summer's over, school will start on Monday. I'm sitting in the dark. The white chair is placed, as usual, in the alcove of my room. When an occasional car passes, light reflects off my silver trophy, resting next to the tape recorder on the edge of my desk. I glance at my prize with pleasure, reminding myself that Pride is all mine. My worry over Snaky is no longer a factor. I smile, and recall seeing him trying to ring the bell at the fair. I'll bet he never did in front of all his bigshot friends.

Even the bid seems months away. Seated in front of my window, I glance in the direction of the old homestead. I have fond memories of Uncle Bill and not so fond memories of Orla—her golden locket and prediction about the black heart.

"Dusty." Maggie speaks softly, as she walks in my room.

I jump out of my chair. "Whew, you scared me!"

She's laughing. "What are you doing, all alone in the dark?"

"Oh, just thinking about the past, high school, the fair and, of course, you." I chuckle.

"High school? That's no big deal, we've been in the same building since seventh grade."

"Yeah, right, but it's school."

"Oh, well, let's enjoy the night." Maggie pulls up a chair by me. "Do you ever look at the stars?"

"Not much!"

"Papa and I used to stand outside on a starry night. He taught me a lot. Let's pull our chairs closer to the window so we can see more of the sky. There's the Big Dipper, and the North Star." Our heads are pressing on the window. "There's the Little Dipper, too."

"Yeah, I see."

"Isn't this romantic? You and I under the stars."

"Yeah." We slide closer with arms around each other. The feel of her hair is like silk. I love it.

We gaze at the sky for a while, and then I sit back in my chair. She pulls back, drawing me close for a kiss. "I'm going to decide what I'm wearing for school."

I laugh. "Jeans and a shirt."

"You're a guy!" She leaves.

Monday morning, on schedule, the bus stops at the farm. When Maggie and I board, I recognize most of the riders as being in senior high, and most have that glum look of not wanting to end their summer vacation.

We take adjoining seats. Maggie reaches over and holds my hand. "You sure look sharp today."

I smile. "Oh, you think so? Maybe you have blinders on. You aren't so bad-looking yourself." We squeeze hands.

"Oh, by the way, I won't be coming home until late tonight. Zelda is picking me up at school, and we're going to a mum show."

"Oh, okay. Zelda must think a lot of you."

"I like doing things with her. Her language is awful and she smokes continuously, but other than that, she's fun to be with."

"If you say so."

As the bus breezes along the flats, I admire our cornfield that's soon to be cut. The remainder of the meadow hasn't changed—it's dead and abandoned as usual. The bid again crosses my mind. Zelda is waiting for the I-vest development plan.

The bus slows and stops at Zelda's house. We both crane our necks to see why. Maggie says, "Oh, no. I think it's Orla."

I let go of Maggie's hand and cover my face, mumbling, "This is bad news!"

Orla comes walking from her house in regal strides as if she's a queen making her grand entrance. She's wearing a turban, dangling earrings, a crimson-colored shawl, and a wrap-around bright red dress. The golden chain and locket vividly stand out.

I nudge Maggie and whisper, "How weird!"

She doesn't comment. As Orla boards the bus, Maggie stands and waves, "Orla, you're back!"

Orla beams, forgets her affected entrance, and rushes to meet Maggie. They lock arms and Orla says, "It's great to see you!"

151

They're standing right beside me and both take a seat. Orla sits across the aisle from me. "Who's this hunk of a guy all grown up?"

"Hi, Orla." I can't bring myself to say, "Glad to see you" or anything similar. She's changed. Her brown eyes are still deeply set in deep dark pools, but they sure aren't filled with happiness. On the contrary, the expression around her eyes and mouth is sad. She's used eye shadow and pencil to accentuate her most unattractive features. She's also gained a few pounds, no doubt due to fried carnival food.

She and Maggie seem excited to meet again. Maggie being Maggie, she doesn't seem bothered by Orla's bizarre appearance. As they talk, I lean forward with my head down, studying the rubber matting on the floor. Being on the aisle, I'm caught between the two, who talk in animated tones. They sound like two woodpeckers drumming on either side of a tin can—only *I'm* the can. Besides the chatter, I feel Orla's presence, knowing she's scanning every inch of me. Her voice elevates into her high-pitched tone; that hasn't changed. "Dusty, what a heartthrob! I'll bet the girls are waiting in line for you."

Her drooling over my looks, plus her loud voice, embarrass me. Continuing to bend forward with my elbows resting on my knees, I freeze in place. I don't answer. She jabs me in the ribs. I jump about six inches off the seat. What to say? It flashes through my mind that I could be rude and totally turn her off, but for her mother's part in the meadow. I don't want to alienate an O'Neil. I temper my question, "How long are you home for?"

She reaches over and holds my forearm, slightly shaking it. "Oh, I'm here to stay."

I conceal my disappointment. "Really!" I glance away. Her haunting dark eyes give me the shivers. "What about the S-man and the carnival?"

Knowing she has an audience of nearly a bus full of kids, she leaves her seat and puffs out her bosom for the benefit of all. "He's a creep. He strutted around the midway with his shirt unbuttoned and the tails flapping." She glances to see if she's attracted the attention of everyone. "He loved to show off his sweet-and-sour tattoos, acting like the grand ruler." She slides back in her seat. "I learned how to read palms, had my own show, and was making good money. You know, guys half drunk on a Saturday night. I'd lure them into my tent, read their palms, and then shove them out after getting a good fee with tips." She puts on a self-satisfied smile. "Well, at closing time, the lord and master himself would come in and demand all the money. Last Saturday night he did the same. While hiding behind a curtain at the entrance, I whacked him over the head with a baseball bat. You might say I hit a homerun." She squeezes her lips with a nod of accomplishment. "He collapsed like a popped balloon. With a bus ticket in my pocket and my bags packed, I left the grounds carrying a wad of money." She spreads her arms. "Ta-da, now, here I am!"

A chill goes through me. "What if you killed him?"

She puts on a smug expression. "I hope I did. He deserved it."

I grimace. "But what if the law comes after you?"

"It won't happen. We gypsies have our own rules. Everybody hates him, the clan will be happy to see him gone." She nods her head in affirmation.

Speechless, I sense Maggie's shocked as well. In her absence, Orla's changed not only in appearance, but in her personality as well. She's downright scary. Since Maggie's planning to be gone for the afternoon, I dread the bus ride home.

—— CHAPTER TWENTY-FIVE ——

After school, there's no way to avoid Orla. She snags me, pulling on the sleeve of my jacket, leading me onto the bus. She's delighted we're together. After the bus starts, and we're seated side by side, she leans into me. "How about stopping at the house and I'll read your palm?"

"What?" I turn my head and watch the storefronts pass.

"I've studied palmistry and can tell what will happen in the future."

"You can? There's no need to know. My future's all planned." Leaning forward with elbows on knees, and head in hands, I try to escape into my own world.

Her hand slides over my back. She tips forward to get my attention. "This will be an experience you'll never forget."

I sit up and rest my open hand on my knee. "Well, do it right here."

"I can't. It has to be in a special setting." She slides closer. "And anyway, you don't know about the future. If I stay, and I plan to, my mother's moving out to live in Boston to be near her other businesses. Maggie will run the shop; and if my mother wins the bid, I'll have the say as to what happens to the meadow."

"Orla, you're full of it! Geez, you girls are only fourteen." I know she's lying. She just came home. How could all this have been planned in such a short time? From what I've seen of Zelda, she's not turning her business over to a couple of kids. But, on the other hand, mother and daughter don't get along. Maybe there's been a fight or angry words and a threat from Zelda to move, distancing herself from her nutty daughter. Whatever the case, I can't take the chance of having a conflict over the meadow, so I give in. She sits back with a smug expression, knowing she has me hooked.

"Okay, I'll let you read my palm."

She bounces in her seat. "This will be fun!"

We leave the bus and go to the house. True to my memory, it's only a shell with a few pieces of furniture scattered around. She points to an overstuffed chair. "Take a seat. It'll take me a few minutes to get ready." Her palmistry stuffs in a bag that she carries to a back room.

I wait, not believing that I've given my okay. I keep running the same idea through my head like a broken record: she's using the meadow to get her way.

Her obsession over me is equal to my obsession over the meadow. Not a good situation, because she'll always be the winner.

From the back room she calls, "Dusty, I'm ready."

I walk into a space off the kitchen that I think is a pantry. A scarlet drape hangs, creating a wall. I'm guessing she pulled it from her bag. At a small table, two chairs are placed side by side. Candles flicker in an unmatched pair of brass holders. They're the only source of light. A tiny glow of incense burns in a dish. Two glasses placed on a table are next to what looks like a bottle of wine.

"Take a seat."

She's wearing a skimpy outfit—a knee-length flimsy robe. She's let her long hair flow down her back. I sit facing the scarlet drape. Other than the incense, the room has an odd smell unfamiliar to me. Soft music plays, coming from somewhere. She holds what looks like a rolled cigarette between her fingers while she pours the wine. "Have a drink. It'll take a while to get ready for the reading."

"I've got to go home for chores. I hope this doesn't take long." I sit and sip the wine. The drink makes my whole insides feel like a blast of summer. I take a second sip, and fall for the feeling.

She takes a short puff on what looks like something homemade, then holds the smoke, slowly releasing it. "Here, do the same, you'll get to like it."

The third swallow goes down. "I don't like to smoke. You know that."

"Don't inhale, that'll come later."

A few minutes pass and a wave of relaxation comes over me. She holds the cigarette to my mouth, and I take a drag. It's okay. I release the smoke and try another.

The fourth swallow of wine slides down. Chores start to lose their urgency. My mind is glazed with well-being and a feeling that I'm floating. The second glass is poured, and in a while the third. The music, the dim light, the incense, the puffs of her cigarette, and the wine put me in another world. In my new place there's no awareness of responsibility. "Ta hell with chores." The next drag on her cigarette, I try inhaling a little. It's different. Moments later, I try some more, but cough slightly. "What is this stuff?"

She laughs. "You like it? It's Orla's own secret recipe. We gypsies know how to make life seem a little sweeter."

Seated side by side, we both drunkenly laugh. She puts her arm around me and draws me closer, giving me a wet kiss. I like it. Not the kiss—but the taste of the warm sweet wine. She gives me a second kiss, leaving more of the taste. I lean closer, wanting a third, and she obliges.

A lull comes in our game. There's the snap of a desk lamp being switched on. The light burns. She quickly pulls it down to within inches of my open palm. She removes the locket from her neck and holds it. In the other hand, she holds a sharp pointer the size of a short knitting needle. "You are right-handed, aren't you?"

"Yeah." The glass is in my left hand. I splurge with another giant swallow.

"In the lines of your palm I see future happiness, but conflict. These two lines at the base of your little finger tell me you'll have two lovers. You must choose wisely or your life will be strewn with heartache. You see these lines bisecting low in your palm? They also show conflict and a shortened life if you don't love the right woman."

I laugh. "You're full of it."

But she's dead serious. "I have two gifts: I'm a reader of palms and a clairvoyant." She continues in a quiet contemplative mood, pointing the needle at various line configurations. I'm so numb that I feel like flopping on the table. Finally she says, "Remember the black heart? We need to see if it's still there. By looking at it, and the sign in your palm, I'll be able to tell what's ahead for you." She drains the bottle into her glass and swallows the last of the wine.

I continue a silly laugh.

With one hand resting on my shoulder, she gently shakes me. "Stop laughing! This is serious!"

"I want more wine!" My hands hold either side of her face. When doing so, my fingers weave into her long black hair. Her lips are buried in mine. The warm wine—it's delicious. She kisses and I kiss for more. Holding her, I pull her toward me, wanting even more.

She slips the chain and locket over her head, turns off the desk lamp and helps me stand. I'm unsteady. With her arm around my waist, she pulls the scarlet drape and nudges me onto a studio couch. I fall face up and flat out. My head's in a spin, but it feels good to relax. In moments, her weight's on me. I'm out of it. My mind's in a fog. She kisses, trying to restart our game, but I can't react. Time slips by. My hands slide down her back to her waistline—all skin. She, again, tries to revive my interest with wet kisses, but I remain dazed in a faraway place. It's no use, I can't react.

"I love you, Dusty—always have and always will. I want to be a Murray. I want it so badly."

A hazy thought drifts through my head to lie—give her some satisfaction. I mumble, "I love you, too." I can't believe my loose words. They have no meaning. My head and my heart are traveling in different directions.

The next few moments are a fog to me. What is she doing? She jars me to attention. Being shaken, I vaguely remember my responsibilities.

Black hair is on my face and in my mouth. It's hard to breathe—her weight presses on my chest. My shirt is open. I don't recall unbuttoning it. We stick like warm paste. I push on her shoulders and we separate. She sits up, hysterically laughing, making no effort to cover herself. I don't remember the past few minutes or maybe an hour. I don't have a clue. I feel I'm waking from a bad dream.

I sit beside her. She puts her head on my shoulder. My arm lies limp over her back. I'm still in a haze, but there's chores to do. Who knows how long I've been here? She shakes me and I foggily come to attention. I ask, "What time is it? It must be late." I stand and feel weak, but weave my way out of the house. On the back step, I button and tuck in my shirt. I still hear her laughing from inside the house. She now knows my weakness: wine. It's also scary—the affect of her concoction of drugs.

The night air revives me enough to stagger, but I know where to go, and start gaining my senses. Reality grips me in fear as I head toward the road. The coolness on my face continues to wake me. In the evening dusk, I can see enough to know that I've reached the edge of Murray's Flats.

Suddenly, a pickup truck, coming out of nowhere, stops right in front of me. It's Clyde Shanks, the artificial inseminator. He does our breeding, since he has the best conception rate among his competitors. That's the only reason we hire him, because he's also the most unlikable man I know. Breeding a cow with thawed semen takes skill. Clyde brags that he's the best, and he is.

I hesitantly open the truck door and pull myself onto the seat. He always wears his baseball cap forward. Instead of lifting the brim to talk, he tips his head back with a superior air, looking down at the lesser folks he's talking to.

"Where have you been? Your grandfather's worried himself sick wondering, and sent me lookin' for you. Hell, I've got all the time in the world, ridin' the roads lookin' for some lost kid that's been in drinkin' with the O'Neil girl. I know she's home. My kid told me she was in school today."

My vocabulary surfaces from the deep darkness. The words don't form, but I ponder: What a jerk! I choose what to say carefully, trying not to slur. "I just stopped by to say hello."

"Sure, to say hello! You smell like a full-blown winery. I'll tell you, Thad's frantic. Addie's been sent to the hospital. Cooner's with her. Hell, your grandfather's a fish outta water when it comes to milking those cows." He pulls the shifting lever into first gear. We roll ahead. I can feel his eyes equally on me as on the road.

I ask, "Addie's sick?" A wave of guilt hits me. Who could ever love me more than Addie? And look how I handle myself. Cooner and Grandpa have done all they can to help me reach my goal, and I return thanks by absolutely going off the deep end. I feel like crying, running to Addie and climbing onto her lap, getting lost in her mothering comfort. Stupid drunk!

Clyde's eyes are consuming me. "Boy, you surprise me, off gettin' tangled with that O'Neil girl. Even as young as she is, she has a reputation, you know." He shifts again, and turns my way. "She's scary, I tell you, she's scary.

"When the carnival was down in Clarenton last week, this young farmer I breed for went Saturday night with his wife and family. On the midway he spotted this banner hangin' outside a tent: *Clairvoyant and Palmistry.*" Clyde pulls the shifting lever into third and leans my way again. "The O'Neil girl stood in her gypsy outfit beside the sign."

"Her name's Orla."

"Oh—well this farmer had been lookin' for his grandfather's watch. He went up to her and said somethin' like, 'Can you tell me where I can find my watch?'" The truck wanders onto the shoulder of the road. He yanks the wheel. "This O'Neil girl motioned for him to enter her tent. 'Come in and we'll see.'"

"Her name's Orla."

"Oh—well, the wife and kids stood outside waitin'. They took forever in that tent. After a fashion he came out having been given the works, but also she told him where he could find the watch."

He again leans my way, as if I'm supposed to be impressed.

"Seeing the shape he was in, his wife was ripped. To calm her, he claimed Orla took the palm of his hand and pointed with a needle to an imaginary field that had just been hayed. She followed a line in his palm and said, 'I see cattails on the edge of a field. You'll find the watch near there.'"

I manage a "Yeah."

"He went home, remembering he'd had a breakdown in that spot. While crawling under his baler, the watch apparently slipped from a pocket."

"Yeah."

"After the palm reading, he reached for his wallet. It was empty."

We're nearing the farm and my head is beginning to pound with pain, worried over Grandpa, to say nothing about Addie, and the drink. I don't comment on Clyde's story because I already know Orla's no ordinary girl.

I leave the truck, desperately wanting *not* to stagger toward the barn. I burst through the door. Grandpa's trying his best to milk, something he hasn't done since before he hired Cooner. Acting disoriented, he's standing in the aisle behind the cows. I can see relief wash over his face. "Uh…where in all thunder have you been—comin' home way past chore time." He steps toward me; but then he stops and stands erect, shaking his head. "My prodigal grandson!"

"I—I'm sorry, Grandpa. I couldn't help it."

He reacts with an expression full of question marks. "Help it? Ain't you got a backbone?" He grimaces, and his face reddens in anger. "Get goin'!" He takes off a milking machine. "Damnation, boy!"

"How's Addie?"

"It don't look good. We should be headin' for the hospital."

My dizziness lingers as I lunge, grabbing a cow's tail. "I'll milk." I don't bother changing my school clothes. Grandpa starts graining and haying the cows.

Clyde has his sleeved arm up to his elbow in the cow he's serving. "She's in a strong heat all right." He's carefully moving the breeding catheter in several directions. "She should settle. It only takes one of these little devils. He'll soon be wiggling his tail, ready to dive into her egg."

He's talking to me as if I'm captivated. I'm not. I'm resting my head against a cow's flank.

"Probably the same thing's happening right now with the O'Neil girl." Looking out from beneath the brim of his cap, he directs his remark toward me and laughs.

The creep! I'm ready to take a machine off. I yell, "Her name's Orla!"

He jumps at my reaction. "Take it easy, boy. So her name's Orla."

"I've only told you that about five times!"

He packs his breeding kit and leaves, saying, "If I have to come tomorrow night, I'll know where to find you." He laughs again and leaves.

There's an empty Coke bottle resting on the windowsill. I grab it and wildly sling it at the door to the milk room. It harmlessly bounces off into the gutter. In the next twenty-four hours, he'll have my screw-up spread all over the county. I hate him. My only redeeming thought is that few will believe him. I've admitted to nothing.

By seven o'clock, we've done a half-baked job of completing chores: no bedding, milk dishes not washed, no silage fed, and only enough hay to last until we return.

With no supper and a quick change of clothes, we're on our way to the hospital. Grandpa's silent in the car. I know he's due some sort of an explanation. Finally he says, "Uh...you ain't pullin' such a stunt like that again. You're the only reason I'm keepin' the cows. I can see I was a fool to buy that calf." He's drawn first blood while concentrating on his driving. He hasn't driven at night since I can remember.

I try to gather my thoughts to win back some respect. "Orla has returned. She claims her mother may give her control over the meadow." In the dim light, I can see Grandpa has a pinched-up expression. He's waiting for more.

"So?" He turns toward me. "Uh...we ain't even bought the place yet."

"What if Orla controls the property?"

"What kind of idiot do you think Zelda is?" He pauses. "The girl's just a kid."

"I know, but she claims someday she'll have control."

"Uh...you let some floozy lead you over fool's hill on the threat of *someday*?"

He doesn't understand, because I don't understand myself, especially liking the wine. "Trust me, it won't happen again."

"Uh... it won't! If it does, the cows and that calf's goin' down the road!"

— CHAPTER TWENTY-SIX —

As the car pulls into the hospital parking lot, neither of us say a word. Cooner often says: "There's a time to speak and a time to say nothing." *Nothing* wins out. I'm quietly analyzing myself. Grandpa, I'm sure, continues to be dumbfounded by my behavior. If he knew more of what really happened at Orla's, it would only make matters worse. Guilt pumps through me as we leave the car, heading toward the hospital.

I haven't even given much thought to the two people that raised and cared for me. By the time Grandpa and I enter the hospital doors, I'm saturated with shame.

We locate Addie's room. The light is dim when we enter. Cooner is by her bed with his head buried in the sheeting. He hears us and sits up. In a low voice almost a whisper, he says, "Addie has had a heart attack."

She's pale, sleeping with her mouth open. She's never been sick, always been the same, always there for me. I'm in disbelief.

He stands and reaches for my hand. "She's so proud of you, Dusty."

My grief is overwhelming; tears burst through broken flood gates. I'm lost for words. Grandpa sits in silence. In some respects, I'm fortunate because Addie's illness gives me an outlet to cry for all sorts of reasons—Maggie for one. If she finds out about my time with Orla, she'll dump me for sure.

Maggie returns late from the mum show, after Grandpa and I come home. She offers to get up for morning chores since Cooner stayed at the hospital. Plus, the nighttime trip to and from the hospital, and the late hour, has pooped Grandpa.

I have a terrible night's sleep, full of worry over my afternoon with Orla. The four-thirty alarm rings too soon. I wake Maggie and head for the barn. I feel lifeless as I start to milk, trying to have as little conversation with Maggie as possible. I'm a zombie, milking the cows by rote, carrying the milk in pails to the milk house, half realizing what I'm doing. Maggie walks down the aisle. "Are you okay, Dusty?" She watches me as I begin to blubber. "Let me hold you. Life has to go on." She hugs me. "Dusty, I'm so sorry. I know Addie means a lot to you, but the doctor told Cooner that the chances of recovery are good."

"I know." I wipe my face with a handkerchief.

She holds me at arm's length with her hands on my shoulders. I drop my head, not wanting to face her. She says, "I don't get it. You're acting different somehow. Is there something else?"

"Orla snagged me." I shrug and start to turn away to tend to the milking.

She pulls me back. "What happened last night after school?"

"I've got to finish." I step between two cows.

She moves closer to the cow I'm milking, and bends forward to get my attention. "What happened?"

I yank the machine off the adjoining cow, stand, and yell, "Geez, Maggie, do you have to know everything?"

"Yes!" She backs away with her hands on her hips.

"Geez!" I empty the milk into a pail and put the machine on the next cow. "We'll talk later."

Maggie's expression is tense. She turns off the vacuum on the two machines, pulls the teat cups off the cows, and pushes me up against the barn wall. "We'll talk right now!"

I gulp and run my fingers through my hair.

"'Snagged'! Just what does that mean?"

"Well, well, she...she did a palm reading."

"And?"

"She—she gave me some wine."

"And you drank it?" Maggie keeps her intense focus on me.

"Ya, y—yes." I can feel myself lifting on the balls of my feet.

"Too much?"

"Yeah, uh, yeah. The dope and wine knocked me out."

"Dope! What next?"

"I woke lying on a couch."

"With Orla?"

"Ye—ah."

Maggie grabs me by the shirt. "Did you or didn't you?"

"I don't think so."

She yells, "This is awful!" and yanks my shirt sideways to the point that I almost fall. "You don't know for sure? You make a good pair—a couple of liars."

She turns and runs toward the milk room, crying. She pulls the door with such force, it nearly comes off the hinges.

After chores, and letting the cows out to pasture, I really don't want to go to the house and face Maggie and Grandpa. Outside the barn door, Slue leaves her doghouse, stretches her legs, and wags her tail. She rubs her head against my knee. "You have a good night's sleep?"

She whines, loving my attention.

I step back into the barn for dog food and water. When I put the dishes down, she ignores them, wanting more attention. "You sure love to be loved."

I walk across the yard, dreading the next scene. I change my clothes in the entry and open the door to silence. Grandpa's holding Maggie's hand. They're sitting at a corner of the table. Her face is streaked with tears. Seeing me, he leaves the table, heading for the door. It slams.

I cautiously pull my chair away from the table and sit.

"Get your own stupid breakfast. I'm not lifting a finger for you!"

"Okay."

A car roars into the yard. I hear the door slam. Maggie goes to the sink and wipes her face. Her back is turned. The kitchen door flies open. "Hi. I've come for breakfast!"

It's Orla. She's immediately aware she's walked into a tense situation and freezes in the middle of the floor. Having discarded her gypsy garb, she's wearing a very tight white sweater and black slacks. Her long hair is pinned in a bun. She looks very mature.

An unbelievable stillness and calm fills our space; all three of us are silently locked in the moment. I hear the click of the electric clock. A cluster fly is buzzing against the window over the sink. The kitchen faucet drips: *splat, splat.*

The fuse of an imaginary cherry bomb is hissing. Tensions are about to explode. Maggie whips around and throws a wadded dish rag at Orla—a perfect strike. It hits her in the face.

Shocked, Orla slugs it back, but misses. "What in hell's wrong with you?"

"You know!" Maggie's eyes squint with her face full of tension.

"Oh, you poor thing! I had your impotent peach-fuzz love for the afternoon!"

"You whore!" Maggie moves toward Orla. Uncombed strands of hair lie in disarray against Maggie's face. "I don't ever want to see you again! And I don't care about *him* either!"

"Oh, he's some prize! Passing out with the blink of an eye! A little wine and he's worthless!" Orla pushes Maggie back on her heels. "So the golden girl can't stand a little competition."

"You slut!" Maggie has Orla by the throat, backing her all the way across the room. "Leave. Get out!" Maggie opens the door and shoves her. "I hope you get arrested—driving illegally."

Orla cries, "You'll pay. I have ways!"

Maggie slams the door.

I haven't moved from my seat. "I'm sorry."

"Sorry? Sorry? That's all you can say?"

CHAPTER TWENTY-SEVEN

Maggie, Orla, and I ride in separate seats on the bus. Maggie won't sit with me. Orla would like to, but I won't let her. Maggie quits 4-H to avoid us, explaining to Shirley that she has too much to do, which sounds logical but, of course, is not the real reason. Tonight, Maggie's cooking the supper meal. Cooner and I come in from the barn. When I enter, I can feel her mood change. She turns her back on me, mashing potatoes in a cooker. The hard *clank, clank* of the masher against the metal reminds me of a hammer hitting a huge spike. The sound brings us to attention.

Grandpa comes through the door and takes a seat. He looks at Maggie. "Uh…how's our cook tonight?"

"Fine!" She moves to the stove to continue frying hamburgers. They fly in the air as she flips them with a spatula.

Grandpa turns my way with an angry expression of the old mad Thad I grew up knowing. In recent months, he's mellowed. Not tonight, not with me anyway.

Addie's returned home. She's not her usual self as she spends a lot of time in bed. "Goodness, I don't have any life," she says. "I just sit while Maggie does all the work." She's seated at the kitchen table in her bathrobe. Her face has lost its color and her hair seems grayer.

Cooner and I come from the bathroom after washing up. Cooner rests his hand on Addie. "How are you feelin'?"

"Dead on my feet." She lifts her head and glances at Cooner. "The doctor said it would take time to regain my strength. I don't know what I'd do without Maggie."

Maggie places a plate of hamburgers on the table. She actually smiles, saying to Addie, "I'm happy to do it—for *you*."

I take a chair and blush.

Cooner turns my way. "What's goin' on with you two?"

Maggie bangs a bowl of mashed potatoes on the table and shoves it. The dish crashes into the centerpiece of fake roses.

Cooner and Addie stare at me. Cooner says, "Looks like the chickens have come home to roost."

I want to run, hide—bury my face.

Grandpa, seated next to me, says nothing. He's reaching for the hamburgers, takes one, and angrily shoves the plate toward me without a word.

I flinch in my chair. The plate of hamburgers slips from my hand. A few spill. The plate clatters onto the table. Cooner, sitting across from me, quickly puts them back and takes one for himself. He frowns at me as our eyes meet. "What's goin' on?"

I look down at my plate.

Maggie steps to the table and spears a hamburger with her fork. She slaps on a spoonful of potato. Going to the sink and standing, she bangs her plate on the drain board. With her back turned, she yells, "It's Orla!" She slams the plate in the sink. It shatters. She yanks at her neck—throws the silver heart in my face. "Take your junk jewelry!" She runs for the stairs.

Grandpa rests his head in the palm of his hand and stares at the table.

Cooner sniffs and blows his nose.

Addie stiffens. "Oh, dear!"

I head for the barn.

In the days that follow into late September, my dilemma with Grandpa and Maggie doesn't improve. I quit taking the bus to school and ride my bike. I don't want to be anywhere near Orla, and seeing Maggie just makes me feel too sad. I snitch food other than at mealtime, staying in the barn during supper. Addie usually leaves me a plate. It's cold, but I think of it as punishment—doing time.

I devise ways to avoid both girls in classes such as Algebra, English, and U.S. History. I enter, sit close to the door, and leave by the back of the room.

At the farm, I turn my full attention to cutting corn. I rush home on my bike, usually beating the bus. When I breeze past Orla's house, I notice she has a cloth sign on the lawn: *Clairvoyant and Palmistry.* With Clyde Shanks spreading the word of Orla's powers, I'm sure she'll have plenty of business.

Grandpa gets permission from the court to borrow Uncle Bill's old John Deere corn chopper, unloading wagon, and blower—a promise to loan had already been given Cooner before Uncle Bill's death.

We've just finished unloading a wagon of chopped corn. It's chore time. Cooner leans on the side of the wagon and says, "Corn cuttin's a lot easier than it used to be. Years back, we had the old corn binder and handled corn in bundles. The chopper and blower were parked at the silo. We fed the bundles into the machine. The whirlin' knives and paddles sent the corn up into the silo." He reaches for a pinch of tobacco. "Thad grew good corn. The bundles were heavy and hard to handle. I don't know who wore out first, the equipment or Thad." He spits tobacco juice. "Years back, he quit growin' corn, and bought better haying equipment."

We're heading toward the barn. Cooner rests his hand on me. "After milkin', that silo needs to be leveled and packed." He spits again. "That'll give you a good excuse to miss supper again."

"Okay."

"Don't you think it's about time to make amends with Thad and Maggie?" He walks through the milk house door and I follow. "Your antics hit and bruised them pretty hard. Now, after a spell, the swellin's gone some. You need to start healin' wounds."

"Yeah, but how?"

"That's for you to figure out."

The silo job takes more than an hour to level and pack. I'm walking in circles treading it, feeling each step sink into the green corn. It smells sugar sweet. After a while, I start feeling a firm footing.

I have lots of time to think how to go about healing wounds, but time doesn't give me a solution. Maggie's the key. I know that. If she felt better toward me, Grandpa would mellow. Cooner's right, I need to straighten the mess. The deadline for the bid on the meadow is coming soon. I've got to prove to Grandpa that I'm an okay kid. Sure, he can see I'm working hard, and that I'm interested in the farm; but my working hard doesn't impress him. It's Maggie that matters.

I'm still pondering my dilemma as I leave the barn. Slue greets me. She whines as I rub her head and back. For the time being, I'm living a dog's life—or less than a dog, prowling around in the dark for food, acting like a rat. After taking off my barn clothes in the entry, I enter a darkened kitchen. Only the nightlight over the sink is on. The plate of food at my place is there with a glass of milk. I'm eager to eat.

"Dusty! Finally!"

"Addie, you're still up?"

She's sitting in darkness at the head of the table. "Yes, we need to talk."

"Yeah, I know." I gingerly take my seat—forgetting my food.

"Cooner and I raised you to be honorable. Just lately, you've been acting like a coward. I don't like it!"

In the shadows, I can't see her expression. But I know her too well. She's not condemning me, but forcing me to stand up to the situation. "I don't like it either."

"We all make mistakes. You aren't alone. Go to Maggie. You may be surprised. Act like you're somebody and take your licks." She gets up with effort and heads for her room. "I want an end to this sneakin' around."

"I'll try." I sit, eating the cold chicken, cold potato, and rubbery peas. I gulp the glass of milk, stand, burp, and head for Maggie's room. I creep up the stairs in the dark, wondering what to say. Her last words ring in my ears: Sorry? Sorry! That's all you can say?

Light filters through cracks around her door. She has on the hit record by Simon and Garfunkel, "Bridge Over Troubled Waters."

—— CHAPTER TWENTY-EIGHT ——

I stand in front of Maggie's door, wondering what's next. Before I knock, Napoleon and courage cross my mind. Addie's words also remind me to act as if I'm somebody: everyone makes mistakes.

The knock echoes down the hallway. The door swings open. "Dusty!" She reacts more in surprise than anger.

"Yeah, it's me."

"Well, stranger." Her serious expression sends chills up my back.

"Can I—I come in?" Fingers slide through my hair. My hand continues to pat the top of my head.

"I guess so."

"Well, isn't it time we at least became friends again?"

"Come in." She turns off the record player. Her room's much like mine: small with an alcove and big windows. She's decorated the walls with pictures of movie stars and pop recording stars. She motions toward the side of her bed. "Pull up that chair."

I place it at the side of her desk. It's about the size of the ones we have at school. I must look kind of stupid because I'm lost for words. Saying I'm sorry comes to mind, but I've worn that one out. I fold my hands and rest them on the desk, next to an open book and spiral notebook. 'Dusty', written in lead pencil at the top edge of her desk, catches my eye. I open my hands and run a finger over my name. "Was that written before or after?" I glance at her.

"What do you think?" Her face flushes.

"Yeah, that was a stupid question."

"Where have you been lately?"

"In hiding." I'm not giving her eye contact. My finger continues to nervously rub the desk over my name. Then I look up. "Maggie, my feelings for you haven't changed. I miss you." I glance again at the desk. "My time with Orla was a huge mistake."

"I guess!"

"I want you to be my girl. Orla surely isn't."

170

Our eyes meet.

She breaks into a smile. "Well, I guess you're at least worth a warm meal." She laughs. "Start eating with us again."

"I'd like that."

"Listen to this record. It's my favorite." The music of "Can't Stop Loving You", fills the room. "Let's dance." She pulls my hand.

She snuggles into my arms. I feel a shower of relief. My nose is buried in her golden hair. Her fragrance makes my knees go weak. After the music stops, we tightly hug. She gently shoves me. "I'll see you. Get lost." She laughs again.

I leave the room and draw a big breath of relief.

The next morning, when we come in from the barn, Maggie's at the stove frying eggs. She's dressed for school in a powder blue sweater and navy slacks. Her wavy blond hair is pinned with a dark blue velvet ribbon. The breakfast sounds: the crack of eggshells on the edge of the big pan, the sizzling of bacon, and the aroma of coffee, make me hungry. She's softly sings, "Can't Stop Loving You."

We're all seated. She has her usual glow when she places the platter of fried eggs on the table. Grandpa stares at her. "Uh…our cook's lookin' pretty."

Cooner says, "Singin' like a canary."

Maggie smiles while she reaches for the coffee pot and a platter of toast. She places them on the table. "It's a great day."

All three adults stare at me. I blush.

Cooner clears his throat and changes the subject. "When I went to the store last night, Orla sure had a slew of cars at her place."

Maggie takes her seat. "With a bunch of riff-raff in town."

"Goodness, that girl's trouble," says Addie. "And she hasn't even turned fifteen."

Maggie adds, "Things will change when her mother comes home."

"I hope so." Addie puts her stray hair in place. "A young girl left to her own devices. It just isn't right."

Within a few days, Zelda does return home. Orla's sign is no longer on their front lawn. The clash of mother and daughter must have been something else.

On Saturday, Maggie comes home mid-morning with the word that the I-vest plan for the meadow is complete. Zelda wants to meet with Grandpa.

Maggie's in the kitchen cooking a dinner of sliced ham, peas and carrots, muffins, tea, and coffee. She's preparing for the arrival of Zelda. Cooner has taken Addie to the doctor and plans to go shopping in the early afternoon, wanting no part of a meal with Zelda O'Neil. Grandpa and I are in the living room waiting. He's seated in an easy chair looking straight ahead. "Uh...I see Maggie's her old self."

I'm sitting in a ladder-back chair, looking in the same direction, feeling as stiff as the chair. "Yeah."

Cooner's advice comes to mind: There's a time to speak and a time to say nothing. I figure the less said the better.

"Uh...see's it stays that way."

"I'll do my best."

"Uh...I'm springin' a bid on the meadow for *you*. It sure ain't for *me*."

"Thanks...I realize."

A car roars into the yard. A door slams. Maggie yells from the kitchen, "Dusty, go out and meet Zelda."

Of course, I'm the one chosen. Maggie's busy, and Grandpa's Grandpa. Folks come to see him.

I meet her in the entry. She's carrying a quantity of rolled papers about three feet long. I assume they're the development plans. "Hi, come in."

She turns and throws her lighted cigarette out the door, and jerks her head backward. "Dusty!" She coughs lightly. "Your grandfather here?"

"Yeah, but Maggie has a meal planned."

"Oh, that girl. She's just too much." She brushes past me. Her business suit reeks of cigarette smoke. She gushes toward Maggie, "My dear, you shouldn't have!"

"I wanted to. It'll give you a chance to get to know Uncle Thad."

In a low gravelly voice she says, "From years back, and from what I remember of him—no one gets to know Thad Murray."

Maggie doesn't smile. "Well, re-acquainted then." I'm still standing by the door. "Dusty, take Zelda to the living room. Dinner will be ready soon."

Zelda leads the way, since she's barged ahead not acknowledging me.

Grandpa stays seated. He's never cracked the book of good manners that Addie's taught me. "Uh…Zelda. Take a seat."

She sits on an old broken-down couch, facing him, and says, "Maggie tells me you're ready to submit a bid on Bill's property."

"Uh…just the meadow. We need to get movin'. The bid deadline's the ninth."

"You realize the meadow's the most valuable piece of the estate."

"Uh…yup."

In a few minutes, Maggie stands in the archway of the living room. "Dinner's ready."

"Zelda, you can sit here next to Uncle Thad." Maggie stands in back of her chair.

We're all seated. Dishes of food are being passed. Zelda says, "My dear, you are so capable. I wish Orla had just *some* of your ability."

"Orla's talents run in a different direction."

"She seems determined to continue her palmistry, claiming her clairvoyant powers," Zelda says. "She's attracting all sorts of unsavory characters. I can't live in the same house with her." She turns toward Grandpa. "Bidding on Bill's estate is timely for me. I want Orla out of my house. She can do her business at the homestead."

"Uh… well, the bid will have to be more than a hundred and fifty grand. Erickson will go that high."

"What I've brought to show you will make that possible."

Grandpa stuffs in a mouthful of ham. He glances at the roll of paper and scowls.

"What a wonderful meal!" Zelda says as she raises her cup.

I notice the yellowing of nicotine between her fingers. She seems to have aged considerably since the day we walked the meadow. Her face has the same smoker's veil of gray, but today it seems even more so. Her graying hair appears lifeless.

After eating lightly, and having a small piece of pie, she stands and picks up the long roll of stiff paper. "I have a proposal that I want you all to see. Maggie, we need to clear the table."

Grandpa says, "Uh…I got to eat my pie." He munches slowly, glancing suspiciously at the roll.

I have an idea what's coming, but I dread seeing it. I never told him of our walk in the meadow, figuring his surprise reaction will put Zelda in her place. I want no part of the discussion.

Grandpa finishes and the table's cleared. She rolls out a print of the approximate boundary lines of Uncle Bill's property. "This parcel of land is approximately two hundred acres, which includes the meadow, pasture, pines and woodland. Thad, we're sitting on a gold mine."

"Uh…I—I don't understand."

"I-vest Engineering, a company from Boston, has presented me with a plan for the development of this property. They think the Huntersville area is situated for future growth. With the completion of the interstate highway system, this land has a huge potential." She lifts the two-by-three-foot paper from a second sheet she's referring to as a preliminary plot plan. "The elevation of most of the meadow is out of the floodplain. The soils also lend themselves to establishing suitable in-ground septic systems. In fact, this plan is so large that it might offer Huntersville an opportunity to have its own sewage treatment plant."

Grandpa sits stone-faced. Never having seen a plot plan, it appears to be a big blur for him. Blue lines apparently are a road leading to the woods, pasture, and pines. Quarter-acre plots are designated for the ridge overlooking the Blue. There are at least a hundred units. The meadow is sliced into sections like a pan of gingerbread for commercial and residential development. There's a huge shopping mall. The pivotal store is a gigantic supermarket. "Thad, if this is handled right, you'll be set for life."

"Uh…this ain't my thinkin'."

"What do you mean?"

"Uh…I'll have no part of this."

"Well, I'm not bidding over a hundred thousand for a bunch of broken-down buildings and five acres."

"Uh...so be it. I ain't bein' a party to any such thing as this."

"I should have known. Farmers don't have an ounce of business sense."

"Uh...and folks like you ain't got no sense at all."

"Let's not get nasty." She fumbles in her pocketbook. "I need a cigarette."

"You ain't smokin' in here!"

She leaves and slams the door. The meeting is going much worse than I thought. I suggest, "Maybe we should call Steven Iverson. He could own half of the meadow. Then the three of you could out-bid Erickson."

"Uh...yup. That looks to be our only chance. If that bitch will buy into it."

Zelda returns. "I think we need to cool down."

"Uh...yup. Why don't Steven Iverson, you, and me bid? You bid what you might, including all the stuff in the house and barns. Iverson and I'll make up the difference for a hundred and sixty-five thousand."

"If I want that house for Orla, I don't have a choice." She coughs. "I sure don't have the cash or the will to go it alone."

Zelda calls Steven. "Thad Murray and I want to see you about the bid for Bill's estate...okay, see you in twenty minutes."

"Maggie, can you help me in the barn for a while since Cooner's not here?" I ask. "There's a few chores to do."

"Sure."

—— CHAPTER TWENTY-NINE ——

From the barn, I notice Steven Iverson's truck. Maggie and I clean the stable, bed the cows, and clean calf pens. When we're finished, just before milking time, we go to the house for a break. Zelda has left. Grandpa reports, "Uh…Iverson agreed on a bid of sixty thousand for fifty acres of the meadow. I agreed on forty thousand for the rest of it. I'm satisfied. That will be enough land."

"Yeah, thanks, Grandpa."

"Uh…it ain't perfect. But it's the best I can do." He gets up to leave. "Zelda's biddin' sixty-five grand for the buildings and five acres. She's demandin' her name will be on the whole of the property. The bitch, she won't give up on that development plan for the meadow."

October begins with a downpour of cold rain. Wednesday morning, Maggie and I make a mad dash for the bus. We sit together, which seems like a small thing, but for me it's huge. I thought that things would never be the same between us, but they are. I slide my hand in my pocket and pull out the tin heart. "I wondered if you wanted to wear this again." I dangle it in front her.

She smiles. "Sure. It's so sweet." She examines it closely.

Maggie and Dusty. She leans over and nudges me. "I love it."

It's raining so hard that the bus wipers appear to be plowing the water off the glass. I'm gazing out the window imagining what forty acres will look like. That amount of the meadow seems vast compared to the seven acres of corn land. The bus is slowing to pick up Orla. She's not by the road, so we wait and wait. The driver blows the horn.

Maggie puts on a disgusted expression. "She's probably still in bed."

Although Orla's a pain in the neck, I do care. "Here she comes." She's not hurrying at all, allowing herself to get soaked. She mopes onto the bus, looking awful. Beads of water run off her face. Her brown jacket is drenched. Wet jeans cling to her legs with every step. But worse yet, she has a huge black eye, and a red bruise on her chin. With shoulders slumped, she drags up the aisle.

Maggie turns toward the window. Orla's eyes show her pain. "What happened?" I ask.

"I've got to see you." She crashes in a seat behind us.

"About what?"

Maggie jabs me in the side with her sharp elbow, and turns her back against me.

"I'll tell you after." Orla starts to sob.

We file off the bus with Maggie charging on ahead, pushing by other kids. I hold back to see what Orla wants. In my opinion, Maggie's over-reacting. The rain has turned to a light sprinkle. Orla and I stand outside the bus. "What happened to you?"

"Two guys—", she starts to cry and then controls herself. "—tried to rape me."

"Really!" I take a closer look. "You're lucky to be here."

"I know. Snaky's been seeing me some. He was just leaving when these two guys barged through the door." She sniffs.

We walk toward school. "They were big and pushed Snaky out the door and locked it. That gave me time to get my baseball bat. I hit one on the head, but the other came after me and knocked me down. Snaky broke in the door and slugged the guy a good one."

"Geez, Orla, you got to quit seeing these creeps."

"Yeah, I know." She cries some more and blows her nose. "Snaky wants me to stay at his house when Mother isn't home."

"Why don't you?" We pass through the doorway of the school.

"Dusty, I'd like it if you and I could become good friends again. You know, have things the way they used to be." She reaches for my hand. "Walk up to the pines, sit in peace—be away for just a short time."

"Yeah, maybe." I'm thinking of Maggie and Grandpa, but she's looking so sad that I don't want to outright say no.

"We could check to see if that black heart is still there. If it is, we need to get rid of it."

"That was years ago."

"It must be still there. The power of my golden locket has been invaded. Last night was the limit."

"Orla! What are you saying?"

"Evil spirits are killing me."

"Well, the tree doesn't have anything to do with what's been going on with you."

"I think it does. Black is a bad omen, peering down on the land, the cattle, and all of us folks. Did you realize that evil can spread? Plants will turn black, cattle will die, and all their guts will turn black. I feel the power of wickedness has overtaken me like a dark shadow."

"Orla, your imagination has gone wild. That heart has been there for years and I haven't seen any signs of black." I turn to study her expression, wondering if she's gone nuts.

She continues, with teary eyes, in absolute seriousness, "The spirit world and omens of evil can overtake our lives without notice. Evil is always there, but if we can eliminate the black heart, we'll destroy the source."

I can't listen to her any longer and head for my class room. She runs after me and grabs my arm. "Let's go this Saturday. I'll pack a picnic."

I turn away and pick up my pace. She follows. "Watch for black. You'll see. We need to destroy that heart."

I stop and face her, trying to think of a good excuse to ditch her plan. "Saturday's a big day at the farm."

"Come on, Dusty, you can give up two hours!"

"I don't know." I leave.

She raises her voice, "Well, you think about it. Oh, by the way, I talked to Mother about the meadow."

I stop in my tracks.

"She promised if she gets part ownership, she'll give me her share." I quickly turn again toward her. Through the tears and flushed face, I detect a slight smirk. "Remember Saturday." Before I'm out of earshot, she yells, "Watch for black."

I'm being yanked around. There's no way her mother's going to give her share of the meadow to Orla, but the black heart does make me wonder. If we go, the omen will be eliminated. We'll knife and slice the thing right out of the no-good tree, light a fire and burn it, happily watching it go up in flames. All her talk about signs of evil really is baloney—I think.

Despite my doubt, the phrase "watch for black" lingers in my mind, clinging to me like a pesky mosquito. During school, everything black stands out: the blackboard, black pants, black shoes, black hair, black buttons, and black hash marks on the gym floor. The letters in everything I read seem to be darker than I've noticed before. Our teacher is in front of the class reading from a black hard-covered book. I stare, not remembering a thing he reads; but the book becomes larger and larger, blacker and blacker. By the end of the day, I'm in a rush to get home and out of the place. Orla's warning sticks with me: "Omens can seep into our lives without notice."

I want to forget that statement, go to the barn to admire Pride and the cows, and unwind. Orla must have skipped afternoon classes because she isn't on the bus—a relief for me. Riding home, I swear, most of the cars that pass are black. I hurry off the bus, desperately wanting to reconnect to the real world. I glance at the tape recorder in my room. Even the control buttons are black.

As I enter the barn, the smells are relaxing, filtering through a ball of nerves. Phew, this feels good like, I'm out from under a ton of Blue River rocks. I'm skipping school tomorrow, that's for sure; a day away from Orla is a must. I'll work in the barn building a new calving pen: handling lumber, measuring, sawing, feeling the nail, striking the head, all solid stuff. I need relief from quirky ideas—seeing black and sensing omens.

It's Thursday morning. The air's cold and frosty, but it feels like we'll have a nice fall day. Cooner and I meet at the barn door. "Morning, Cooner. What a great day! We're going to work at building the bigger calving pen that Grandpa wants."

He sniffs and pulls his handkerchief from his back pocket and blows. "Thought you had school."

"Well—I—I do, but I want to work on that pen." My hand flies through my hair.

Cooner stops and holds me by the forearm and searches my expression. "That Orla's gnawin' at you again, ain't she? I saw Eddie at the store last night. He claims he had to fight two guys that were after her."

"I didn't even mention Orla!"

"You ain't needin' to. You act as nervous as a snared rabbit."

"Cooner, let's drop the subject. We're working in the barn." I walk away.

He raises his voice, "If you tangle with her, she'll send your thinkin' off track through a month of Sundays."

"Yeah, yeah. Let's get going on chores." Cooner is wise, but sometimes the wisdom he spouts doesn't make any sense.

After chores, I come in the house, wash up, and speak to Maggie. I haven't had a chance to see her since she left the bus in a huff. She's busy with breakfast. We're alone for a short time. "How are you this morning?"

"Fine." She flashes me an angry expression while opening the oven door and sliding out a tin of biscuits. "Orla's got you wrapped around her little finger?"

"No, she hasn't." I need to sound confident when in fact I'm not. "I do feel sorry for her."

"What does she want from you—another party?"

I'm standing next to her by the stove. "Remember, Maggie, you're my girl." I put my arm around her. "I am worried for Orla, though. Her life's out of control."

"It's her own fault."

Cooner, Addie, and Grandpa enter the kitchen.

We both cut our conversation. Maggie bumps me with her hip and smiles. "Sit down or I'll poison your breakfast." She laughs.

I take my seat. "I'm working in the barn today—fixing the pen Grandpa wants changed."

Grandpa stares at me. "Uh…I ain't expectin' you to miss school 'cause of it."

"I know, but it needs doing." I try to stay calm. "Several cows are due to calve."

Addie is at the table. "Goodness, school's important."

"It'll be all right for just one day."

Maggie takes her seat. "Oh, school's a snap for Dusty. He got 75 on his last algebra test."

"Let the boy do as he minds to," Cooner says.

I appreciate Cooner's support, but the pressure of disapproval is too much. I leave for the barn.

Before the door closes, I can hear Maggie say, "It's Orla again."

—— CHAPTER THIRTY ——

I have a lot of fun staying home from school, seeing the new pen take shape. We're working with 2x10 planks pulled from the lumber pile. We're sawing for proper length and driving spikes into uprights. It feels great to see the spikes sink into the wood as I swing the hammer, releasing my frustration.

Cooner yells, "Holy jumped up!" He's dancing around, shaking his hand. "I just hit my thumb. Golly it hurts."

"Let me see." The base of the nail is immediately turning red. "Ouch! You've got yourself a good one."

"Maybe if I keep workin', I'll forget the pain."

The afternoon goes well, and we finish the pen. I stand back. "That's a big improvement. Now we won't have cows cramped for space at calving time."

At night milking, Cooner shows me his thumb. "Golly, this blasted thing hurts. Look, the nail is turning all black." He sits on a stool and with the awl of his knife pierces a hole at the base of the nail to relieve the pressure of blood. I try to ignore the fact that his nail is turning black, but the thought won't leave. He holds his hand near my face.

My head and cap are sunk into the flank of a cow as I wash her udder. I quickly glance. "I see." My remark sounds casual, but the black is a stark reminder that the omen will seep into our lives without notice.

Blood, nearly black, is oozing near the cuticle. He presses the nail, and the dark red rushes faster. "Golly, does that ever feel better."

He takes chewing tobacco from his back pocket, fills his mouth with a big pinch, then licks the shreds from his lips. He's in the aisle watching me put the milker on the next cow. "Boy, you look all worked up over somethin'. What's ailin' you?" He steps closer to try and get my attention. "It's that hocus-pocus witch, ain't it?"

I weakly smile. "I'm okay."

"You ain't actin' right. Orla and her gypsy thinkin' has got a hold on you." He spits a line of juice in the gutter. "Eddie told me what goes on at her place. It ain't good."

My back is turned as I stand between two cows. I'm plugging the machine to the vacuum line. I don't want to lie, not to Cooner. "Snaky can tell stories."

Cooner spits again. "That's for sure."

He shakes his limp hand, walking up the aisle to start feeding. He abruptly stops at Pride's pen. "Your heifer's ailin'."

He reaches to feel an ear. "Cold as a clam." He calls to me, "Come see. Somethin' has hit her hard."

"What could it be?"

"I ain't sure. You've got to get Doc Chambers here. She's dead on her feet."

She stands with head down and ears drooping. "Gosh, she's cold and depressed. Cooner, would you call the vet? I'll keep milking."

Doc Chambers is an older man. Besides doctoring small animals, he's good with cows. Farmers like him as their veterinarian.

Pride's still standing by the time I've finished milking. Who knows why, but she seems near death. Doc comes into the barn, wearing a fedora and dark blue coveralls, carrying his black case which he places in back of the pen. He checks Pride and takes her temperature, which is below normal. He slips on a plastic sleeve, lubricates his hand, and enters her anal track. Pulling his arm out, he closely examines the stiff manure in his gloved hand. "This is entirely black."

"Black!"

"Yeah, you sound surprised."

"Well, what's wrong?"

"The black is old blood." He pinches her hide, checking for dehydration. "This heifer is bleeding to death."

"Really?"

"Yes. She either has an ulcer or a broken blood vessel in her intestines. Our only hope is to give her a large transfusion of blood and pump plenty of water into her. Maybe the bleeding will clot and stop. Let's tie her in a stall and put a healthy cow next to her. We'll start transferring blood. Blood types aren't an issue in bovines."

We tie an older cow next to Pride and start the process. With the two heads and necks tied in opposite directions, Doc puts a large-gauge needle in each animal's neck vein. We are able to fill and empty two 60cc syringes at a fairly rapid rate. Doc remarks, "If she pulls through this, feed her your best hay and only a pound of grain a day. Has she been getting corn silage?"

"Yeah, as much as she can eat." I pull the plunger of the syringe and fill it from the healthy cow.

"Well, stop that." He pushes the plunger, giving Pride another dose. "She's fancy. Is this the heifer that Jimmy Iverson brags about?"

"Yeah, she's the one." I draw the plunger again and watch it fill, and then hand him the syringe. He returns the empty for a refill.

Doc asks, "You pasturing heifers next spring up across the Blue on land your uncle used to use?"

"Yeah, maybe a few. I hate to see it all grow up."

"Those heifers will have to get shots for blackleg. Years ago, I remember going up there and finding several dead."

On the word "black", I drop the empty syringe.

"You got the jitters, boy?"

"Well, that's awful. You found heifers dead?" I wipe the syringe with a wad of alcohol-soaked cotton and resume drawing from the cow, watching blood rush into the cylinder. "Gosh—blackleg? I've never heard of it."

"I hadn't seen a case until that day. At first, I didn't know what it was. I cut one heifer open and all the muscular tissues had turned to thick black syrup."

"Black, huh?" Orla isn't anywhere near me. I haven't seen her in a day and a half, yet I hear her words.

Doc rambles on while I collect blood. "Blackleg is a clostridia disease caused by soil-borne bacteria. It can live in the soil for an undetermined length of time—some reports estimate more than twenty years."

"This donor cow is getting cold."

"Yes, and your heifer is coming around." He goes to his truck and returns with a box in his hand. "Let's pump some warm water and bicarbonate of soda into her. She may have a severe case of acidosis."

We slide a tube down her throat. "A diet of too much corn silage and grain can do that."

I release the old cow's head. She starts eating hay and drinking from the water bowl next to her. "Maybe I won't pasture that land up on the ridge."

"Vaccinate. It should be okay. We humans can get a clostridia disease—tetanus or lockjaw."

"Lockjaw?" I feel the muscle along my jaw and open my mouth. I wonder if I'm next, remembering that the black heart is a bad omen peering down on us. I continue rubbing my face. "Do people's jaws turn black, too?"

Doc throws his balding head back, laughing. "You seem to be really into black tonight."

"Oh, you…think so?" My face turns red. "Well…black blood, blackleg, I…I just wondered."

"I'm not an MD, but I understand the symptoms begin with muscle spasms in the jaw—to the point where it's difficult to open your mouth."

"Oh." My hand runs along my jaw, rubbing my face again. I'm hungry and tense. Maybe that's why I can't open my mouth as wide as usual, or maybe that's the furthest I could ever open it.

The barn door slams. It's Cooner and Maggie. They've finished eating.

Cooner says, "Golly, your heifer's lookin' better. S'pose she'll come around?" He rubs her flank. "Poor critter. We sure don't want to have anything happen to Pride."

I ask Doc, "What're her chances?"

"I'm not sure. Check her in a few hours." He's packing his bag. "If she seems worse, give me a call."

"I sure will!"

Maggie steps between the cows and hands me a warm muffin wrapped in a napkin. "You must be hungry."

"Thanks." I smile. "I need something to eat after Doc's gotten me all worked up over lockjaw and stuff like that." I munch on the soft sweet treat.

Maggie lightens my mood. "Come to my room tonight and I'll give you an algebra lesson."

"Thanks, I'll do that."

"You'll be in the house soon?"

"Yeah, it won't be long." I watch her walk away. "Hey, I liked the muffin."

She raises her hand in a wave.

Doc leaves, and I give Pride the best hay I can find. She grabs a mouthful and starts chewing. The prognosis is hopeful, but only time will tell.

After checking on Pride several times in the night, I'm reassured that she's feeling better. The bleeding, from whatever the source, seems to have stopped. During morning chores, she eats a large quantity of hay, and she's all too eager for the little grain. Cooner assures me, "Pride looks to be normal this morning."

"Yeah, but I'm riding my bike to school. I'll be home during my break to check on her."

He stares at me. "That ain't necessary."

"Well, just in case." I really don't want to see Orla, especially on the bus ride to school.

I've also decided that, on Saturday, I'll take a couple of hours from the morning to check on the black heart without anyone knowing. I don't want to give in to the fact that Orla may have cast a gypsy spell on me.

When I get to school, I try to avoid her, but she knows my schedule. She's waiting for me when the bell rings and classes change. Her black eye's improving, but her sadness and slumped shoulders haven't changed. "Dusty, you ready for tomorrow?"

"You don't have to come."

She pleads, "But I want to." Tears fill her eyes—so much so they begin to run down her face. "Of course, the heart won't be the same as when it was carved several years ago. Wearing my locket, I'll be able to tell if it's the source of evil that's dragging me down."

I stand, wondering what to believe and what not to believe.

"If you go by yourself, you won't recognize the signs of wickedness that's flowing down from the ridge."

I continue staring at her, thinking of Cooner's thumb, Pride's blood, and now discovering that the whole area around the tree may be loaded with blackleg. Maggie will be working. No one has to know

Orla's with me. "I'll meet you across the Blue by the quartz stone at ten. Wear high boots. You'll need them to cross the Blue."

She brightens and leans into me. "Good. I can't wait!"

"We'll follow the river down to the cattle bridge; that's the safest way to go."

Saturday morning I'm reminded of the opening of the bids in a few days. It's just a passing thought, however, because I'm determined to eliminate the black heart. I leave the house quietly. There's been another heavy frost. I hunch and hurry toward the barn. Slue's buried in hay that Cooner put in her house. She doesn't stir when I enter the barn door. I start milking. Cooner comes through the door. "Well, well, you're up and at it early this mornin'."

"Yeah, I want to walk up and take a look at Uncle Bill's old heifer pasture."

"Really?" He gives me a suspicious glance. "That weren't never much of a pasture."

"I know." I hate his staring at me. "Maybe we can cut some brush before snowfall."

"A waste of time." While he watches me, he pinches a wad of tobacco and shoves it in his mouth. His next question sounds as if he has a mouth full of marbles. "What's up with you?"

"Nothing." I turn to put the machine on the next cow. "Don't you think it's about time you started feeding?"

"Yup." He shakes his head and walks up the aisle.

At nine-thirty, I leave the house, heading for the bridge. After a pleasant breakfast, Maggie's left for work. Cooner continues staring at me, trying to figure out why I'm *really* going. He'll never know.

The sun is bright, but frost is still on the shaded bridge planking as I cross. The wild asters and goldenrod are dead and frosty white. I walk along the cow path under the willows, crunching frozen leaves. The quartz stone is in sight outside the corner of the fence next to the river. It's well before ten. I cross the fence and sit on the white stone, waiting for Orla.

The animal path, following the rim of the pit, leads straight up from the edge of the water. The pit opens up fifty feet or so beyond where I'm sitting. The fast moving water laps the bank. Ice crystals have formed on the dead grass at the river's edge.

I watch as Orla walks awkwardly across the meadow with a bag slung over her shoulder. She's wearing fishing boots, held by rubber straps over each shoulder. She waves from the opposite bank before carefully stepping into the surging water on the flat stones of the old ox cart road. The water's at knee level. With outstretched arms, she teeters from the force of the rushing Blue.

Water splashes up to her hips. Finally she reaches me. I kneel on the edge to take her hand. "These waders worked slick, but that water's freezing."

"Where'd you find them?"

She slips the strap of the canvas bag over her head. The edges of a blanket stick out. Bottles clink when she lays the bag on the dead grass. "Some Bill had." She begins taking off the boots. "My sneakers fit perfectly in them, but my feet and legs are frozen."

"You feel free to take Uncle Bill's stuff?"

"Why not? The place isn't locked."

"That's stealing."

"Really, Dusty! A pair of old fishing boots!"

"Well, I wouldn't do it."

She slings the bag strap over her shoulder again. "Let's go."

We face the steep bank at the water's edge and the wildlife path. It follows up the bank about ten feet from the pit's edge. Orla shades her eyes with her hand. "Isn't that the tree up there?"

"Yeah, but we can't reach it on this path." I glance along the edge of the pit to the tree. "What do you think, we're mountain goats?"

"It's the most direct," she says. The Blue rushes behind us and the steep climb lies in front of us. "I'm going this way."

"Orla, we can't! It's too dangerous!"

"Well, animals use it."

"Yeah, with four legs!"

"I don't care. We can do it." She scampers up the bank. "I'll meet you up there."

"Geez, Orla, I can't let you do this alone!"

We start, heading for the pine tree. We have no choice but to crawl; our bellies and legs hug the ground. We creep around saplings and pasture juniper, over and around rocks. Orla stops. Sneaker toes support her. Her heels are just above my head. "We have a way to go yet."

She gasps for a breath. "We're about halfway."

I stretch my neck and glance over the edge. We're at least a hundred feet above the bottom of the pit. "Just stay on the path."

"Don't worry." She stops. "Whew, I need a rest."

"Here, let me have your bag." I'm several feet below her. She's clinging to small trees. We've climbed high above the river.

She takes the strap off her shoulder, and in passing the bag down to me, it slips, smashing on stones. She slides back past me on her stomach. Grabbing a sapling, she regains her footing.

I catch the strap of the bag, and smell wine dripping from the bag. "We can't stop now. Keep climbing. We'll rest on that flat stone up ahead." I reach above and leave the bag. Carefully placing my feet on stones, I climb down to give her a hand. We find the footing to reach the natural shelf and sit. We face the almost vertical bank we've just climbed. The Blue rushes downstream. She checks the bag. "Darn! The wine!"

"Wine! Who cares at this point? Leave your bag here." I throw the strap over a bush.

"I wanted to have a little snack when we reached the tree."

"With wine? No thanks!" I lean and glance to my left over the pit's edge, cringing at the distance to the bottom. "Going this way was *not* a good idea." I turn to check the distance we have yet to climb. "Let's go back. We'll walk to the bridge."

She tightly squeezes my hand. "This *is* scary."

"I know. I told you so. I really don't like what's ahead."

Orla unzips her jacket and holds the locket. "This will keep us safe." She tucks it behind her shirt. She relaxes and pulls her hand from mine. Getting to her feet, she turns. "Let's keep climbing." She heads up the bank.

We continue on, grasping for anything we can find to keep us from falling. Orla's above me. Her feet are within inches of my head. I follow and glance up. Holding to low-growing brush, we keep going. We're almost to the ridge. Suddenly, Orla screams, "My locket!"

The chain is caught in the branches of a small bush. Desperately, she tries to free it. Her feet slip. She hangs by the golden chain. With one hand, I try and give her footing. The chain breaks. She crashes into me. We both fall a few feet. I regain footing and hold on to a small tree. I grab her arm.

She continues screaming, "My locket!" The toes of her sneakers kick at soil-covered stones. She's not trying to gain a foothold on the bank. I keep holding. "Orla! Help me! Help yourself!"

Her free hand feels for the chain that was around her neck. "My locket!" Her knees bang against the bank. Blood runs from under her pants onto her sneakers. Her hand starts to slip from mine. I hold onto her jacket sleeve. Her head slowly drops through the collar of her coat. Her other arm slips out of the jacket. "Orla! Grab something! Grab something!"

She falls—sliding out of control, crashing over small trees. I can't help her. She continues screaming, "My locket!"

Her momentum is so fast she can't possibly stop. She flies over the flat stone, barely touching it, and in less than a second plunges into the fast-moving Blue. The surge of water is too strong. It carries her downstream.

I'm frozen in place. How much time passes, I've no idea. I cling to the bank, hoping what I just saw is not true—then reality kicks in. I scamper and yank the chain and locket free. It's still warm. I slip both into my pocket.

I hurry as fast I dare, sliding, crashing into small trees, being speared by juniper needles. How I reach the bottom safely is beyond me. I jump the fence by the quartz stone and follow the river under the overarching willows. I frantically run, desperate to locate and save her.

I try to see her as I go. Where is she? Where is she? All I hear is the rushing water. Finally, I spot her shirt floating. I run through the cattle resting area to try and catch her at the dam. She's bobbing along near the edge on the opposite side. I charge across the bridge, running toward the dam. Water is roaring over the stones.

I hold on to a root at water's edge and wade to catch her by an arm and pull her onto the bank. Her face is blue. I push her chest. Water bubbles out her mouth. I keep pushing, pushing, hoping for a breath.

190

But nothing comes from her mouth, which is expressionless. "Come on Orla, say something!" She's lifeless. Those deep brown eyes don't focus grief or anger or demand anything. They're just there, sunken into her head. The stare that could derail a train is gone. She's gone. She's dead.

I rush to the house; Cooner and Addie are at the table drinking coffee. "Orla drowned! She's by the dam. Geez!" I plop in a chair and start crying. "The locket!" Tears run down my face. "I tried, geez!"

Addie rushes to the phone. Cooner hurries out the door. I sit in disbelief. I don't know for how long, but it seems in no time the sheriff and state police are standing in front of me. How, why, when, and where are asked in a dozen different ways. They start me believing I was the cause, and maybe I am. After a long grilling, Cooner steps in, "Can't you see the boy's all wrought-up?"

The sheriff backs away. "What was he doing with her kind, anyway?"

I yell, "Her name is Orla!"

After they leave, Cooner pulls up a chair. "That girl got into your head in a big way; but you ain't to blame yourself for what happened."

"I was a part of it."

"But you weren't the cause of her death."

"The golden locket. It didn't protect her like she thought." I reach in my pocket and hold it in my hand. "The chain broke."

The next day, I'm numb to what's going on. At mealtime a wave of grief strikes me. I'm not eating. My fork dabs at the food. The image of Orla lying dead on the bank won't leave me.

Cooner stops eating. "What's the problem?"

I raise my voice in a wobbly tone, holding back tears. "Orla! It's terrible! Zelda hated her. Her father treated her mean. We couldn't stand her most of the time. I'm just sad!" I sniff and wipe my face.

Addie comments, "She was trouble from the day she was born."

"My papa was good to her." Maggie lays her fork down. "She was always at the house. He gave her Rosie's locket."

"Yeah, I know." I reach in my pocket. It slips from my hand and dangles from the broken chain.

"Uh…yup, that's the one Rosie wore." Grandpa reaches for it and opens the locket. "Sure enough, a picture of Rosie and Zelda's mother, Orla O'Neil."

"Keep it in your hand!" I plead with a sound of urgency.

Maggie throws her head back. "Why?"

"It's Orla—her warmth." Everyone stops eating. "I—I yanked it from the bush right when she fell."

Maggie stares at me. "Dusty! Get a hold of yourself!"

"Well, it is her! It's never cooled since her fall."

"Godfrey, Dusty, you've got to come to reason." Cooner holds a napkin and wipes his mouth. "You've looked into the eyes of death before. Nothin' will bring her back. She's dead."

"But none of you knew her mystery like I did." I pause. "The power she claimed to have when she held this locket."

"Baloney!" Maggie pushes away from the table. "That was just an act."

"Well, not completely. She saw things the rest of us couldn't."

"Yup, you're right; she could," Cooner says. "But the locket weren't a part of it. It's like knockin' on wood for good luck. The luck ain't in the wood." He glances my way to see if I'm listening and continues. "Just lately, folks claimed she weren't findin' stuff they'd lost." Cooner makes his point with his elbows resting on the table. "I heard at the store that drinking, drugs, and deadbeat guys were takin' up her time."

"Yeah, well, she claimed the evil of the black heart was the cause." Grandpa passes me the locket. I clutch it in my fist. "This was her good side." Then I open my hand and reach toward the middle of the table. Everyone's attention is drawn toward the locket. "It got smothered in evil."

Grandpa and Addie stare at me.

"Oh my gosh!" Maggie starts clearing the table. "And you fell for that line?"

"None of you knew her!" My voice starts to break again. "I'll admit, I wondered about the black heart."

Cooner reaches across the table for my arm. "Don't you see, the poor girl was lost. She had to blame somethin' for the way she was actin'."

"Yeah, maybe. We never did see if there *is* a black heart."

"Naw, after all this time, the tree has healed."

"Maybe the tree has, but I haven't."

"You need to check it—lay the matter to rest," Cooner suggests.

Maggie stands at the kitchen sink. She gets my attention as I leave. "Just remember, Dusty, Orla doesn't live in that locket."

"Yeah, I guess not. But I still want to check out the tree."

"Okay, we will."

The next day, before the funeral, Maggie and I walk to the ridge following the old skid path. We push through the undergrowth to where the lone pine stands. We both search for the heart. The bark's rough where the heart was carved, but nothing shows. Maggie rubs her hand over the spot. "Cooner knew. It looks just like a human scab."

"All the fuss over the black heart was a waste. Orla's death was a waste. The black heart probably only lasted for a matter of months." I stand staring at the tree feeling both ridiculous and a little disappointed. Maggie, watching my reaction, says, "Let's go." She reaches for my hand to pull me out of my trance.

We hold hands as we walk down the logging skid path. My other hand is shoved in my pocket. My thumb is sliding over the gold piece, massaging the smooth feel. "If I'd only known this locket is really only a piece of jewelry."

"Well, you didn't."

"Do you want it?" We're approaching the bridge. "It belonged to your grandmother."

"It's too much Orla's as far as I'm concerned—a part of her I don't care to remember."

We're on the bridge and stop to look upstream, watching the rush of water spilling over the dam. Foot-long icicles hang on small tree limbs at the river's edge.

We stand in silence. I pull the locket from my pocket and hang it over the water. "The icy water took Orla. So I'm letting it take the locket." It drops from my hand and vanishes in a rush.

Maggie has a startled expression. "You're okay?"

"Yeah. It's time to move on."

The funeral for Orla is held around her grave, dug in hard October ground. Shirley reads a few passages from the Bible. People talk; they visit and offer their sympathy. There's not a person who really misses Orla. Zelda puts on a good front. I hear her say, "Thank you, thank you" to people she hardly knows.

But going through the motions of a funeral can't bring Orla back. In a weird way, for better or worse, I was in her life. Maybe I'm the one that misses her the most. It's hard not to care for somebody who claims they love you. Without thinking, my hand slips in my pocket, feeling for the warm locket. It's gone. Somewhere, it's in the cold Blue River—the water that took Orla's last breath.

— CHAPTER THIRTY-ONE —

I walk off the school bus a couple of days before the bids are to be opened. Buster Erickson is just leaving Grandpa's apartment. He flashes me a satisfied smile, nodding and tugging on the brim of his fedora. I don't return him the favor of a greeting; instead I look at my feet. The crook! What's that cockeyed smile supposed to mean?

During night chores, Grandpa comes to the barn. "Uh…Erickson's goin' to win the bid. The old rascal ain't plannin' to lose."

"How does he know what you bid?"

"He don't, but he fished around to get an idea. He ain't placed his yet."

"Well?" I clear my throat. "Well, what did you tell him?"

"Uh…he asked me, 'What do you figure farmin' land's worth?' I tried to throw him off a little. 'I don't know,' I said. 'This ain't just farmland, it's Murray land.'" Grandpa sits on the milk stool behind the cows. "'Murray land ain't worth no fifteen hundred an acre, is it?' Erickson asked. Uh…hearin' that figure made my eyebrows jump, not meaning to, but it gave him the answer he wanted. I sort of blasted him outta my place, knowin' I'd showed my hand."

"He really doesn't know." I stand in the aisle, eager for an answer.

"No, I didn't have to tell him. The price of farmin' land can't compete with a truckin' outfit. I'll tell you, if we don't win the bid, these cows are goin'. I'm sick of losing money."

"Well, can't you at least wait until spring?"

"There ain't no need to."

As I'm milking, I notice him stopping to check each cow. He's looking at her left side, then her right. Cooner notices him, too. "What's wrong, Thad? What's you lookin' at?"

Grandpa abruptly turns to leave the barn. "Oh, nothin'."

It makes me upset, because I know he's checking the cows to put a price tag on them. At supper, Grandpa shares his thoughts. "Uh…

feedin' corn silage helps, but it ain't enough to make keeping twenty-five cows worth doin'."

Cooner's upset. I can see the change in him. He's lost his laugh and his appetite. Addie keeps watching him with darting, worried eyes. I know they're probably wondering where they can go to find work. He glances over the walls of the kitchen while sitting at the table. No doubt, he's thinking what it will be like to have to move to another farm, but he doesn't say.

That night, I glumly sit in my white chair, just staring off into darkness. I miss the light I used to see at the old homestead. Once in a while, car lights come toward me across the Flats or red taillights go the other way. Big deal.

Cooner's talk of a bumblebee-sting-in-the-butt day doesn't even come close to describing my feelings. A sting goes away, but change has come too fast, and life's only going to get worse. Grandpa talking about losing the bid and selling the cows doesn't give me any hope that I will ever farm the meadow.

Today, October 15, Grandpa, Maggie, and I go to the Huntersville National Bank. Since Emily Ann Gray is the executrix of Uncle Bill's estate, she invited interested parties, as well as those who have bid on the Murray property: Zelda, Steven Iverson, and Buster Erickson. Maggie and I wanted to go to see who wins.

When we walk into Emily Ann Gray's office, her grandfather is sitting behind her desk, greeting us as stiffly as a cornstalk. Emily Ann explains, "I've asked Grandpa Silver to come in and handle the opening of the bids, since I'm too closely connected to the Iverson family."

I can imagine him sitting in my white chair, probably never relaxed. His shoulders and back are erect, with hands on the desk and elbows bent at a perfect right angle. Cooner would say, "He's wearing fancy threads." It looks as though his suit was bought new this morning. After welcoming us, he nervously sits with knitted fingers.

He slides his arms outward, his hands resting on what looks like the bid envelopes. With his thumb and index finger, he feels for the knot of his dark blue tie that squares perfectly against the stiff white collar of his shirt. We sit looking like hungry cows waiting to be fed.

We're in a semicircle around the desk. I'm seated midway in line and can see nearly everyone in the room, except for Grandpa, who is beside me.

Maggie's seated at one end with her back next to a dark-paneled wall. Steven Iverson is at the other, facing the wall and Maggie. Steven is using the opportunity to stare at Maggie. But gosh, she's only fourteen and he's twenty-three or four. However, you'd never know it by his interest in Maggie. She's wearing a white sweater with a maroon silk scarf neatly placed around her neck and draped off each shoulder.

His black curly hair is neatly combed. He has on a light green dress shirt and pressed khaki pants. One might guess they are near the same age, and his interest in her would bear that out.

Her complexion reddens, and that dimple at the edge of her smile is deep red. She nervously pulls on the ends of her scarf, looking down her front, checking for specks that might be nestled in her sweater. She flashes a quick, nervous smile his way—then turns toward her mother for only seconds. Next, she glares at Steven. He seems flustered, looking down at his pants, sweeping his hand across his shirt. They carry on testing the power of their stares over each another. It seems totally out of place to me. After all, this is not some enchanted evening at a dance hall, but serious stuff.

The old man clears his throat. "Usually, I wouldn't think it necessary for interested parties to be present at the opening of bids. However, due to the keen interest from the Murray family, Zelda O'Neil, Buster Erickson, and Steven Iverson, I thought it was wise to do so. I want to make it abundantly clear that I have the authority to reject any or all bids. Under law, I must accept the highest bid, the one benefiting the William Murray estate the most. However, if the highest bidder is unworthy for financial or moral reasons, I can reject the bid."

It's sounding as though Mr. Silver is totally bored—as if reading from some law book. He doesn't look at any of us while talking, but stares straight ahead at the office wall.

He continues, "Standing in for the executrix, I am in control of this estate until the deed is signed and the funds are deposited in a trust fund for Margaret Murray. No one is to set foot on this property until the deed is signed. I want to remind the successful bidder that the baled hay in the barn has been sold separately and is the property of the court until its removal by May 30, 1971."

He pauses, draws a deep breath, and continues, "I have set the date of January 15 for the signing of the deed. This will allow time for the highest bidder to secure the necessary funds. Are there any questions?"

Erickson is wearing a silk shirt with his usual pocketful of cigars. The shell buttons are held by their very edges as the cloth stretches over his big belly. He sits breathing gustily with his mouth open and lower jaw jiggling. "Hiram, I want to ask a question before you open those bids."

Mr. Silver stretches his neck and squints in a frown. "Yes?"

"Can I give you my bill for the taxes I paid?"

"Why, no! We've already discussed this earlier. I need a receipt or some proof that you actually paid William Murray's taxes."

"The proof is sittin' right here in this room. Thad, ain't I the one that paid you money in cash for Bill's taxes?"

"Uh…yup, but you owed Bill for hay that you already took."

Maggie raises her voice, "More like stole. Someone was at the barn loading hay during my papa's funeral."

I'm thinking: good for Maggie. Now we'll see what kind of lies Erickson can tell.

Erickson smiles, showing his brown teeth. In a sappy tone, he says, "Young lady, you know that weren't me. I was at the funeral."

"Maybe not you, but you can hire people to do your dirty work."

I blurt, "Yeah, that's right!"

Erickson jumps to his feet yelling, "You kids are accusin' me of bein' a thief?"

Maggie calmly replies, "My papa was so sick, I don't think he knew what was or wasn't due him. I think you still owed him money for hay you took even before he died, and someone took at least one load during the funeral."

"That's a lie!"

She at least gets him mad, too mad. That's enough proof for me— the crook.

Mr. Silver slaps the desk. "Let's lay this matter to rest. I won't accept a bill or statement of any kind from you, Mr. Erickson. That being settled, let's open the bids."

Erickson wheezes, grumbling as he sits, "I never get beat. The Murrays ain't heard the end of this!"

I feel good, seeing the crook put in his place, but that's the high point of the day. Everything goes sour after that. Buster Erickson wins the bid at one hundred and seventy thousand. Five thousand above Grandpa, Zelda, and Steven Iverson's combined bid.

Erickson sits looking proud, fingering a cigar, removing the cellophane, crumbling the wrapper in his fat hand. Sticking the cigar in his mouth, he's eager to light it up, flipping the cover of his gold lighter.

Maggie says with determination, "I don't want Buster Erickson owning my papa's farm."

"But why? He's offered the most money." Mr. Silver grimaces, shifting in his chair, feeling for the knot of his tie.

"If he buys it, farmers won't be able to use the land. It's always grown crops and I want it to stay that way. Buster Erickson is going to sell it to some big trucking place."

He bites on his cigar, sending it pointing toward the ceiling. "Trans-World Trucking for its New England depot."

I can tell that Mr. Silver doesn't like Buster Erickson because he keeps scowling at him, tightening his lips, and glancing at his fingernails. He draws a deep breath as he says to Maggie, "I'm not free to follow your wishes because you legally aren't an adult. I have to sell to the highest bidder, unless of course there is a good reason not to."

I ask right back, "What's a good reason?"

"Well—well, if you could prove that Mr. Erickson willingly and wrongfully cheated William Murray or his estate—that would be cause."

Buster Erickson laughs and stands to leave the room. "Good luck, kid."

After he leaves, Zelda O'Neil adds, "I know we would be willing to meet Buster Erickson's bid."

Steven Iverson joins in, "Yes, with no problem."

Grandpa keeps quiet.

"I can't allow that, or the bank and I might have a lawsuit on our hands," Mr. Silver says. "There has to be a good reason why I wouldn't honor Buster Erickson's bid."

Maggie weakly smiles. "I'm sorry the meadow will never be farmed again."

"Yeah, that's for sure." I get up to leave. "I guess we all really knew the crook would win out in the end."

The losers drag out of the bank. On the ride home, Grandpa is somber. He says nothing, but that jaw muscle is continuously working.

The loss hits me hard, knowing that the meadow will never be Murray land again.

— CHAPTER THIRTY-TWO —

For the next few days, the weather changes and it warms up, melting most of the early snow. Although it's late fall, it seems like spring. Upstairs in my room, I slide my window open and breathe in the clear cool air. Since the sun has set, a chill comes with the freshness of the night. I can hear the roar of the Blue rushing over the dam. The starry sky is clear. The moonlight casts long dark shadows as it strikes the cluster of buildings in the yard. I can occasionally hear the clank of a cow's stanchion in the barn as she changes her resting position.

A slight nighttime freeze glazes the driveway. The moonlight reflects off ice crystals between the gravel pebbles in our drive. The maple at the edge of the lawn stands motionless with its gray limbs reaching like a hundred hands with a thousand fingers.

I'm warm, wrapped in my blanket, even though the window's still open. Sometime during the night, half awake, I hear a crackling sound in the drive like the sound of popping popcorn. I briefly dream that the maple tree has bloomed white kernels, and it's a giant popcorn ball.

In an instant, I wake with a start. Slue is barking. There's an old car with no lights coasting into the drive. The rolling tires are breaking the surface ice. Two lightly dressed people, hugging themselves against the night chill, hurry to the barn. Through the barn windows, I can see their flashlight cast shafts of bright orange. The light's directed at Pride and the sign over her pen.

Fear of who's in the barn momentarily cripples me. Next, the question: what will happen to Pride? I dress and hurry downstairs to wake Cooner. He groggily comes to the door. "What's the problem?"

"Two people are in the barn."

"Well, go and turn on the lights. I'll be right there."

The car has dented fenders and rust holes looking like Swiss cheese. I draw a deep breath, quietly opening the door. I feel for the inside switch and find it. The *snap* sounds like the shot out of a gun. I jump. While squinting, waiting for my eyes to welcome the light,

201

I hear Cooner's hurried steps behind me. We look down the line of cows. There're two people leaning over the pen gate, talking to Pride. Cooner raises his voice, "Who's there?"

A return, "It's us."

We're within a few feet of them. It's Snaky and his girl. She looks pathetic in a skimpy pink dress and a worn zip-up sweatshirt. She's slight with skinny legs, and shorter than Snaky. She's not even as tall I am since my growth spurt took hold.

Her face is pale from the cold, matching her bare shivering knees. She hugs herself, shaking her humped shoulders, leaning into Snaky's side. "Warm me up, I'm freezing."

He obliges, but fidgets. I notice he's winding the silver chain, hanging by his side, around his finger. This is a Snaky I've never seen. Losing his hot Ford along with his license may have caused him to grow up.

Cooner asks, "What are you doin' here at this hour?"

"We were at my brother's birthday party. Comin' home, my junk car ran out of gas and the battery died." He looks at Pride. "We've been pushin' it to your place. I want to get it off the road because it ain't registered." He runs his hand over Pride's head. "Just the same, if I can get it goin', I'll drive it home."

Cooner offers, "We'll try."

Snaky continues to rub Pride's head. "I wanted to show Queenie the calf that wrecked my car."

Cooner clears his throat. "You wrecked your own car. Don't go blamin' this calf."

"Well, yes—I guess so. I'd sure like to have my car again. This here animal would just about pay for a new car."

"Dusty keeps watch of the place from his bedroom window."

Snaky turns to me. "What, you afraid someone will steal her?"

"I don't take any chances."

"You ain't even to think it," Cooner adds. "This heifer is stayin' right in her pen."

Snaky smiles. "Just foolin'. I guess I'll have to forget about a good car for a while. She is mighty nice, though; I'd sure like to own her."

Pride's long lean neck reaches over the gate. Queenie slides her delicate fingers through the long hair on Pride's head. "She's a friendly one."

I ask, "You want to take a better look?" I realize after the offer that I'm showing possible thieves my pot of gold.

Queenie brightens. "Sure, bring her out of the pen."

I slip on Pride's halter, unhook the gate, and lead her onto the walk. She's growing tall, long and lean, still showing her nice top line.

Queenie runs her hand from Pride's hips to her tailhead. "She's so soft and smooth."

"She handles easily."

Snaky gives me a sarcastic smile. "You weren't leadin' her too good the day she ran into the road."

"I'm sorry she did that—wrecking all those cars—and yours, too." That was kind of a lie. There was a part of me that wasn't too sorry to see his hot Ford off the road.

"Thanks for sayin' that. I guess you folks ain't farmin' here much longer. There won't be any reasons to worry about calves runnin' around."

"I was hoping I could farm here. I could, too, if it wasn't for Buster Erickson wanting the meadow."

Queenie adds, "Buster Erickson is a thief. You know he's been stealin' Bill's hay."

Snaky corrects her, "We think he is; there ain't no proof yet, but I'm workin' on it. I've got a couple of guys I want to see. Just lately, I went to work to deliver a truckload that was sittin' in the yard. The guys that work regular for Erickson didn't know where it came from, but I remembered the small bales."

"I sure would like to catch him stealing hay," I comment. "I'll keep close watch of the place, especially at night." I don't want to say any more because I'm not sure about Snaky, about whose side he's really on—mine or Erickson's.

He adds, "It ain't right, stealin' from a dead man. Bill was a good friend of mine."

Cooner yawns. "Dusty, put Pride back, and get the gas can in the shed. Bring the funnel, too."

I lead Pride into her pen, take off her halter, and swing the gate shut, dropping the hook into the eyelet. Queenie and Snaky are watching me. It makes me nervous.

After we put gas in the old car, Cooner starts his truck. We connect the jumper cables and Snaky's old car starts. He sticks his head out his window. "Thanks, you guys. I'll give you a hand someday."

Queenie waves. "Goodbye, Dusty, I loved seeing Pride."

"Thanks."

As Cooner leaves to go back to bed, he says, "The LaQuines have always been willing to break the law, but they never forget a favor."

"I hope not. Both watched me open and shut that pen gate."

The next couple of days, word travels fast that Thad Murray is selling his cows. Steven Iverson and other buyers come day and night, to see the cows and to see how much milk they give. They check each cow, feeling and poking as they look over the lineup for soundness—pinching and pulling hides. Cooner has told me that a thin loose hide is the sign of a good milker. All of Grandpa's cows have thin hides. Everyone who comes to the barn notices Pride and wants to buy her with the herd. Grandpa tells them, "Uh…she ain't for sale. She belongs to my grandson."

He knows he has good cows, and therefore he's set a high price. He expects that someone at some time will pay his asking price: a thousand a head. Several days pass and a few farmers come for a second look, wanting to be sure the cows will be worth the asking price.

Cooner's worked in the morning, but he doesn't come for night chores. He can't stand seeing what he calls *his* cows being examined as if they were clothes at a rummage sale. On Friday night, Steven Iverson walks in the barn and announces, "I'm buying the herd. I'll have cattle trucks here Monday morning and a check after the bank opens."

Hearing the news, Cooner just lies in bed.

Addie cries, "I don't know what to do for him. There ain't no pills for a broken heart."

During supper, Cooner looks awful. He hasn't shaved in days. His eyes are red as he continually wipes his nose and sips on a cup of tea.

—— CHAPTER THIRTY-THREE ——

Cooner is always saying how smart I am, but I'm sure not smart enough to figure a way to make him happy again. If I could find a way, I'd want to after all he's done for me. Maggie is staying with Zelda for the night, since Addie is able to do housework again.

The night's clear and cold. It seems colder than normal for the end of October. The nearly full moon brightens the sky as it glows from the east, bathing the meadow like a giant spotlight. The land will be paved over for big trucks coming and going where once working hooves walked to till the land. But it will never matter to anyone that Cooner and Addie have to move to find work, or that I'll never get to see my dream-farm come true. All that will be left is a road sign: Murray's Flats.

While sitting in my white chair, I watch the moonlight fill my room. Frost is beginning to build on the window. Only the outline of a picture that's taped to the dresser mirror is visible. I drew it—my future farm—a few years back. I should rip it up, but it's cold, too cold to leave my warm blanket. The tape recorder and trophy also sit on my desk. I haven't used the recorder since my report on Napoleon.

Without warning, for just a second, I notice a flash of light in the barn near Pride's pen. Slue isn't barking and no cars are in the yard. Who or what is it? In a glimmer it comes and goes in seconds. Suddenly, a beam hits my window. I jump. Someone's out there in the shadows.

I'm curious more than scared. It must be something to do with Pride, since that's where I first saw the flash. I jump out of the chair and dress. Grabbing my flashlight, I run out into the cold night toward the barn, open the door, and turn on the lights. The cows are all resting, chewing their cuds. Running to Pride's pen, I notice something strange. The point of the hook on the gate pierces a small piece of brown cardboard. The hook has been slipped back into the eyelet. Pulling the note from the hook, I read: Watch for lights at Bill's. Walk don't ride.

Back in my chair, I ponder the note. It has to have been written by Snaky or Queenie, but a lot of people have been through the barn this week. Then I remember that Cooner told Snaky that I keep watch over Pride. They also saw me slip the hook in the eyelet on the pen gate. Maybe they knew then that they might leave a note.

What a mystery. I haven't done Snaky much of a favor, just pouring a little gas in his tank. He has reason enough to lure me away in order to steal Pride. Then again, he even said he was a good friend of Uncle Bill. But what would he be doing at the old homestead? I don't want to bother Cooner. He's in such tough shape. I wonder: should I follow the directions on the note? While sorting this out, and coming up with no answers, I keep watching in the direction of the old homestead.

It's late. My breath collects on the cold window and frost blocks my view. I put my mouth close to the window and blow. The frost melts. With my fingernail, I scrape a round circle of slush off the glass. The moon is much higher in the sky.

I'm getting tired of looking in one place, seeing nothing. It occurs to me that this might be a trick to lure me away from the farm. Then they can drive into the yard, load Pride, and be gone. Nothing's at our barn and it's all dark at the old homestead. Keeping up this back and forth business is tiresome. Every half minute or so, I have to rub the window to clear the frost.

Sometime during this intense watch, I fall asleep—then wake with a start. The window's thick with frost. I repeat the blowing of hot breath on the golf-ball-size circle, then scraping the ice. I'm worried that I might have missed something. Maybe Snaky calling me from the house and me not showing is a good thing. The thought almost makes me chuckle, but not quite.

I rub my face with my hands to rest my eyes, and then I refocus. A flash of light catches my eye. I look closer through the round frost-free hole. My breath clouds the glass. My pajama cuff wipes it clear again. Lights are moving past the No Trespassing signs at the old homestead.

Cooner wouldn't walk in the middle of the frigid night to the old homestead, nor would he let me. I remember courage again, but I don't have a white horse. However, Napoleon didn't have Slue and I do. She'll be better than a horse if I need her protection.

Searching in the dark for clothes, I pull my pants on over my pajamas, button a shirt, and slip on two sweaters. I take the tape recorder, just in case there's a chance to use it. In the moonlight downstairs, I continue to dress. I slide the recorder between my two sweaters, tuck them under my belt and tighten it, then pull on my insulated pack boots and overcoat, and put on my wool hat and mittens. I'm out the door. A deep breath tells me it's cold—very cold for the end of October.

I run to get Slue. I hear every step crunch on the frozen ground. She's deep in her bed of hay. Only a cluster of frost the size of a small snowball clings to the hay, giving the clue that a live animal is buried. I speak in a low voice, "Slue." She backs out of her bed, wagging her tail.

Hurrying across the flats, all I can hear are the click of her toe nails on the pavement and the *clomp* of my boots. Up ahead the old homestead is dark. Has the vehicle left the yard? I'm still wondering if this might be a Snaky trick—a decoy to lure me away from the barn.

Turning around and walking backward for a few steps, I see no lights at the farm, and it's totally dark up ahead. If anything's going on, it's being done in darkness. The cold continues to sting my nose and cheeks. I hold my mittens on my face, walking blind, only peeking now and then to keep my direction.

I'm coming closer to the old homestead. There's a faint light through the open haymow door. Cooner has turned the power off. It must be a lamp of some sort. The outline of a hay truck parked under the door is barely visible. I stop to listen—there's not a sound. Walking on the frozen drive is not a good idea. The crunch of my boots will be heard. I take hold of Slue's collar and lead her to the back of a shed. The building blocks my view of the truck, but it gives me a chance to get closer, unnoticed. At the corner of the shed, there're shadows of bales being thrown out of the mow door. Whoever's stacking the truck must be working furiously. The person moving on top of the hay truck is impossible to see because of the barn's shadow. I move closer to the corner of the barn. From my new position, the light from the moon is enough to see the truck nearly loaded—stacked in layers six bales high.

The thumping of my heart pounds in my ears. The next move is important. Waiting to be sure of what to do, I swallow to clear my dry throat—all the time holding tightly to Slue's collar. Cooner has trained her not to open in a bark unless she's free to sniff a hot trail. She's shaking from the cold. Maybe she's sensing danger. Probably we're equally frightened.

We slowly move toward the truck, inching along the side of the barn. My hand continues to tightly grip Slue's collar. We are at the back end of the truck—hidden. Since the thieves are almost finished loading, soon someone will be standing on the ground to rope the hay.

Slue and I crawl under the truck. We lie in the center. If the truck moves, we won't be crushed by the tires. Slue's shaking hard now. The frozen ground draws our body heat. The tape recorder must be kept warm. Rolling on my side, I pull Slue close to me.

People jump to the ground, grunting while pulling on ropes. All that can be heard are the grunts and the chug of rope, being bound tightly through steel rings on the side of the truck. There's no talking. These people are obviously haulers of hay, making it unnecessary to give instructions to each other.

My tape recorder is worthless. What use will it be to record grunts and groans? We're getting colder and colder. I can barely feel my feet and both of us are shaking. I keep my mouth shut so no one can hear my teeth chatter.

I'm hoping they'll hurry and drive out of the yard. My daring adventure is a flop. Finally, the truck doors slam. The cold groan of the engine turns slow, then slower, then slower yet. It moans to a stop. The truck doors open and the hood latch clicks. In the faint light, I count three sets of feet and legs in front of the truck.

"Whatta we do now?" someone asks.

"I don't know—the boss should be here any minute. He wants to inspect to make sure all the evidence is covered."

I forget about being cold as I hear the conversation. I wonder who's the boss? Just in case it's Buster Erickson, I pull my recorder from under my coat, feel for the Record button, and press.

"We need jumper cables," a voice flatly announces.

In moments, lights flash in the yard. A door slams. "You guys get a move on before we get caught."

It's Erickson's voice. By the car lights, I can see four sets of legs standing in front of the truck.

"We can't, Buster. It ain't startin'." I recognize Snaky's voice.

"You idiots! I told you to keep the truck runnin' while you loaded."

"Snaky told me to shut it off. He couldn't stand the exhaust."

There's enough evidence if the recorder works, but will it work in cold weather? Somehow the truck needs to be prevented from moving. But with jumper cables, it will be gone in just a few minutes. There's no other option; the truck has to be disabled. Then I'll get absolute proof that Erickson's behind the plan to steal this load of hay.

Shaking Slue's collar, I command, "Sic 'em."

She lets out a loud string of ferocious barks from under the truck. For a second, feet and legs are airborne as her sharp voice stings the quiet night. A man falls. A set of legs pump skyward. It's Erickson. Slue has him by the pants while setting her paws in frozen ground. Rolling to his hands and knees, he's crawling toward the car. Slue grabs for another bite, pulling and slipping his pants to his knees.

He's able to stand, yelling, "Help! Help!" Pulling on the band of his underwear, he covers his rear from the frosty air and lunges to his open car door. The other three are already inside. I yell, "Slue, stop!" She sits by the car as lights continue to shine on the side of the truck. I place the recorder, still running, under the truck, then crawl out to stand.

I hear Erickson's voice. "It's the Murray kid!"

Kneeling by the right tire of the truck, I remove the stem cap, and turn it upside down to start unscrewing the valve inside the stem as Slue sits guarding me. None of the men dare leave the car.

Erickson yells from his open window, "Hey, quit that! You're nothin' but trouble! Get away from that truck or I'm rammin' you!"

I continue unscrewing the valve. He races his Cadillac backward and gets in line to run me over. Pressure from the tire blows the valve in the air. I dive toward the other front tire as Erickson's car crashes into the truck. The radiator blows fluid in a mass of steam. The car stalls in a groan. It missed me by several feet.

On the other front wheel of the truck, I start the same process. My hand is too shaky to connect the groove of the cap to the stem. Erickson's two helpers are out of the car. One has a folded umbrella in his hand and tries to hit Slue, but she's too quick. His attempted blows keep missing. She leaps with her front paws, hitting him in the chest, sending him stumbling to the ground.

The groove finally slips into the valve. With my index finger and thumb, I start turning. Suddenly, an arm is around my neck. I hold tightly to the tire with one hand as the arm closes, choking me. A howl of pain breaks into the night air. The arm instantly releases. I glance and see Slue's teeth are momentarily sunken into the guy's leg.

She's busy barking and charging at the men. Finally the stem flies into the air; but by now, the guy with the umbrella has reached me. There's a sting on my head. I fall in a daze, but hear Slue's growl. She apparently chased the guy back to the car.

It takes just a moment for my head to clear. Erickson is screaming, "Do something, Snaky! You idiot! Do something!"

The four sit helplessly in the car. Slue keeps them at bay. She's panting, and steam is pouring from her open jaws. Saliva drips off her tongue. I stumble to my feet, still feeling dizzy, unable to move.

Erickson's door flies open. He charges toward me with a tire iron. Slue lunges for him, but he keeps coming, blowing big gusts of air. I back up and fall to the ground. Snaky leaps from the car. He pushes Erickson aside and yanks the iron from his hand.

I dive for the tape recorder under the truck, slipping it under my sweater. Erickson yells, "We're comin' back to get you!"

The tire air whistles a slow steady tune. Snaky's at my side urging, "Let's get outta here!" He lets out his donkey laugh as he slaps me on the back. "Good goin', kid."

I run as fast as possible across the flats, charging in the house, with Slue right behind. I bang on Cooner and Addie's door. "I got him! I got him!"

A big *boom* shakes the house. Apparently Cooner fell out of bed. Startled, he opens his door. "What is it?"

"Come quick!"

I place the recorder on the table. As he's coming, I hit Rewind, and then press Play. The whole conversation blares in the kitchen. Cooner stands, laughing. "Addie, call the sheriff! They're stealin' hay at Bill's place!"

Slue flops next to the woodstove. Cooner runs his hand over her head as her tail slaps the floor.

Grandpa, Zelda, and Steven went to the bank today to sign papers, giving them ownership of Uncle Bill's place.

We're at the supper table. Grandpa stops eating. He pauses and grins. "Uh...now, with the meadow, I guess it's time we rearranged the barns. We'll make room for some more good cows."

"Yeah." I smile.

Maggie leaves the table to help Addie. Together, they both stand holding a big cake and announce: "It's time to celebrate."

We all clap, even Grandpa. We enjoy the cake, mutually agreeing that the impossible is for real: Grandpa now owns nearly half of the meadow.

After supper, I head for my room, feeling great. I dive for my chair and run my hands over the fuzzy armrests. It's snowing. Lights from on-coming traffic shine through the flakes. Snow is collecting on my windowsill. I hear footsteps coming toward me. "Hi, Maggie."

She stands in front of the window. "Isn't the snow pretty?"

"Yeah, it sure is."

We both stare into the storm. The meadow will sleep under a white winter blanket. In time, as the months pass, the sun will wake the soil. We'll work the land, sow the seeds, and plant the corn. During the warm days of summer, the meadow will grow lush alfalfa. By fall, the corn will be ready for harvest.

I can't wait for spring.

Date Due

1/27/11			
FEB 0 5 2011			
Ill due 3/25/11			
MAR 1 6 2011			
AUG 2 4 2011			

Breinigsville, PA USA
13 May 2010
237998BV00002B/2/P